CAPTIVES OF ARGAN

By the same author:

ELAINE
THE ICE QUEEN
THE FINISHING SCHOOL
WARRIOR WOMEN

CAPTIVES OF ARGAN

Stephen Ferris

This book is a work of fiction.
In real life, make sure you practise safe sex.

First published in 1997 by
Nexus
332 Ladbroke Grove
London W10 5AH

Copyright © Stephen Ferris 1997

Typeset by TW Typesetting, Plymouth, Devon

Printed and bound by
BPC Paperbacks Ltd, Aylesbury, Bucks

ISBN 0 352 33145 3

One

In the palace's great hall, where once there had been light and music, there was now near darkness, relieved only by the narrow streaks of light that leaked through the shutters. On a wide, low dais, the golden throne with its encrustation of precious stones dwarfed the two figures huddled beside it. Princess Nerina and her only remaining servant, Leah, little older than her own 19 years, had listened in horror for days to the distant sounds of battle. At first, there had been some hope of victory. Commanders, counsellors and ministers had come to the princess with reassurance and to seek her authority for the commands which had dictated the strategy of the fight against the invaders. Today, no one had come into the room and the eerie silence was somehow more menacing than had been the noises of conflict.

For the fiftieth time Leah asked, 'Do you think there is any hope, Highness?'

For the fiftieth time Nerina replied, 'There is always hope.' On this occasion she added, 'But it is now a very small one I fear.'

'What will they do with us?'

Nerina laid a comforting hand on Leah's arm. 'Imprison us, certainly. Torture us, perhaps. No doubt they would like to take their pleasure with our bodies but I have a means of preventing all those things. In the great ring of State on my finger there is enough poison for us both. I will not allow you to be ravished, any more than I would permit it to happen to me.'

Leah was wise enough to say nothing. She was well aware that her mistress had no experience of men. It was therefore quite likely that she meant it when she said that death would be preferable to sex. Leah, on the other hand, had sufficient experience of casual couplings with many of the palace's male staff to know that there was a certain pleasure to be had from them. She had no experience at all of death and could not see any possible joy in it.

She changed the subject. 'I still don't see, Highness, why Prince Argan would want to attack us.'

'It has all been explained to me by my counsellors, Leah. My mother's kingdom of Isingore is large, while Argan's principality of Paradon is small. This palace is full of treasure, which is reason enough for any thief. Too cowardly to launch an attack while my mother lived, he waited until her death brought me to the throne then, thinking he was dealing only with a weak and feeble girl, he launched his treacherous assault on a land which had never threatened him or given offence in any way. Now I fear evil has triumphed. I expect at any moment that Prince Argan's troops will burst in on us.'

The princess rose and squared her shoulders. 'Come Leah!' she said. 'If that is what is to happen, let them not find us cowering in the darkness. I shall greet them with the dignity of a ruler. Help me to light the candles.'

She crossed the floor of the great throne-room, her brocaded shoes soundless on the carpet; only the rustling of her floor-length silk dress marked her progress. At a side wall, she took a crank from a bracket and fitted it into a socket in the wall. She disengaged the pawl and, as she wound on the handle, a windlass concealed in the wall let out the rope that led to one of the great chandeliers high up against the ceiling. She continued to wind until the chandelier was within a foot or so of the carpet then locked off the windlass. There were tapers and matches in a niche. She lit a taper and gave it to Leah then lit one for herself. Together they circled the chandelier, lighting the candles at the centre first then working towards the outside until a hundred or so gave off light. Raising the chandelier again was more difficult and it took their combined strength to wind the handle.

At last the princess was satisfied. She took her seat on the throne and arranged her dress with care then waited tensely with Leah at her side. The wait was a long one and her pose hard to maintain. She had slept little for the past few nights and from time to time her head drooped as sleep stole upon her.

Half-dozing, she recalled another occasion she had witnessed in that room and another use for the windlass in the wall. It seemed a hundred years ago but was in reality only a matter of months since Leah had shown her the peep-hole which allowed them to look down into the great hall and see what took place when serfs were brought before her mother to be judged for some misdemeanour. What she had seen had made her mother, Queen Lavinia, seem even more remote. They had never had a close relationship. Nerina had been brought up by Dorcas, a faithful wet-nurse who had become in turn her nanny and then her governess. Dorcas had been more of a mother-figure to her than the Queen. Her passing had caused the princess intense grief which she still felt much more keenly than the more recent death of her natural mother, who had always seemed too busy with affairs of state and with prolonged drinking bouts to bother much with her daughter.

At the peep-hole with Leah, she had seen that the Queen was already a little the worse for drink, despite the fact that it was not late in the evening. Her face was unnaturally flushed and she took regular gulps from a silver chalice which she waved unsteadily when she wished to emphasise something she said. All about her in a semi-circle sat the wealthiest and most powerful in the land – barons and their ladies – so that the grey hall seemed to be illuminated by the splendour of their rich clothing and jewellery as much as by the chandeliers.

The Queen clapped her hands and the great double doors at the end of the hall opened to admit two uniformed guards. Between them was a man whose hands were bound behind him. He was naked to the waist and wore only a pair of moleskin breeches. Each holding him by the upper arm, the guards propelled him forward until he stood before the Queen; then they forced him to his knees.

'Who is this?' Queen Lavinia asked.

One of the guards took a piece of paper from his pocket and consulted it. 'Luther, tithing man of the hamlet of Altdorf, Majesty,' he said.

'Ah yes! I remember.' Lavinia stared at the kneeling figure. 'Your people have paid less than half the tithes I set. Why?'

The kneeling man met her gaze unflinchingly. 'The answer is simple, Majesty. The tithes are set too high. In an exceptionally good year we might meet them, even though that would mean that babies starved because of it. In this year, when the weather has not been exceptional, the amount was impossible to find.'

'There is no such word as impossible!'

4

Luther stared at her. 'Perhaps not in your vocabulary, Majesty, but among the people of my village it is common currency.'

'You are an impertinent fellow, Luther. And why do you stare so?'

'Majesty, every day I see about me poverty, disease and distress. When I get the opportunity, it pleases me to look at the cause of those evils.'

The Queen half rose from her throne, flushing red with anger. 'You move from impertinence to arrogance,' she exclaimed. Controlling herself with an effort, she sat down again, smiling without warmth. 'In my experience,' she said, 'arrogance increases with the amount of clothing worn. You! Guards! Take those breeches off him and let's see how brave he is when he is naked.'

Luther threw himself forward and rolled on to his back so that he could kick out at the guards, but, with his hands bound behind him, there was little he could do to prevent them from stripping him. They worked with swift efficiency, unfastening his belt and grasping the legs of his breeches to up-end him so that they did not so much remove his breeches as empty him out of them.

Watching, Nerina could see that her mother, if not just, was at least a good judge of a man's reaction to nudity. No longer proud and upright, Luther sprawled on his belly, frantically trying to hide his private parts from view. There was no mercy in the Queen's voice as she ordered, 'Raise him up and let's see what he is so ashamed of.'

The guards dragged him to his feet and held him there. He flushed and turned his head away, closing his eyes so that he should not see Lavinia's eyes fixed on his manhood. His penis and testicles were of great interest to Nerina as well. She had never seen a naked man before. Leah, beside her, had seen such things on many occasions and giggled audibly.

'Take him round and show him off to the ladies of the court,' the Queen said.

Again Luther struggled and threw his body about in an effort to prevent what was to come but the guards had no difficulty in marching him over to stand before a large group of well-dressed women, evoking a little buzz of excitement among them as they tittered and pointed.

As Luther was being dragged into the required position, Nerina had her first good frontal view of his body and she stared intently. The sight of his penis was completely fascinating. Thick, long and white, it hung down from a thatch of dark pubic hair, dividing the testicles hanging below. She felt her face growing hot as she suddenly became acutely aware of her own private parts. Even as she watched, Luther's penis twitched and jumped a little, as if operated by invisible strings, then began to lengthen and erect itself as the shaming impact of so many female eyes made itself felt through the medium of his brain, almost as a tangible force. Aware of what was happening to him, Luther turned his head up and away in denial and humiliation. By chance, that look was directed at Nerina's peep-hole and she shrank back in embarrassment for a moment or two until she realised that it would be quite impossible for him to see her.

Queen Lavinia had also noticed the change in his body. 'Well!' she said. 'What have we here? A man ready for sport? If I am not to have my tithes then at least we ought to have some entertainment in exchange. Bring in the wench!'

The woman in question had obviously been detained just outside the door in anticipation of the Queen's command, for it was only a few moments after her order that the doors opened again to admit another two guards. This time they held between them a dark-haired girl of about 25 who shrank back in alarm when she first saw the assembled nobles and the bright lights. Her feet were bare and her simple, grey woollen dress was torn at the neck, revealing one graceful shoulder and the upper part of one breast. Elsewhere, the dress clung to the curves of her body and those curves were so voluptuous that a spontaneous ripple of applause greeted her appearance.

The guards marched the girl to a place in front of the throne and thrust her to her knees, holding her there while she peered apprehensively at Lavinia.

The Queen stared at her impassively. 'You are Gerda, then?'

'Yes, Majesty, if it please you.'

'And you are of the village of Altdorf, too? I have not been misinformed?'

'No, Majesty. I mean, yes, Majesty. I mean that I am from Altdorf and Luther is my tithing-man.'

Lavinia smiled slightly. 'And just your tithing-man? No more than that? You know that I hear all the gossip.'

Gerda blushed bright red. 'No, no!' she protested. 'I haven't . . . I mean we haven't . . .'

The Queen leant forward and her stare intensified. 'But you'd like to, wouldn't you, Gerda? That is what gossip says.'

If it had been possible, Gerda's face would have become even more scarlet and she shook her head, unable to speak for embarrassment. From where he stood across the room, still held upright by his guards, Luther shouted, 'Leave her alone! Your quarrel is with me, not her. She has done nothing. Punish me if you must but there is no need to torment Gerda.'

Lavinia transferred her gaze to him. 'Ah, but there is need, Luther, if you are to be cured of your rebelliousness. Rest assured though that I shall punish you, as you suggest. Guards! Position him for a whipping!'

The guards pushed Luther back towards the centre of the room and placed him below one of the great chandeliers which hung from the raftered ceiling. At the Queen's signal it descended slowly on its suspending rope until it could be reached. Another soldier tied a length of rope to the centre of it then knotted the dangling end to the cords around Luther's wrists. Lavinia signed again and the chandelier began to ascend. As it did so, the guards holding his arms released him. He pulled frantically at his bonds but there was nothing he could do to prevent what was happening. As the upward pull on his bound hands increased, he was forced to bend forward to relieve the pressure until he was stooping most uncomfortably on tiptoe, his arms stretched straight up behind and above him, the muscles in them betokening the strain and pain he felt.

Gerda looked on in mesmerised horror as Queen Lavinia produced a long, coiled whip from beside her throne. She rose and, with a flick, uncurled the length of it so that it landed on the floor beside Gerda. Another flick and the lash jumped and cracked with a report that echoed around the room.

The Queen's smile was icy. 'So, Gerda, would you like to watch while I flay the skin off that rebel backside with this?'

Gerda flung herself forward, grasping the Queen's knees through her embroidered dress. 'Please, Majesty! Spare him, I beg you!'

Lavinia waved an arm at the crowded room. 'But we must be entertained. If you deprive us of the spectacle of a whipping, do you have an interesting alternative to offer?'

Gerda looked up with tear-filled eyes. 'Majesty, I don't understand what you mean.'

'It's perfectly simple. I won't whip the man you love if you can provide a show which is equally diverting.'

'But I have nothing to offer; no entertaining skills.'

'On the contrary, you do have something to offer. What about your body? That looks to be attractive.'

Gerda continued to look at her uncomprehendingly, so the Queen elaborated. 'If you were to remove your clothes and stand naked in front of my guests, that might please them.'

Gerda blushed red again and Luther, for all his doubled up position, contrived to make his voice loud enough to be heard. 'No, Gerda! You must not do it! Not for me.'

Gerda looked around and was reminded of his helpless vulnerability. 'I'm sorry, Luther,' she said. 'I must.'

He continued to struggle and voice his protests as Gerda rose to her feet. With quiet dignity, she drew off her dress over her head and cast it aside before standing, quite nude, in front of the throne, her head bent and her hands clasped together in front of her, hiding her genital area.

Lavinia sat down again and put down her whip. 'Head up, girl!' she commanded. As Gerda obeyed, the Queen allowed her gaze to wander over the bare body in front of her in a manner which made no secret of the fact that she was doing so in order to embarrass her victim.

'Put your hands at your sides!' Obedience to that order meant that the patch of dark pubic hair at the junction of belly and thighs was fully revealed, and

9

the fact that Gerda shuffled uneasily from foot to foot showed that she was well aware that Lavinia's scrutiny could now include that secret place. From her watching place, Nerina also inspected Gerda's nakedness and found her heart thumping a little harder as she tried to imagine what it must be like to be shamefully exposed to so many gloating eyes. Gerda's breasts were full and firm so that they seemed to tilt upwards to her brown nipples. The rest of her body fulfilled the promise it had shown beneath her clothes. A narrow waist and long, flat belly gave way to the swelling curves of hips and thighs, while her buttocks were twin moons of perfection, womanly in their rounded appeal yet as taut and firm as youth and healthy exercise could make them.

Lavinia nodded approvingly so that Gerda was encouraged to ask hopefully 'May I put my dress on again now please, Majesty?'

The Queen's look of approval gave way to a frown. 'No! Not yet. My guests would like to admire you more closely.' She nodded across the room. 'Walk over there, close to them, and allow them to look and touch.'

For a moment it seemed as though Gerda would refuse but after hesitating for only a few seconds she turned away and crossed the hall to present herself as she had been bidden to the assembled nobles. They rose as one and crowded around her, men and women alike; touching, feeling, sniggering and talking among themselves while Gerda stood quiescent, allowing them to do what they would with her body.

When Lavinia clapped her hands to demand attention, the guests sat down again and Gerda came back to stand once more in front of the throne. 'Majesty,' she said, 'I have done what you asked of me. May we go now?'

'Not just yet, Gerda. Did you like that?'

Gerda hung her head. 'No, Majesty. I was ashamed.'

'No reason to be ashamed of such a body, Gerda,' the Queen said. 'But if you didn't like it, why are your nipples now erect and long? No, don't cover them with your hands like that. Everyone has already seen your excited state. You have done well and I feel it would not be fair to allow you to leave in this state of mind without having had the opportunity to sample the love-making you have been dreaming about. Today I feel in a match-making mood. You and Luther shall pleasure each other here and now while we watch.'

The emotions that chased one another across Gerda's face were a delight to the Queen and exciting to Nerina, looking on from her vantage point. Gerda's mouth fell open while she considered whether or not she had heard aright. Deciding that she had, confusion, embarrassment and alarm etched themselves one after the other on her features. Finally, though, came the expression the Queen had been looking for. There was definitely a trace of excited expectancy there, even as Gerda shook her head vehemently.

'No! No, Majesty. Not with all these people. I couldn't.'

Lavinia reached down and picked up her whip again. 'What a pity,' she sneered. 'Are you quite sure it's impossible?'

Gerda looked desperately around for some way out of her predicament. She stared hard at Luther, now groaning slightly from the discomfort of his enforced stoop, understanding only too well what could happen to his bare body. She looked again at the whip and her gaze travelled back to Lavinia's face, reading

11

there only implacable determination to carry out her threat.

Gerda nodded, resigned. 'I will try, Majesty,' she murmured, hanging her head.

'Good!' The Queen clapped her hands again. 'Take him down and attach him to that pillar.'

Luther struggled again as the chandelier was let down and his hands were untied. The length of time he had spent in that position had cramped and weakened his arms so that he was no match for the burly guards as they took him across to the slender pillar Lavinia had indicated. They set his back against it, then pulled his arms around behind the pillar before lashing his wrists again.

'On his knees, I think,' Lavinia commanded. The soldiers grasped his ankles and dragged them backwards, one on either side of the pillar, so that he fell to his knees with a thud, scarcely able to break his descent by gripping the pillar behind him with his arms. They tied his ankles together then passed another rope around his chest, binding him to his support so that he could not bend forward.

The Queen nodded, satisfied. 'Good. Now, my dear, you may fulfil your sweet ambition. Go and kneel down in front of him.'

Gerda did as she was told and stared at Luther, searching his face with her eyes. He stared back. 'Don't do this thing, Gerda,' he said. 'Not to save me. Let them do what they will with me. I will not have you so shamed.'

She put out her hand and touched his face, allowing her finger to wander down the deep crease at the side of his mouth. 'Only tell me one thing,' she said. 'Do you feel as I do? Do you desire me as I desire you?'

He twisted his head from side to side with closed

12

eyes, knowing that the massive erection of his penis gave the answer before he spoke. 'Yes, my love. I have felt like that for a long while but have been afraid to speak. But not like this! Not with these animals watching. I cannot allow you to so degrade your sweet body.'

'And I cannot allow harm to come to the person I love so much when it lies in my power to prevent it. At any other time I would be obedient but at this moment I must disregard what you say.' She smiled encouragingly and stroked his face again. 'Don't mind them. If we love one another enough, it matters not who watches. We can still be alone and private in our minds.'

He began to protest again but she stilled his voice by kissing him full on the lips then allowed her kisses to trail down his body and over his chest while her hands sought and found his penis. She drew in her breath sharply at the excitement of holding this treasured part of him at last and he, in his turn, echoed that sound with a great gasp of arousal. She sat back on her haunches and inspected his organ while she manipulated it, rubbing it gently while she felt below and took the weight of his testicles in her other hand. She shuffled backwards a little then leant right forward and he felt her breath on his inflamed flesh.

'No, Gerda. You mustn't!' he cried, as her lips closed around the glowing tip of his manhood. 'Oh! Ah! Yes!'

Nerina, in her hiding place, felt a slight movement beside her and turned to see that Leah was moving in a curious way. Her right hand was up underneath her skirt and there was a blissful expression on her face.

'Leah! What are you doing?'

Leah did not interrupt her movements. 'Princess, I

am pleasuring myself. Do you not feel the need to do the same?'

'I don't understand what you mean.'

'Oh Princess,' Leah said. 'I knew that you had not been with a man but I did not realise that you had not found your special places either.'

Nerina regarded her gyrating companion in astonishment. 'I don't know what your are talking about,' she said. 'And stop doing whatever it is that you're doing at once!'

'Just one moment more, Highness, I beg you,' Leah answered, panting a little, her face screwed up in intense concentration as she remained glued to her position at the peep-hole. 'Ah! Oh! Mm!' she breathed, then her whole body seemed to melt into relaxation. Her hand came out from under her skirt and she puffed out her cheeks as she blew a stray lock of hair out of her eyes. 'That's better!'

Nerina was about to ask for further explanation but loud groans from the hall below drew her attention back to the two figures by the pillar. Gerda was sucking vigorously on Luther's penis now, her naked posterior high in the air as she rocked back and forth in her efforts to encompass the whole length of him. For his part, Luther was straining violently upwards, the tendons of his neck standing out as he sought to hold out against what was being done to him. His expression reminded Nerina of that she had just seen on Leah's face.

'Enough pleasure for him!' Lavinia called. 'Now it is your turn, Gerda!'

'Oh yes, Majesty!' Gerda answered with deepest sincerity, allowing Luther's huge erect organ to emerge from her mouth. She swiftly reversed her position so that her buttocks and exposed sex were presented to his interested gaze. She crawled backwards, her legs spread on either side of his knees, until she could reach back between her thighs and grasp his penis to guide it to the place which was now so hot and wet, ready to receive it. She centred the head of his manhood between her soft, pink labia then, with a moan of pleasure, thrust herself hard towards him so that she was impaled upon him. Her head shot back, her mouth opened and a little scream of joy emerged, then she was rocking furiously back and forth, massaging his whole length with her body.

'You may stop now, if you want to,' Lavinia said.

Gerda turned her head in the direction of the sound, glazed eyes unseeing. 'No! No! No!' she panted, in time with her rocking.

'What about you, Luther? Wouldn't you like to stop?'

It was unlikely that Luther heard what the Queen said. If he did he took no notice. His lips drawn back from his teeth in an animal snarl, he was jerking his hips as far as his restraint permitted, thrusting forward as Gerda pushed backwards so that their bodies made a slapping sound as they met, his testicles banging against the backs of her bare thighs. In a crescendo of lust, their body movements increased in force and pace until Gerda, with a shrill cry, strained her head violently upwards as she reached her peak, just as Luther came too, great spurts of his semen pumping into her with all the force of his youth and love.

Nerina and Leah had stolen away at that point and saw no more, but Nerina had never been able to enter the great hall after that without a mental image of what she had seen done there and the use to which the pillar and the chandelier had been put. Those images whirled before her tired eyes now as she watched and awaited her fate with Leah, halfway between sleeping and waking.

When the heavy doors were flung open with a crash, it came as a surprise to Nerina; she gave an undignified squeak of alarm and started in a manner that ill became a Princess. By the time she had gathered her wits the intruders were in the room; a double line of dragoons, their silver helmets, breastplates and black, thigh-length boots gleaming while the sky-blue of their tunics and plumes proclaimed their allegiance to Prince Argan.

They did not rush upon their victims as Nerina had expected but turned inwards to face one another, forming an avenue along which advanced a young man in a spotless, white, double-breasted uniform with a very high, closed-neck collar which most perfectly set off his lithe physique. Leah, still standing beside the Princess, stirred uneasily as she took in his gold braid and buttons, the heavy gold epaulettes and high-fronted cap. These things, she thought, paled into insignificance when compared to his face. Lean, brown and lantern-jawed, there was yet a gentle humour lurking in the depths of his blue eyes, even though one of them was partly concealed by a monocle.

Princess Nerina rose haughtily. 'You dare to come into my presence unannounced?'

The young man came to a halt, nodded a formal court bow and clicked his heels. 'Forgive me, Highness,' he said. 'Allow me to present myself. I am Michael, Count of Selfingen, one of the smaller estates of Paradon. I am aide to Prince Argan and leader of his armies. I know that it is customary for your High Chancellor to introduce visitors. Unfortunately, he was hiding under a table. The part of him sticking out was not recognisable and the soldier who tried to winkle him out was a little too enthusiastic with the point of his bayonet, so that he is now indisposed. His wound is slight. Please be reassured that he will live to hide again.'

Beside her, Leah giggled audibly and Nerina was annoyed as much by that as by the realisation that she was also amused. To conceal what she felt, she assumed a dramatic pose, looking up and away to one side with one hand at her throat. 'Very well, monster!' she cried. 'Do your worst! Imprison me! Torture me! Ravish me! You shall never have my soul!'

Count Michael smiled slightly. 'Highness, if your soul is only one half as beautiful as the body it inhabits, it is a matter of the bitterest regret that I shall never possess it. The magnanimity of your other invitations overwhelms me, but I must decline them. My purpose in intruding upon your privacy was to satisfy myself, on behalf of Prince Argan, that you had come to no harm and to invite you to visit him as a guest in his home at Perlestadt, Paradon's capital.'

'Invite me? Guest? What sort of invitation is it that comes backed by armed men?'

'A perfectly genuine one. You have only to say the word and I will withdraw, taking my troops with me, then you will have the palace to yourself.'

Nerina drew breath to speak but Count Michael hadn't finished. 'Before you decide, may I be impertinent enough to enquire if you can cook, Highness?'

The unexpectedness of the question startled Nerina into a reply before she could stop herself.

'No.'

'Ah! That will cause a difficulty for you. When I said you would have the palace to yourself, that's exactly what I meant. All your staff have left.'

'Nonsense!' the princess protested. 'They wouldn't. I know that my people fought valiantly against Prince

17

Argan's treacherous invasion. They would not desert me now.'

'Did you see or hear them fighting to prevent my entry into the palace?'

Nerina bit her lip, recalling the days of eerie silence.

'Much as it pains me to do so, Highness, I have to tell you the truth about your mother, the late Queen of Isingore. She was a brutal and greedy tyrant. When the people could not tolerate any more they appealed to Prince Argan to save them and he responded by undertaking a campaign of liberation, not unwanted invasion. Your army came over to our side in droves and the whole countryside rose up and joined us in driving out the few barons who shared your mother's weaknesses.'

The princess recalled her mother's enjoyment of the indignities inflicted upon innocent flesh in that very room and bit her lip again.

The Count drove the point home remorselessly. 'Look at me! Look at my men! Do we look as though we have been engaged in a furious battle with a loyal army determined to die for you? You know in your heart that there is nothing for you here, or anywhere in Isingore, except starvation and the hatred of your people.' His expression softened and he grinned engagingly. 'Come, won't you accept my Master's kind invitation, made with respect and admiration for a fellow ruler, to take refuge with him? Or would you rather try to cook the food you won't find in a kitchen without even fuel for the stove?'

Nerina made one last attempt at a refusal. She indicated her companion. 'Why, as for cooking, Leah can . . .' She broke off as Leah opened her eyes wide, shaking her head in denial and shrugging while she spread her hands with palms outwards in a gesture eloquent of her lack of culinary expertise.

The princess capitulated with dignity. She inclined her head. 'Count Michael, you may tell your master, Prince Argan of Paradon, that the Princess Nerina of Isingore is pleased to accept his invitation to stay for a short while.'

The Count's bow was lower and more courtly this time. 'Your Highness is most gracious. May I have the privilege and pleasure of escorting you myself? I have a fine carriage waiting outside.'

Nerina inclined her head again. 'Very well. Come Leah.' She stepped down from the dais and walked across the room. Count Michael offered her his arm and she took it. Together, they passed down the avenue of dragoons and out of the door, Leah following a little way to the rear. Behind Leah, the dragoons turned and marched in solemn step, forming quite a little procession. In the past few days, Nerina had often imagined herself being taken into captivity. None of the methods of capture she had envisaged had been anything like this.

In the cobbled courtyard at the foot of the wide, shallow steps down which the procession trooped, a four-in-hand coach was waiting, its glossy blackness almost matched by the coats of the horses. On the door was emblazoned in rich gold and blue what Nerina recognised as the personal insignia of Prince Argan. She was a little flattered that he should have sent one of his own vehicles to fetch her. The cloaked, top-hatted coachman got down from the driving seat. Opening the door, he unfolded the built-in steps, then positioned a small wooden stool, so as to make it easy for her to reach them. Count Michael extended a steadying hand and she took it, allowing him to usher her inside. She noticed with slight surprise that he was equally courteous to Leah, who followed her. He handed her in with exactly the same deference, even though she was only a servant.

19

As the dragoons mounted their horses and formed themselves into an escort to the front and rear of the coach, Count Michael got in with Nerina and Leah, settling himself on the seat opposite them. 'Highness,' he said. 'I regret that I must ask your leave to draw the blinds before we set off.'

Nerina regarded him with disdain. 'Are you then so ashamed of what you have done? Imprisoning two defenceless women is what I might have expected of such a villain as Prince Argan. At least let the people see his beastliness.'

Count Michael smiled broadly. 'I can only repeat that neither of you are prisoners, but guests of my master. Any time you ask me to stop the coach and allow you to get out, I will do so at once. Please believe me, though, when I tell you that the purpose of drawing the blinds is for your protection. If your people recognised you they would throw things. Such is their hatred for your regime that if they proved to be strong enough in number, even my soldiers would not be able to prevent them from dragging you out. What they would do then is a matter of conjecture but I imagine it would involve more than throwing mud.' He reached across to either side of the coach and drew down the blinds, leaving as illumination only the glass trap which enabled passengers to communicate with the driver.

The coach jolted and lurched on its way for a little while and Nerina thought over what she had heard. 'But how can the people possibly hate me?' she asked. 'They hardly know me. I have done nothing to harm them.'

'I believe that you are convinced of that, Highness,' the Count said. 'Yours is a sin of omission, rather than deliberate malice.'

'What do you mean by that?'

'In the admittedly short period during which you have been ruler, you have not bothered to find out what your advisers, your ministers and counsellors, were doing in your name.'

'What did you expect? My mother, the Queen, taught me nothing of affairs of state. I left everything to those I trusted.'

'Did you never read the papers they asked you to sign?'

'No. I don't think I would have understood them, anyway. All I know is that everything appeared to be going along as normal until Prince Argan made his treacherous attack on our kingdom.'

Michael laughed again. 'Ah! Normal for Isingore, perhaps. Many of the papers you signed were warrants and orders. Have you any idea what your signatures authorised?'

'No.'

'Death, Highness!' He leant forward and tapped his forefinger on Nerina's knee to emphasise his words. 'Disease, Highness!' He tapped again. 'Poverty, dispossession, theft and misery, Highness!' Each of these accusations was accompanied by another tap until Nerina felt her eyes prickling with tears at such injustice and she knocked his hand away.

'Sir! You go too far. If you were the gentleman you claim to be you would not treat a lady so.'

He sat back in his seat. 'And if you'd had something other than girlish fluff between your ears, Princess, you would not have signed something you had not read.'

Silence prevailed in the coach as it rattled on its way, Michael's born of complacency and Nerina's of fury. She felt Leah's hand steal into her lap to pat her own, consolingly, but snatched it away with an angry glance. She was not in the mood to be patronised by a mere serving wench. She thought about Michael's claim that they were not prisoners and his offer to permit them to get out of the coach whenever they wished. That is what she would do, she decided. That would show him. She would demand to be released. She and Leah could find some friendly homestead, or even an inn where they would be welcome.

She was about to make her demand when the coach lurched alarmingly and stopped. There was a clatter of hooves as the dragoons behind them surged up alongside, borne on by their momentum, followed by an excited shouting and chattering. Count Michael reached up to the trap above his head and opened it.

'What's happening, Konrad?'

The coachman's red face appeared in the opening. 'Just a broken trace, Sir. It will take a few minutes to repair it.'

'Very well.'

Nerina hooked a finger into the blind beside her and eased it towards her to make a crack to peek through. They appeared to be in the middle of a village street, but which village, she had no idea. Nerina had left the palace only once or twice in her whole life, so the opportunity to see another habitation was something of a novelty. It was just as depressing as the few others she had seen: drab and ill cared for. Few doors boasted any paint at all and those that did were cracked and peeling. An open drain in the centre of the street gave off an offensive odour which was apparent to her even in the enclosed environment of the coach. Everywhere, thin rotting thatch and rickety grey walls echoed the thin, grey listlessness of the people.

Already, a crowd of villagers was gathering, attracted by the stark contrast provided by the bright colours of the uniforms and the novelty of such a magnificent equipage. By squinting a little, she could just see the coachman and the postilion attending to the harness, assisted by a couple of dragoons who had dismounted for the purpose.

A red-haired woman with an equally red-haired baby on her hip, evidently bolder than the rest, stepped forward. Her dress was ragged and her feet were bare. From one corner of her mouth dangled an empty clay pipe, broken and stained. She addressed herself to the coachman, jerking her head towards the coach. 'Who've you got in there?'

'Count Michael of Selfingen, leader of Prince Argan's armies.'

Turning, the woman called to the crowd, 'Count Michael! It's Count Michael himself!'

The assembled mob broke into a ragged cheer. 'Hooray! Hooray for Count Michael! Long live Prince Argan, our saviour!' They surged forward, pressing against the side of the coach in spite of the fact that the dragoons spurred their horses among them in an effort to keep them at a distance. 'Come out, sir, please. Come out and show yourself, won't you?' Hands reached for the door handle and Michael leant forward quickly to snick the bolt across.

The clamour increased and the count glanced apologetically at Nerina and Leah. 'I'm sorry,' he said. 'I must. Bolt the door behind me and don't open it until you hear my voice asking you to.' He shuffled across the coach, opened the door facing away from the crowd and got out quickly, closing it behind him.

Nerina had thought that the noise of the mob could not have got any louder, but when Michael emerged from behind the coach, flicking at his immaculate uniform with one white glove, the sound became deafening. The people swarmed around him,

23

clapping him on the back. Several women tried to kiss his hand.

The captain of the dragoons urged his horse into the crowd to get close to his master, sabre in hand. 'Get back! Get back, damn your eyes! Here, you men. Get in here with me and give 'em the flat of your blades!'

The count held up a restraining hand. 'Please, captain! These good people are our friends.' He held up both hands and made pushing motions in the air. 'Only give me a little air, kind folk, and I will speak to you.'

Such was the force of his personality that the mob fell back obediently into a semi-circle and waited. He cleared his throat. 'Good people of . . .' Out of the corner of his mouth, he spoke to the captain, 'What is this place?'

'Kuhfeld, sir.'

'Good people of Kuhfeld. I bring affectionate greetings from your cousin, Prince Argan. He asks me to tell you that with your own brave help his army has been completely successful in overthrowing the tyrant. From now on, he promises that there will be truth and justice for all. He cannot guarantee good harvests and healthy cattle. What he can guarantee is that, however much or little there may be, all will share it equally as does brother with brother. That is the way of Paradon, as you know, and in the future that will also be the way of Isingore!'

This provoked another bout of cheering, louder even than before, until Michael held up his hand again for silence. 'And now I see, my friends, that my coach is repaired and I must, regretfully, continue my journey.'

The red-haired woman spoke up. 'Before you go, sir, tell us what has happened to that devil's spawn, Nerina? Have you taken her prisoner?'

Nerina withdrew her finger from the blind as though it had suddenly become red hot, allowing it to fall back into place while she sat, rigid with terror and embarrassment, listening while the conversation outside continued.

'I am a truthful man,' Michael said, 'So I cannot speak the words you so badly want to hear. I have to say that I have been to the palace and there is no one there. I have not taken Nerina prisoner and I cannot tell you where she is.'

The groan of disappointment this statement evoked sent chills through Nerina. She heard the red-haired woman's voice again. 'When you catch her, sir, give her to us. We'll have a bonfire of faggots ready for her!'

'I will remember what you say.' Michael passed behind the coach again and knocked on the far door. 'Quick! Let me in before they come round this side!'

Leah unbolted the door and he hastily scrambled in, bolting it behind him before sinking back on to his seat and mopping his brow. 'Phew! That was close!' He reached up and rapped on the glass trap. 'Drive on quickly!'

As the coach lurched into motion again, Nerina sat deathly pale and still. Only when she was certain that they had cleared the village did she relax just a little. 'You lied for me,' she said.

'Princess, I am hurt. I spoke only the truth. I have been to the palace. There is now no one there. True?'

Nerina nodded. 'I suppose so.'

'I told you that you were not a prisoner. You don't believe me, but that's not my fault. As for telling them where you were, I just couldn't bring myself to do that. By the way, just before we stopped, I had the feeling that you wanted to leave. Still want to do that?'

Dumbly, the princess shook her head. If there was one thing she was now certain of, it was that the last thing she would consider would be leaving the safety of that coach.

Two

Princess Nerina, still desperately short of sleep, was
aroused from an uneasy doze by a change in the
sound of the horse's hooves. Instead of clattering on
a hard road, they now made a hollow noise like the
rumble of thunder. Count Michael lifted the bottom
of a blind, then raised it all the way to the top.
Reaching across the coach, he did the same to the
blind on the other side, admitting a stream of sunlight
that made both women wince and blink.

'You're quite safe, now, Highness,' he said. 'This is
the bridge over the Regus, which marks the border
between Isingore and Paradon. No one in Paradon
will harm you.'

For one so little travelled as Nerina, an excursion into
another State was such an exciting diversion that she
forgot her fatigue and stared out of the window with
fresh interest. They were passing through rich farm
country. All around, the Alpine meadows between the
well-kept hedges and walls were resplendent with the
colours of summer's flowers. Already, hay was being
harvested. Now and again, she saw lines of men
advancing with swinging scythes and, even at a distance,
the smell of the new-mown crop permeated the air. Now
and again, they passed a traveller on the road. Nerina, in
her previous travels, had been accustomed to peasants
who took off their hats and bowed low as she passed in

her coach. If they were too poor to have hats, they pulled their forelocks instead. Some of them knelt. These travellers were different. On sighting the coach, they made way for it, smiled and raised a hand in casual greeting, calling, '*Gruss Gott!*'

At first, Nerina imagined that it must have been the coachman and postilion that they were addressing, until she noticed that Count Michael raised his hand to return their salutes and smiled back.

She could not contain her curiosity. 'These people show you no respect, Count Michael. Why is that?'

'What you mean is that they exhibit no fear of me,' he said. 'I would be very worried if they did. Instead, they show warmth, friendliness and, perhaps, affection. Which would you rather have?'

Nerina did not know how to answer that, so she changed the subject. 'Will the journey be much longer?' she asked. 'It is a while since I have eaten.'

Michael was all contrition. 'Forgive me, Highness. How thoughtless of me.' To Leah, he said, 'You must be hungry, too.'

Leah beamed at him. 'Oh yes, sir!' she said. 'Very hungry!'

'Then we'll stop and get a little refreshment.' He rapped on the glass trap and opened it. 'Konrad! Stop at the inn in Selfingendorf.'

Nerina was a little put out. The man obviously didn't realise it, but he had made it sound as though he would not have stopped for food if Leah had not been hungry as well. Who, she wondered, was more important to him – a princess or a maid?

Michael continued to speak, apparently unaware of her disapproval. 'We are on my own estate, so I can guarantee the quality of the food.' He smiled at Leah who returned his smile in full measure. That really was most irritating, Nerina thought.

28

Presently the coach clattered into a very different village from the last one Nerina had seen. The cottages were well-tended, their walls gleaming with limewash and their thatches intact. Doors, windows and shutters were painted in gay colours, while window-boxes sprouted an exuberance of flowers. The people they passed were well-dressed, pink of complexion and sturdy or plump of frame. Everyone raised a hand in a positive chorus of '*Gruss Gott!*' Some eschewed even that degree of formality, simply waving and calling, 'Michael!'

Outside the timbered inn, the coachman reined in the horses, climbed down and adjusted the steps. Michael got out and handed out each of the ladies in turn. A ruddy-faced man wearing a leather apron emerged from the front door of the hostelry.

'Joseph, you old scoundrel!' Michael called, advancing with hand outstretched.

'Michael! How good to see you again, sir.' They shook hands then, to Nerina's astonishment, embraced warmly, clapping one another on the back.

Michael disengaged himself. 'Now, Joseph. Ask young Ernst to be good enough to look after the horses. My dragoon's horses need a drink, too. It might even be that the dragoons themselves might be tempted to sip some of your beer if you asked them nicely.' He turned to pull the two women forward. 'This is Leah and this is Nerina. They are both faint with hunger and thirst. Some of your good wife's crusty bread and ham should see to their hunger, while a couple of steins of your best cider will top that off nicely.'

'At once, sir!' Joseph turned and bustled away into the inn, calling, 'Emma! Ernst! Michael is here.'

Nerina allowed the anger which had been building inside her to erupt. 'Sir! You forget who I am. Not only do you put horses and soldiers before me, you neglect to mention my proper rank and put my maid first, too. Is it your intention to insult?'

Michael's slow smile was infuriating in the extreme. 'Without horses, we could not continue our journey. Without soldiers, we would lack protection. Without you . . .' He allowed the rest of the sentence to go unspoken, leaving Nerina to draw the obvious conclusion. 'As to your rank, of what are you now Princess? And did you really want me to announce to the world that you were once the hated tyrant of Isingore?'

Nerina bit her lip as the force of his argument was borne in upon her. 'But putting Leah before me!' she protested.

'Is Leah, then, less hungry than you?'

'No, but . . .'

'So we have two equally hungry young women, neither of them the ruler of anything. One of them has learnt to be useful to others by fetching and carrying, at least. The other has learnt nothing. Who, then, should come first?'

Nerina gave up. With a toss of her head, she said, 'Just show me to my dining room.'

'Dining room?' Michael regarded her quizzically, then indicated the rustic table and benches outside the inn at which a few villagers were sitting. 'It's a beautiful day. What could be more pleasant than to eat here?' He spoke to the group at the table, 'Friends!' he said. 'Can you find room for three hungry travellers?'

'Gladly, Michael.' The villagers shuffled about, leaving space on the benches on either side of the table.

The count offered Nerina his hand. 'You first.' Unbelievably irritated, the princess allowed herself to be seated beside a stout farmer and watched as Michael handed Leah to a place beside her before going around the table and sitting down, facing them.

At once, Leah got up. 'Forgive me,' she said. 'You are too squashed.' She scooted rapidly around the table and hitched her skirt in a most unladylike manner so that she could squeeze in between Michael and his neighbour. Nerina looked daggers at her, but she appeared not to notice.

When the food came, it was as delicious as Michael's description had made it sound, while the cider was like nectar. Nerina forced herself to eat slowly and with dignity, watching Michael and listening to the way he exchanged idle gossip with the villagers, all of whom he seemed to know by their first names. Her meal was somewhat spoilt by Leah's behaviour. She took every opportunity to touch Michael's hand and arm while moving her body against his in a manner which could only be described as snuggling. Nerina maintained what she hoped was a regal silence until the meal was finished and they were back in the coach.

'I have to tell you, Count Michael, that I am displeased. I do not understand the ways of Paradon.'

He shrugged. 'I know you don't,' he said. 'But you will.'

It was growing dark before Count Michael invited Nerina to look out of the window for her first glimpse of their destination. She peered in vain for some sight of an imposing castle. The only building in sight was a large villa built in the Romanesque style and surrounded by pleasant green lawns.

'I do not see Prince Argan's castle,' she said.

'His castle? Why should you suppose that he lives in a castle?'

'A palace then. Some sort of fortified place.'

He shook his head sorrowfully. 'There are only two reasons for fortifications. One is to keep people out and the other is to keep people in. Neither of those things is necessary for my prince.'

'You mean that is his home?'

'Of course.'

Nerina sniffed. 'Pooh!' she said. 'It is not very grand at all. I would have thought that the ruler of even such a small land as Paradon would have built something more in keeping with his status. My palace in Isingore . . .'

Michael completed the sentence for her. '. . . Was built and maintained with taxes stolen from the people, who starved in consequence. Prince Argan's home was built with money he earned by honest labour and its upkeep is provided in the same manner.'

The princess blinked several times, this extraordinary concept being rather difficult to absorb. 'Labour? You mean that Prince Argan works to earn money?'

'Indeed he does, as do we all, myself included. In addition to managing his farm, he travels extensively abroad, procuring orders for Paradon produce and arranging the import of those things we cannot make ourselves.'

Nerina was truly aghast. 'Prince Argan is a merchant? He is in Trade?' The emphasis she placed on this last word was such as to make the capital letter obvious and to equate that occupation with halitosis and warts.

'As I am and as was Mohammed, the prophet,' Michael said, equably. 'Christ himself was related to a carpenter. My master is not displeased to be in such good company. As for me, I manage to live with the shame.'

The princess bit her lip in vexation. Nothing, it seemed, could disconcert this annoying man who could even find reason for pride in being a common dealer in commodities. The coach turned in through a pair of handsome gates and crunched up the long gravel drive which led to the house. At the verandahed entrance, it stopped and Michael helped both women out, as before.

A dark-haired woman of about thirty years, wearing a simple, Grecian style dress which left one shoulder bare, came out to meet them.

Count Michael clicked his heels and nodded a bow to her. 'Good evening, Alcina,' he said. 'May I introduce my companions?' With an exaggerated movement, he reached past Leah and took Nerina's hand. 'This is her recent Highness, the Princess Nerina of Isingore.'

This heavy irony was not lost upon Nerina, who ground her teeth with rage before extending her hand, palm down, to Alcina, expecting it to be kissed. Instead, Alcina grasped it firmly as would an equal and, without even a hint of a curtsey, said, 'Welcome, Nerina, to Prince Argan's home.'

Nerina opened her mouth to protest, but Michael was already pulling Leah forward. 'Also come and meet the delightful Leah,' he said. Leah blushed and smiled as Alcina greeted her in exactly the same fashion as she had Nerina.

'Watch out for her,' Michael said. 'She giggles a lot!'

Leah proved the truth of his words by giggling, in spite of the fact that Nerina was glaring at her furiously.

Michael pointed at Nerina. 'And watch out for that one. I get the feeling she would like to bite someone.' He bowed to all three women. 'Now I must take my

33

leave of you. Alcina will show you where to go and take care of all your needs.'

Leah stepped forward impulsively and grasped his hand, pressing it to her breast. 'Sir! Oh sir!' she said. 'Will I see you again?'

He freed his hand with difficulty and kissed her lightly on the forehead. 'If a tree falls on me and kills me on the way home, probably not. Failing that, I don't see how it can be prevented.' He clambered into the coach and set off back down the drive, his mounted escort scrunching in front and behind.

Alcina turned and went into the house. 'Follow me,' she said, over her shoulder. Nerina and Leah followed her into the spacious entrance hall and up the broad staircase. On the first floor, a long wide corridor appeared to traverse the whole length of the building, to judge from the windows at either end. Alcina opened a panelled door and stood back to allow them to enter. The bedroom was large, deeply carpeted and looked comfortable. The mellow flames of several lamps added warmth to the scene. A large four-poster bed dominated the room, its green damask curtains and counterpane blending subtly with the window coverings and the hue of the carpet. Alcina led the way to an inner door and threw it open. 'Bathroom,' she said, indicating the mahogany panelled water closet and bath.

There was also, Nerina noticed, one of the new-fangled douches which were just becoming fashionable and had only recently been installed in her own palace. They went back into the bedroom. 'Thank you,' she said. 'This room will serve tolerably well.'

Alcina stared at her. 'This is not your room, Nerina. It is Leah's.'

'Leah's!' Nerina looked about her at the gilded dressing table with its huge mirror and at the comfortable armchairs. All this for a servant? Her own room must be truly splendid.

'Leah, you stay here. Nerina, follow me,' Alcina said as she led the way back into the corridor. She stopped at the next door, opened it and stepped aside. Nerina, entering, saw at once that it was almost an exact image of Leah's room except that the colour scheme was pink, instead of green.

Nerina turned to Alcina. 'There must be some mistake,' she said. 'This is no better than Leah's room.'

'And why should it be?'

Surely, Nerina thought, this woman must be remarkably dense. 'Because she is my maid,' she said.

'She is a guest of my master, Prince Argan, just as you are, Nerina and, as such, is entitled to the normal privileges accorded to a guest.'

'And that's another thing,' Nerina exclaimed. 'I have noticed that you have not addressed me with proper respect but have overlooked it, thinking that perhaps you knew no better. You will, in future, address me as "Princess", or "Highness". You may send my maid to me, now.'

'For what purpose, Nerina?'

Such a flagrant disregard of her command did not go unnoticed, but Nerina kept her temper. 'Because my journey has wearied me. I wish to retire.'

'And what has Leah to do with that wish?'

Nerina was shocked. 'Why . . . why . . . I must be undressed, of course, and my hair must be brushed!'

Alcina smile was mocking. 'Have you injured your hands and arms in some way?'

'No, of course not.'

'Then what prevents you from undressing yourself and brushing your own hair?'

To Nerina's shock was added astonishment. It was

35

hard to know how to deal with such ignorance. 'I . . . I . . .' she stammered, but Alcina held up a soothing hand.

'Never mind, I will undress you, if that is what you want.'

Much mollified, Nerina graciously inclined her head. 'Very well,' she said and turned her back. 'This dress has buttons at the back which are tiresome to reach. Be especially careful with them. They are French and . . .' She let out a little yelp of dismay as she felt Alcina grab both sides of the back of her dress and rip it apart in a shower of precious buttons, pulling it down as far as her elbows. Alcina yanked again, splitting the dress to below the waist, then spun her around and ripped at the buttons on her sleeves, detaching them as well so that, before Nerina could stop her, she had pulled on the sleeves to allow the dress to slide to the floor, leaving her victim in chemise, drawers, stockings and shoes.

Nerina clasped her arms across her bosom and shrank away as Alcina came at her again. 'No! No! Keep away!' she screamed, but Alcina took not the slightest notice. Her fingernails scraped against Nerina's tender white skin as she grasped the broad lacy straps of the chemise and, with one swift jerk, tore it apart, the material ripping with a loud noise. Nerina twisted away, leaving herself naked to the waist, the remnants of her chemise in Alcina's hands. Alcina's glittering eyes were now fixed upon her lower garment and Nerina ran from her, putting the four-poster bed between them. For a few seconds, they dodged from foot to foot, measuring each other up, then Alcina feinted to come around the foot of the bed. Nerina tried to jump up and run across it, but Alcina launched herself in a headlong dive over the footboard and tackled her around the waist when she was only half-way across, bringing her thumping down on her stomach with a force that made the mattress bounce.

'No! No! Oh God! Not that!' Nerina screamed again, more loudly this time as she felt a questing hand in the waistband of her drawers. A rending sound and a sudden draught of cold air told her that the unthinkable had happened. She made the mistake of attempting to wriggle forward but, as Alcina had a firm grip on the linen of her drawers, all that happened was that she wriggled out of them completely.

She felt Alcina's hands on both her ankles, dragging her back into the centre of the bed, and tried ineffectually to resist, clutching at the counterpane. Suddenly, the whole weight of Alcina's upper body was across her back and she was helplessly pinned under her arm. She flailed her legs, but that did not prevent each ankle in turn being held in a steely grip while her shoes were removed. Still pinning her in the same way, Alcina disposed of her stockings and the accompanying garters, leaving her completely naked.

Alcina got off her and she lay there, sobbing, with her face in her hands so that she did not see her tormentor cross to the dressing table and return with a hairbrush, which she threw on the bed beside Nerina's heaving nakedness. The first inkling she had that the assault was to be renewed came when Alcina buried both hands in her hair and dragged her forward off the bed, lifted her to her feet, then pushed her backwards so that her knees caught on the edge of the bed and she sat down with a bump. Alcina tore at her hair savagely, scattering pins everywhere, until the long black tresses flowed like a river down her back and over her shoulders.

'You wanted your hair brushed,' Alcina said.

37

Taking a firm grip on the back of Nerina's neck and forcing her head down towards her knees, she plied the brush lustily, tugging at the tangles.

'Ow! Ow! Stop!' Nerina tried feebly to raise her hands to ward off her attacker but Alcina easily knocked them away and continued to brush.

'Ouch! Ooh! Stop! Please stop, I beg you!'

Alcina let her go and stepped back, panting a little. 'Do I understand that you don't want your hair brushed after all?'

Nerina shook her head, her face again buried in her hands. 'No,' she said, in a muffled voice.

'No? Don't you mean, "No, thank you"?'

Nerina took away her hands and looked up, regarding Alcina with tear-filled eyes, cowering a little. 'No, thank you,' she recited, dutifully.

'Sure you don't want me to help you any more? With your nightdress, for instance?'

'No! I mean, no thank you,' Nerina mumbled, correcting herself hastily.

'Very well, I'll leave you to sleep. You will find everything you need for washing or cosmetic purposes, either in the bathroom or in the drawers of your dressing table. Make your bed when you get up and remember to leave your room tidy.' Alcina tapped the hairbrush meaningfully on the palm of her hand. 'These things have uses other than for brushing hair,' she said, then put the brush back on the dressing table and went out, closing the door behind her.

Nerina sat where she was for a few minutes, regaining some of her composure before rising and going into the bathroom to wash perfunctorily. She put on the starched linen nightdress she found under the pillow, then sat at the dressing table and tried to rectify some of the havoc which had been wreaked

38

upon her hair, wincing slightly as her brush strokes passed over sore places.

She thought about what had happened to her that day. Obviously, in spite of Count Michael's protestations, she was indeed a prisoner and was to be maltreated. This room, so pleasant in appearance, was to be her prison. Certainly, Alcina must have locked her in, so there was no point in trying to escape. Anyway, she was tired. She stopped brushing and went over to the bed. Turning back the covers, she crawled in, finding it extremely comfortable. She lay back on the pillows. She must make a careful plan for the future. With a little thought and determination, surely she could . . .

She slept.

The sun was already at full strength and leaking through the gaps in the curtains before Nerina woke again. For a moment, she could not recollect where she was, then she remembered and shuddered at the memory. A sound which she could not identify was coming from outside her window and she got up to investigate. Drawing back the curtains, she blinked at the sudden influx of light and it took a moment or two before her eyes adjusted to it. She found herself looking down on what seemed to be one of the gardens at the rear of the house. The lawn was green and trimmed, bordered by bright flowers. In one corner, an ornamental fountain played, its output making attractive patterns on the surface of the pool that surrounded it. She noticed these things with only half her mind. Her eyes were drawn to the source of the noise which, now that she could see as well as hear it, resolved itself into laughter and happy shrieks originating from a group of ten or so young women who were disporting themselves on the grass. They were all dressed as

Alcina had been, with one shoulder left bare, except that whereas her dress had been of blue silk, their clothing was white and seemed to be cotton or linen. Four of the girls were playing a game Nerina had never seen. Each had a stringed racquet and they were batting a feathered object to each other over a high net strung between two poles – an occupation which seemed to call for a great deal of laughter, whether or not a shot was missed. The others were playing Blind Man's Buff, one of their number groping and stumbling after the others with outstretched arms – something else that seemed to require a lot of giggling. Such spontaneous enjoyment was infectious and Nerina found herself smiling with the girls. She was still smiling when she heard her bedroom door open. She whirled around, her hand rising instinctively to clutch her nightdress to her throat as Alcina came in.

Alcina saw the gesture and smiled. 'Don't worry. I haven't come to undress you again, just to bring you clothes and to enquire whether you slept well.' She laid a small bundle of material on the bed.

Nerina eyed her warily, trying to assess how far she could go with this woman without provoking the sort of embarrassing reprisal to which she had been subjected the previous night. 'Why should you care how a prisoner sleeps?' she asked, with a fraction less haughtiness than she would have liked to employ.

Alcina laughed. 'Prisoner? What makes you think that you are a prisoner?'

'Being locked in one's room usually indicates that status, does it not?' Nerina enquired with heavy sarcasm.

Alcina came towards her. 'Come with me,' she commanded, taking Nerina's wrist and pulling her forward.

A most unpleasant falling sensation occurred in the pit of Nerina's stomach. She had pushed too far and now this mad woman was going to drag her off to some dungeon, strip her naked again, beat her and subject her to unimaginably horrible indignities!

Alcina opened the bedroom door, then stopped and released Nerina's wrist. 'Look,' she said. 'Look at the door. Do you see a lock or a bolt, inside or outside?'

Nerina's voice was so small that it could hardly climb out of her throat. She gulped. 'No,' she said.

'How, then, do you suppose that I locked you in?'

Nerina's voice shrank even further. 'I suppose you couldn't have done,' she murmured.

Alcina's grey eyes bored into her, forcing home the truth. 'So your accusation was quite false and unjust?'

Nerina felt like a little girl caught with her fingers in the honey jar. She looked down and kicked at the carpet with one bare toe, unable to meet those eyes. She nodded.

'And have you nothing to say to the innocent person whose character you have so lightly besmirched?'

Nerina hung her head still further. 'Sorry,' she mumbled.

'What? I didn't quite catch that.'

Nerina raised her head and stared desperately around the room, taking in the ceiling, the walls and the furniture, anything rather than those eyes. A delicate blush coloured her cheeks. 'Sorry,' she said at last, the sibilant word forced from her lips by compressed embarrassment.

Alcina nodded. 'I accept your apology. Now come back to the window with me.'

They went together to the window and Nerina looked again at the happy crowd below. Alcina said,

41

'Those are the only sort of captives you will find at Prince Argan's home. They are the prisoners of their contentment with their lives.'

Nerina's curiosity was piqued. 'Who are they? How do they come to be here?'

'They work here.'

'You mean they are servants?' If true, that was incredible. Nerina had never seen servants playing happy games.

Alcina smiled tolerantly. 'No, they are not servants. Their work is here. The fact that the work consists of cooking, cleaning, making beds and lighting fires does not make them servants in the sense you mean. If that were true, one could as easily describe Prince Argan as their servant, since he works in order to provide them with money and a nice place to live.'

Nerina shook her head in bewilderment. 'I don't understand.'

Alcina patted her hand. 'That's because you do not have the knowledge and experience which would give you that understanding. Don't worry about that. It will be given to you before you leave here.'

'Leave? You mean that my captivity is not permanent?'

Alcina pursed her lips. 'How many more times? You are free to leave at any time. Now, if you wish.' Nerina opened her mouth to speak, but Alcina went on, 'But think about it before you decide. In Paradon, everyone works. Everyone, without exception. What are you trained to do? How would you support yourself? Where would you live? Would you go back to Isingore, for instance?'

Nerina shook her head vehemently, recalling the appalling fate the red-haired woman had in store for her.

'What would you say if I told you that, one day, you would return to Isingore?'

42

'Go back? I can't!'

'Yet you will, because it is Prince Argan's wish that you do. You will rule Isingore again, but not until you have learnt how to do it in the Paradon way: fairly and with justice for all. This is all a little too much for you to absorb at once, I know, but it will become clearer as time goes on. For now, there are more immediate things to think about. I see that you have not made your bed or tidied your room as I asked.'

Nerina blushed again and shuffled her feet. 'I do not know how,' she said. 'I have never made a bed.'

'Leah has made many. Would you like me to ask her if she will come and show you how?'

Nerina brightened considerably. 'Yes please,' she said. 'Send Leah to me.'

'No, no,' Alcina said, reprovingly. 'It is not a matter of sending her to you. Remember that there are no servants here. No doubt she will be employed here and it may be that part of her work will be bed-making. Whether or not she makes yours will depend on the roster I make out. If she comes at all, it will be as a friend, willingly helping another friend. That must be clear in your mind, otherwise I will not pass on your request.'

'I see,' Nerina said, slowly, trying to wrap her mind round the concept of Leah as a friend. She shrugged. If that would get her bed made for her, why not? 'Very well,' she said. 'Please ask her for her help as a friend.'

'Good. Now put on your clothes and I will go and find her.'

When she had gone, Nerina washed her face before sitting down at the dressing table to get the night's tangles out of her hair. There were pins aplenty in a dish but she had never pinned up her own hair and, after struggling with it for a while, she gave up in despair. She went over and inspected the clothing on the bed. The dress seemed to be an exact copy of those worn by the girls in the garden. There were no stockings and no chemise – just a pair of light, silk slippers and one other garment. She held this up to examine it. So alien was the design that it was several seconds before she realised that what she was holding purported to be a pair of drawers. She was accustomed to these being of heavy linen and all-enveloping, split at the crotch and reaching well below the knees. These things were of flimsy silk, undivided and almost transparent. The legs would come only a short way down her thighs and would not grip at all, being very wide and edged with a band of delicate lace. There was not even a secure draw-string at the waist, just some sort of stretchy arrangement. She blushed fiery red and hid the sinful item behind her back for a moment while she recovered her poise.

After a moment or two, she shrugged. Her own underwear had been ripped to shreds. It was either these things or nothing. Raising her nightie a little, she stepped into them and pulled them up, wriggling them up underneath until they settled about her waist. She moved her buttocks and thighs experimentally. There was no doubt that the silk against her skin was delightfully cool. Maybe they were not so bad after all. She pulled her night-dress off over her head and went over to the dressing table so that she could inspect herself in its mirror. The drawers clung to her in a most embarrassing way, emphasising, rather than concealing, curves and crevices. Worst of all, the transparency of them meant that she could quite clearly see the darkness of her pubic hair through the material. She blushed again and went hastily back to the bed, seeking to cover her shame with the dress.

44

She was still struggling with it when there was a tap at the door and Leah came in, now dressed in imitation of the other women. 'Good morning, Nerina,' she said.

In her exasperation with the dress, which now enveloped her head and arms, Nerina did not even notice the familiarity. 'Oh good,' she said. 'Come and help me with this wretched thing. I can't understand what's wrong with it.'

Leah came across and inspected her handiwork, sorting through layers of material. 'Oh, I see what it is,' she said. 'You've got your head stuck in the armhole. Look – put this hand there. Now give me your other hand. No – the other hand. That's right! That goes through there, like so and your head goes here, like so. There!' she gave a few tugs at the dress, which settled itself into place like magic, leaving one shoulder bare in the approved style.

'That's better,' Nerina said. 'Now you may do my hair.'

Leah hesitated. 'Forgive me, Highness,' she said. 'I have been given very strict instructions.'

Nerina sighed. 'By Alcina, I suppose?'

Leah nodded. 'She has told me that I may help you as a friend, but am not to allow you to treat me as a maid. It's very difficult. I am not even allowed to call you "Highness", Highness.'

Nerina gave a snort of laughter before she could stop herself. 'Very well. You'd better do as you're told. Tell me, friend Leah, will you please help me with my hair?'

'Gladly, High . . . I mean, friend Nerina.'

As Leah expertly dealt with the tangled mass of black hair, rapidly reducing it to pinned order, she kept up a continuous babble of chatter which embraced the richness of her room, the respect with

45

which she had been treated and, most especially, the attractive qualities of Count Michael, whose name cropped up over and over again.

'I am led to believe that he will visit this very afternoon. I have been given permission to play in the garden with the other serv . . . with the other girls. Do you think he will notice me?'

'If you behave as you did yesterday, I don't see how he could miss you,' Nerina said drily. 'Now, what about the bed?'

'I was told that I could not make it for you, but only show you how to make it yourself.' Leah looked about her, then lowered her voice to a conspiratorial whisper. 'No one is looking, though. We could make it together and no one would be any the wiser.'

The bed made, they gathered up the torn remnants of Nerina's clothing and made a pretence at flicking dust, then Leah said, 'Are you hungry? I could bring you some breakfast. It is past the right hour but Jacob, the chef, gave me a pomegranate in exchange for a kiss, this morning. I'm sure I could get him to scramble an egg for you.'

'Two eggs,' Nerina said. 'And some toast and hot chocolate. If you can get so much without surrendering your virtue altogether, friend Leah,' she added.

Leah giggled and left. Nerina resumed her position by the window, leaning with her knuckles on the sill. When she heard the door open again, she thought it was Leah returning and did not bother to turn round. 'They look so happy,' she said. 'It might even be nice to go down there with them and learn to play that strange game.'

Alcina's voice made her jump. 'I don't think that would be advisable, just yet.'

Nerina turned to face her, somewhat disconcerted. 'Oh? Why not?'

46

'You are not ready yet. The games you see are not the only ones they play. Here, in Paradon, attitudes to sex are very different. It is part of what makes our society work so well. It is my understanding that you are not only a virgin, but have yet to discover the joy of any sort of sexual fulfilment. Is that true?'

Nerina blushed scarlet to the roots of her hair, quite unable to make any reply.

'I see,' Alcina said, looking at her closely. 'Your face tells me all I need to know. Look into the garden again.'

Nerina did and saw that there were now several young men mingling with the women. There was a lot of smiling and touching going on. 'I don't understand what you want me to look at,' she said.

'Pay close attention. You see that girl with the really red hair?'

'Yes.'

'See how she is holding out her hand towards that young man.'

Nerina observed that the girl in question had her hand stretched out in front of her, palm upwards, with her thumb unnaturally strained away from her fingers, forming a right angle. 'Yes, I see that, but what of it'

'Watch as the man comes toward her. See how he stretches out his forefinger and touches the base of her thumb. Her hand is symbolic of her body. She spreads it as she would spread her legs. His finger symbolises his penis. He accepts her offer. Soon they will go away and be private together. Over there, see that other man with the dark curly hair. He raises his finger to point at the blonde. Ah! She closes her hand into a fist. She refuses him. Wait, though. Now she raises her own finger to her lips. She rejects the full sexual act, but consents to oral stimulation. For one

47

versed in our ways, these transactions are wonderfully simple, with no embarrassing words to be spoken. Simple offers, followed by acceptance or rejection with no hurt feelings. In your unenlightened state, you could not deal with such things. You have to know and understand the pleasure to be had. When you feel ready, I will teach you all you need to know.'

'You? Teach me? Oh no! I couldn't!'

'You would like to be restored to the throne of Isingore?'

'Of course.'

Alcina smiled. 'Prince Argan will not permit that until he is satisfied that you are fit for the office. That means adopting the attitudes and customs of Paradon. It means learning to put yourself in the position of those you hope to rule; learning how to take and give pleasure, freely and willingly. Power over others may be used for good or for evil. My master has to be sure that, confronted by those choices, your instinct will always be to choose the good. When you feel ready to accept what I can teach you, the development of that instinct can begin. Final proof of your readiness to rule will come when you can willingly offer yourself and your virginity to the Prince in a full sexual encounter and satisfy him completely.'

Nerina was staggered at the enormity of this concept. 'What? I don't believe that you could suggest . . . Never! Never!'

Alcina shrugged. 'The choice is entirely yours. You may accept or reject the idea. No one will force you to do anything. I repeat that you are free to leave at any time, or you may stay here as long as you like. I will not even forbid you to go into the garden. I will, however, repeat my advice that it would be unwise in your unprepared state.'

48

At this point, Leah came back into the room with a tray of food and Alcina turned away. 'Take all the time you like to think about it,' she said. 'My offer to teach you what you must know remains open in perpetuity.'

Three

Nerina had several days in which to think about the situation in which she found herself. During that time, Leah came to see her frequently so that the erstwhile Princess became accustomed to the idea that she was now a friend and not a servant. Leah, for her part, never completely adjusted to the change. It was with the greatest difficulty that she remembered to address Nerina by name and not as 'Highness'.

One day, they were sitting together by the window in Nerina's room. Leah was demonstrating the correct technique for sewing on a button, a task for which her pupil showed no aptitude at all.

'Bother!' Nerina exclaimed, not for the first time, as she pricked her finger. She examined the injury, then put her finger into her mouth to suck away the tiny spot of blood.

Leah tittered. 'Better not do that if you go into the garden,' she said.

Nerina blinked. 'Why not?' As understanding came, she blushed. 'Oh! Oh! What a dreadful thing to say. As if I would . . .' Then the humour of the thing struck her and she tittered, too, rather guiltily.

'Remember when we saw such a thing together, Leah?'

'I remember.'

Nerina glanced about her as though to make sure

that they were alone. 'That's the only time I have seen
... I've seen ... You know what.'

'I'm sure it was. Not for me, though,' Leah said,
smugly. 'Closer than that, too.' She reached across
and guided Nerina's hands. 'Look – like this. You go
round three times with the thread, then pull through,
see?'

With a petulant gesture, Nerina dropped her work
into her lap and stared at Leah. 'Are you telling me
that you've actually done ... it?'

'Of course.'

'Why?'

Leah stared blankly. 'Because it's fun, silly ...
Sorry! I mean High ... Sorry! I mean Nerina.'

'It didn't look like fun. It looked quite painful.'

'It's not. You just sort of have to pull faces at the
time, that's all.'

Nerina called to her mind's eye the strained, intent
expression on the face of Luther and of Gerda in
particular. 'I don't understand. Why do you have to
pull faces? Is it some sort of ritual?'

Leah shook her head. 'No. You just can't help it.
I can't explain if you've never felt it yourself.'

'Tell me what it feels like.'

Leah shook her head. 'I mustn't. Alcina said so.'

'Well, Alcina's not here now.'

'All right, then. I'm dying to tell someone, anyway.
You must promise not to report me to Alcina, though.'

'I won't.'

'Well.' Leah hitched her chair a little closer and
lowered her voice. 'Yesterday, I actually did it with
Count Michael.'

'With Count Michael?'

'Ssh! Not so loud!'

Nerina dropped her voice. 'With that beastly man.
But he's so arrogant and rude.'

51

'No he's not. He's lovely. If you're going to be nasty about him, I won't tell you any more.'

'Oh, very well, Leah. He's a lovely man, if you say so. Go on. Tell me about it.'

'I was playing in the garden with the other girls. Michael just appeared. He came straight past all the other girls and pointed at me. I nearly fainted with pleasure.'

'You knew what that meant, then?'

'Oh yes. I learnt that on the first day. I put out my hand and he touched me. Just there!' She put her finger on the mound at the base of her thumb. 'It burned like fire.' She examined her hand. 'I'm surprised there isn't still a mark there. Well, I just took him by the hand and brought him straight up to my bedroom.'

'Here? Next door?'

'Where else? Oh, Nerina! He was so gentle and so kind, yet at the same time strong and not to be denied. It was wonderful!'

'Surely you can go into more detail than that?'

Leah needed little urging. She wiggled as though to settle herself more firmly in her chair and her voice became a conspiratorial whisper. 'First he kissed me. It was a very long and very special kiss, with tongues and everything.'

'What do you mean, with tongues?'

'We put our tongues in each other's mouths.'

Nerina wrinkled her nose. 'Disgusting! Sorry, I shouldn't interrupt. What happened then?'

'All the time, he was squeezing my breasts through my dress, so I said, "Would you like me to take it off?" and he said, "Yes, please!" so I did. I was so pleased that I was wearing my new knickers instead of those ugly drawers. "Knickers" – that's what they call them here. They come all the way from Paris.

Prince Argan had them made to his design. Our dresses, too. Did you get some?'

'Never mind about my underwear. Go on. You'd just taken your dress off . . .'

'He kissed my breasts, one at a time, then he took one of my nipples in his mouth and sucked it.' Absent-mindedly, her hands strayed to her breasts and she scraped her thumbs across her nipples. 'He hugged me again and I told him his medals were cold, so he took off his jacket. Then he took off everything else too. Oh, Nerina! He was so beautiful to look at that I nearly fainted again. His penis was so long and thick! He picked me up in his arms and carried me to the bed just in time, before I fell down. I lay on my back, but I kept my legs closed. To tell you the truth, I was so wet that I was afraid the stain would show if I opened them.'

'What do you mean, you were wet?'

'Down there. Between my legs. You know . . . No, of course you don't.'

That was not entirely true. As she had listened to Leah's account, Nerina had herself become aware of a certain moistness in that place.

'Michael solved the problem, though. He pulled my knickers down and took them off. He didn't rip at them impatiently, as some men do. He took his time and it was lovely to feel that silk sliding down my legs. I opened my legs very wide for him and held out my arms, but he didn't come to me right away. He sat down beside me and kissed my special place.' Leah's hand was pressed into her lap, moving a little.

Nerina was appalled. 'You can't mean that he . . . that he kissed you there! He put his mouth in that place?'

'Surely! It was lovely. Not enough men do that. Only the ones who care about their lover's pleasure

53

just as much as they care about their own. He knew exactly how to do it, too. I peaked almost at once.'

'I don't understand what you mean.'

'I know you don't. You won't until you've felt it yourself. That was just the first of many. When he came into me, it was perfect. Nice and slow at first, then faster and faster. Such a master! Such a superb lover! I peaked again and again. And when he came, his sperm was so hot inside me and made me feel so good that I . . . Oh, Nerina! I can't tell you any more. I'm getting too worked up, just thinking about it. I love him; that's all. If I didn't see him again, I think I should die.'

Nerina was not unhappy that Leah would tell her no more. She had found herself so strangely moved by the recitation that she felt obliged to move about in her chair in an attempt to alleviate a certain warm unease, a discomfort that was not a discomfort and was located in no particular place.

'How can you say you love him?' she demanded. 'You have known him for such a short time.'

'I loved him the instant I first saw him,' Leah replied. 'For some people, it happens like that. It was meant to be.'

Nerina thought about this for a few moments. 'Tell me, friend, Leah,' she said. 'Do you know what Prince Argan intends for me?'

'Rumour says that he wants to put you back on the throne of Isingore.'

'He does. But do you know the price I have to pay?'

'No.'

'I have to learn about things such as you have just told me. Experience them myself, I mean.'

Leah sniffed. 'If you were a proper woman, you would have learnt that long ago. I'm sorry, Highness.

I intended no offence,' she continued, seeing the look on Nerina's face.

'You think I should, then? Alcina has offered to teach me.'

'I would, but I am not you. Still, unless your body is defective in some way, you will enjoy it.'

'Do you think so? Perhaps there is something the matter with me. Perhaps I am not as others are.'

'There's only one way to find out.'

'I suppose so. There is more though. Prince Argan expects to have his way with me. To take my virginity.'

Leah was shrewdly practical. 'A small enough price for a throne, perhaps. It's going to happen some time. Why not with Prince Argan?'

'Because I would hate it. He must be old and fat if he has to obtain a virgin in that way.'

'You don't know that, do you? He might be as nice as Michael.'

Nerina did not say so, for fear of offending Leah's sensibilities regarding her lover, but privately thought that having to surrender herself to someone as insufferably patronising as the count would be an ordeal she could not stomach. All the same, what Leah had described to her had given her a great deal to think about during the time she was alone in her room, which was often. It was not many days before she found that regimen intensely boring. She spent long hours staring out of the window, particularly when the other inhabitants of the house were at play. She found herself longing to be able to join that happy band. Not, she hastily told herself, because she had any interest in joining in their sexual antics, but just for the laughter and the company.

Alcina visited her every day, which relieved the boredom a little. At each visit, she expounded a little more on the subject of Paradon's way of handling affairs of state. Nerina could not make up her mind quite how she felt about Alcina. She was still wary of her, mindful of her first lesson in the perils of haughtiness. Nevertheless, it was difficult not to begin to like this mature woman, who showed every sign of being willing to devote time and trouble to Nerina's education.

One day, as they were sitting by the window, Nerina said, 'You told me yesterday that Prince Argan was not a ruler in the sense in which I would understand that word. Surely, as Prince of Paradon, he must be?'

Alcina nodded. 'He is the prince, of course, but the people rule themselves.'

'How can they do that?'

'Very easily. Each town and village elects one of their number every year to be a deputy to the council. It is the deputy's task to know everything about his own community and the people in it, therefore he has to be well-respected and trusted by all. For example, Joseph, the innkeeper at Selfingendorf, whom you have met, has been their deputy for many years. The council meets once a month and the deputies have the chance to bring to attention any problems. If the solution to the problem is to enact a law, then the council has the power to do so.'

'The deputies must be well-paid.'

Alcina looked shocked. 'No! Of course not. It is considered to be an honour to serve the community in this way. To be paid would be intolerable and would lead to competition for the post for the wrong reasons.'

'Then Prince Argan presides over these council meetings?'

'Seldom. He receives reports of their doings, of

course, but he attends only when there is a matter of foreign policy to be discussed. He informs the council of the facts and they decide what to do about them. It was they, not Prince Argan, who decided to respond to the pleas of your people and send the army into Isingore.'

'But there must be tithes. Who pays for your army?'

'Of course there are taxes, but they are decided by the people who pay them. They understand that defence is necessary. We have only a small core of regular soldiers. Almost every able-bodied Paradon man has his own uniform and arms at home. They give up some of their time for training. They do so, partly because they know it minimises their taxes and partly because it is a matter of pride and status in Paradon to be ready to defend it.'

Nerina said, wonderingly, 'And this works?'

'Assuredly. Because each citizen, without exception, supports himself and gives his talent, free of charge, to Paradon when required, taxes can be used for the good of the people – to provide a welfare fund to aid a particular village that is in difficulties for some unavoidable reason, or to help those who have trouble with doctor's bills.'

'So Prince Argan makes no decisions at all?'

'Rarely. It sometimes happens that there is a deadlock and the council cannot agree. Then they ask Prince Argan to adjudicate and he does so. In order for that to be acceptable, he has to be a man who has never been known to lie; a man rich enough in his own right to seek no financial advantage for himself, generous and kind in spirit and wise in the ways of the world.'

'And is Prince Argan all these things?'

'All and more, as you will come to know.'

Nerina was intensely curious about the paragon of virtue thus described. 'When shall I meet him?'

Alcina smiled. 'When you are ready. I have explained why you are not ready, yet.'

'Then at least tell me what he looks like.'

Alcina nodded towards the window. 'See for yourself,' she said. 'The prince came back from his travels last night.'

Nerina jumped up and pressed her face against the window pane. There was the usual crowd in the garden below, but this time there was a new figure among them. Nerina stared at the stranger and her heart missed a beat. He was very tall and slender; his thick, curly hair was so fair as to be almost white. He wore a simple white shirt, open almost to the waist, so that his blonde chest-hair was clearly visible, while his long legs were encased in tight-fitting black trousers and black riding boots. A black sash at his waist completed the outfit. His clothes were certainly not magnificent or opulent, Nerina thought, neither could he be described as handsome in the classical tradition, although his features were regular enough. It was something else, she decided, that was making her gulp with excitement and causing her stomach to feel so peculiar. It was as though he were surrounded by a golden light which shone principally from his head and particularly from his eyes.

She watched him as he made his way through the girls, a feat accomplished only with difficulty as they waylaid him and tried to detain him. Many stretched out their hands in the gesture of sexual offer Nerina had come to understand. When one did, the prince would smile, take her wrist in one hand and use the other gently to close her palm into a fist before stroking her cheek, kissing her lightly on the forehead, or making some other contact which would indicate his approval and affection.

Nerina found herself a little out of breath, as though through climbing stairs rapidly. Without her knowledge, her own hand reached out, palm upwards and thumb extended.

Alcina noticed the gesture and, copying the prince, took Nerina's open hand and closed it into a fist, saying, 'Not yet. You are not ready.'

Nerina started guiltily, blushing. 'No! I wasn't thinking . . . I mean, I wasn't . . .'

Alcina smiled knowingly, her eyes softer than Nerina had ever seen them. 'Don't be ashamed. My Prince has that effect on most women.' She reached out and stroked Nerina's heated cheek. 'I have experienced it myself so many times, yet it does not dim with repetition. I would lay down my life for the opportunity you have to be alone and private with him.'

Nerina gulped. 'But before that can happen, I must learn what you can teach me?'

'Indeed you must.'

'I am ready. Teach me.'

Alcina laughed aloud, then rapidly collected herself. 'I'm sorry, Nerina. I wasn't really laughing at you, but with pleasure at the way you reacted to seeing the prince. However, I won't begin your lessons today.'

Nerina's disappointment was evident. 'Oh? Why not?'

'It would not be fair, so soon after such an experience. It must be rather like being struck by lightning. I want you to arrive at the decision in a more settled frame of mind. I will come to you again tomorrow. If you still feel the same way, we can begin then.'

That night, Nerina hardly slept at all. Her mind was in a ferment. It was hard to decide whether she felt eager anticipation or dread at what the morrow might bring. She tossed and turned, her head filled with an assortment of erotic fantasies. Soaring above them all was the golden halo of Prince Argan. Cost what it may, she had to go through whatever training was necessary to enable her to meet him.

Finally, towards dawn, she fell asleep and in consequence was still asleep when Alcina came to her. She roused her by shaking her shoulder gently. Nerina started up in bed, her hair tousled. 'What? What is it?'

'It's all right,' Alcina soothed. 'You merely slept a little late. Have you thought about our conversation yesterday?'

Nerina had thought of little else. 'Oh yes!'

'And have you changed your mind?'

'Oh no! I am a little afraid, though.'

'Don't be. Nothing will happen without your full consent and approval.'

Nerina hesitated. 'That was only part of my concern. I am afraid that there is something the matter with me. That I am somehow different from other women so that I will never understand what they find so pleasurable.'

'I'm quite sure that is not the case,' Alcina said.

Somewhat reassured, Nerina made haste to get out of bed, wash and dress. 'How do we begin,' she asked.

'Very gently and very simply. First we will bathe together. Come with me.'

She took Nerina out of the room and down the stairs. In the back part of the house, she opened a door and they went in. Nerina found herself in a large, tiled room which appeared to be a communal bathing place, to judge by the warm, steamy atmosphere and the raised, tiled plinths covered with towels.

She was intensely embarrassed to see that there were two other women in the room and that they were completely naked. Gerda was the only woman, apart from herself, that she had ever seen naked and she found it hard to resist staring at their bodies. They were very young, hardly older than herself, and they were both very beautiful. One was fair and the other dark. The blonde had small pink nipples and very sparse, golden pubic hair; not much more than a few curls which did nothing to conceal the division of her sex. The brunette's nipples were longer and brown, while her pubic hair was a regular forest at her crotch. Nerina found herself wondering whether those characteristics were typical of persons with that particular hair colour, or whether they were random.

'This is Helga,' Alcina said, indicating the blonde. 'And this is Mai.' Both girls smiled and nodded. 'They will help us to undress.'

'I have to take my clothes off while they are here?'

Alcina took Nerina's hand and squeezed it encouragingly. 'Don't be afraid or ashamed. This is their work and they are well used to seeing bare bodies. I will let them undress me first while you watch, then you will see that there is nothing to it.'

The two girls came to Alcina and unfastened the belt at her waist. She raised her arms and they lifted her dress off over her head. Her breasts, when they came in view, were quite splendid, Nerina thought. Large and firm, they stood out from her body in what was almost an aggressive manner, their tips adorned with very dark, very long nipples which were already fully erect. Her perfect skin had a silky quality and a slightly olive tint. She kicked off her slippers and Mai knelt to pull down her knickers and help her to step out of them. Completely nude, she turned to face Nerina squarely, spreading her arms widely away

61

from her body so that they concealed nothing. The lower half of her mature body was as perfect as the upper part. Strong, tanned, tapering thighs led down past delightfully dimpled knees to slender ankles and delicate toes. Her pubic hair was as black as that on her head, yet subtly different from that of either of the other girls. Dense lower down, it rose in a distinct line up her stomach, from which lateral curls extended as though they were branches of a small tree. The general effect was most becoming, Nerina thought. As she stared, Alcina rotated, her arms still spread, so as to afford a view of her back and buttocks.

'Now you,' she said.

Nerina tensed and shivered a little as the girls came to her. Now her trepidation at the prospect of being undressed was mingled with a certain unease because of her suspicion that her own body would not compare favourably with the magnificent specimens in whose company she found herself. She felt her belt being loosened and raised her arms as Alcina had done to facilitate the removal of her dress. She kicked off her slippers and, almost simultaneously, felt the soft stroking of silk against her skin as her knickers were drawn down over her buttocks and thighs. She raised her feet mechanically, one after another, as in a dream. She was naked! Automatically, she hung her head and hunched a little, shielding herself with her hands.

'No, no,' Alcina chided. 'You have nothing to be ashamed of. You are beautiful. Stand tall and proud so that all may admire God's handiwork. That's right! Chin up. Shoulders back. Better – much better!' She took Nerina's hand. 'Don't be afraid. They are just going to wash us, that's all.'

She indicated two wooden stools. 'Sit there and I

will sit opposite you. Now relax and just let the girls do their work.'

Nerina jumped as she felt a touch on her back, but relaxed as she realised that it was only a wash-cloth. Plied by Helga, it travelled to and fro and up and down, spreading soapy lather over her skin. It was pleasantly warm. She had not been washed in this way since her beloved Dorcas had done it for her when she was a little girl. The pleasant memories that thought evoked helped her to forget any embarrassment so that even when the wash-cloth moved from the back of her body to the front and passed across her breasts she did not flinch. Looking across at Alcina, she saw that Mai was doing the same thing to her. The creamy lather clung to her body in a way which made it even more attractive, if that were possible.

Helga said, 'You have to raise yourself on your hands a little and open your legs so that I can wash your underneath parts.'

'Can't I do that?' Nerina enquired, a little nervously. Catching Alcina's eye, she observed her shaking her head in sad disapproval. 'I'm sorry,' she said and raised herself as instructed.

Being washed in such intimate places was difficult, but there was nothing remotely suggestive or sexual in the way in which Helga went about the task. That was very calming and Nerina submitted to her ministrations with good grace. Having her face and ears washed was actually rather amusing and tickled a little so that she was smiling by the time the lathering was completed.

'Keep your eyes closed,' Alcina ordered.

Nerina did so and gasped a little as a pail of warm scented water was poured over her head. She wiped her face with her hands in time to see that Alcina was receiving exactly the same treatment. That the ordeal she had feared so much was over and that it had been such a pleasant experience made Nerina smile across at Alcina and open her mouth to say as much.

'Ugh!' Taken unawares, a second bucket of water caught her in mid-grin and some went in her mouth. She spluttered, spat it out and laughed aloud. Thus warned, she paid more attention to what Helga was doing and did not open her mouth again until she was certain that all the lather was washed away and there were no more pails to come.

As Helga wrapped her in a large towel and began to pat her dry, Nerina was surprised to find herself saying, 'Thank you.' She could not recall having spontaneously thanked a servant before.

Alcina said, 'That, at least, should answer one of your questions.'

'What do you mean?'

'Open your towel and look at your breasts. You may have doubts about your body, but it has none about itself. Your nipples have reacted to the treatment they have received, just as the rest of your body will dance to nature's tune when it is played in the right key.'

Nerina stared down at herself, noting the firm outline of her brown teats as they protruded from the equally brown aureolae, then, recalling her modesty, drew the towel closed again.

'Now we have a massage,' Alcina said as Mai removed her towel. Helga took away Nerina's, too, and all four moved towards two plinths which were side by side.

'I've never had a massage before,' Nerina said. 'Is it nice?'

'Delightful. You'll enjoy it. Lie down like this.' Alcina got on to one plinth and lay down on the towel, face down, resting her head on her arms. Nerina copied her exactly, turning her head so that she could see what was going on next door. She saw Mai take a small glass phial and empty something into her hand before smoothing it onto Alcina's long back.

'What's that?'

'Aromatic oil. Mm. Very soothing.'

Nerina jumped a little as she felt Helga doing the same thing to her own back, then she was lost in the stimulating sensation of having her back rubbed. Up and down went Helga's skilled hands, expertly soothing and moulding muscles Nerina had not known she had. It was wonderful. Something quite alien was happening to her body and she struggled to identify it. She felt sleepy and happy, but at the same time there was a strange unease, rather like that which she had first felt when Leah had described her encounter with Michael. Mingled with it was a kind of tense expectancy. She wondered, idly, if she would have to turn over so that the front part of her could be reached, then flushed guiltily as she realised that her sense of expectancy stemmed from that. She was actually looking forward to the sensation of oily hands passing across her breasts and belly, perhaps even . . . No, no! She turned her mind quickly away from that sinful thought.

When she saw Alcina raise herself on her elbow, then roll on to her back with her hands under her head, Nerina's stomach lurched in a strange way before she did the same and lay there, trembling slightly in anticipation. She was vaguely disappointed when Helga massaged her feet and legs, then her neck and shoulders. She glanced sharply at the girl, but could see no sign of teasing on her face; just a serious concentration on her work. Looking across at Alcina, she could see that her body was being dealt with by Mai in exactly the same fashion, so she closed her eyes and relaxed, vaguely disappointed.

At the first pass of Helga's hands across her nipples, she opened her eyes wide and gasped aloud. Although she suppressed it at once she saw that Alcina had noticed the sound and was staring intently at her. Ashamed, she tried to pretend indifference to the massage and managed to restrain further sounds, even when Helga's fingers explored her navel and came close to her pubic region.

When all the oil had been rubbed in, so that her skin was soft and dry, the treatment came to an end. Alcina got up from her plinth and indicated that Nerina should do the same. Helga and Mai helped them to dress, then Alcina thanked them and led the way back to Nerina's bedroom.

She did not speak until they were safely inside, then she said, 'There! What did you think of your first lesson?'

'Lesson?' Nerina was puzzled. 'But I learnt nothing.'

'On the contrary, you learnt how to be naked, yet unashamed, in the presence of others, equally naked. You learnt how pleasurable close physical contact with another human being can be. You learned that your body responds to certain stimuli.'

'Oh yes, those things. But I thought the lessons were to be about sex.'

'Are you so certain, then, that thoughts of a carnal nature never entered your mind?'

Nerina coloured slightly, remembering that Alcina had heard and seen her reaction to having her breasts massaged. 'Perhaps,' she admitted, grudgingly.

'Then that is a start. Tomorrow we will bathe together again. Then every day after that until I feel you are ready to advance a little. Today you took from Helga. You can have no idea of the pleasure she derived from giving to you. Later on, you will give as well as take, so learning how to double your enjoyment.'

Four

'Routine' was too harsh a word to use for an experience as delightful as the daily washing and massage
ritual, yet Nerina was sorely tempted. At every visit
to the bath-house, she hoped that this would be the
occasion on which some further knowledge would be
imparted, but each time she knew disappointment. So
used to it had she become that when the pattern
finally did change, it took her by surprise, as Alcina
intended that it should.

They had completed the usual ceremony and risen
from their plinths. Normally, they would have been
assisted to dress at that point but Alcina laid a
detaining hand on Nerina's arm.

'Wait,' she said. 'This is the day we move on a
stage.'

Nerina found her heart thudding and her voice
revealingly shaky. 'Oh?'

'Yes. Come over here and let us sit on our stools
again.' Alcina drew the low wooden supports so close
together that, when they sat facing one another, their
knees were almost touching.

'First, we will touch one another with our eyes,'
Alcina said. 'I have watched you taking sly peeks at
my body and at Helga and Mai. It's all right,' she
hastened to add, as Nerina showed signs of embarrassment. 'Such curiosity is perfectly natural and

healthy. Now you shall satisfy it by staring openly at me, while I feast my eyes on you.'

Alcina parted her knees and put her hands at her sides, resting on the stool so that they concealed nothing. Desperately shy, Nerina clamped her thighs together and looked everywhere but at her companion.

'Come now. That won't do at all,' Alcina said in reproof. 'You must look at me.' More gently, she went on, 'I give you permission. I would like you to look. Am I so ugly that you do not care to?'

'No! Of course not.' Nerina forced herself to gaze at Alcina's body, keeping her eyes strictly to the area above her waist.

Alcina noticed this self-imposed restriction and smiled slightly. She parted her legs even more until her pink labia were clearly visible in their nest of black hair. 'Look everywhere!' she insisted.

Nerina obeyed and found herself blushing hotly. At the same time, the now familiar feeling of expectant unease surged through her stomach.

'Now you,' Alcina commanded. 'It's only fair. Put your hands down on the stool. That's right. Now spread your legs as I have spread mine. Can you feel my eyes on you?'

Nerina nodded, unable to speak. It was true. Alcina's stare was like a thousand tiny fingers crawling over her skin, invading her breasts, her nipples, her stomach and, most especially, her private place between her legs which now seemed to become the centre for all she was feeling.

'Look into my eyes. Now touch me. Go on. Reach out and feel my breasts. That's right. Don't they feel good? Lift the weight of them. See how your touch makes my nipples stiff. Touch them, too. Feel how springy they are. Now I am going to touch yours. Keep looking into my eyes. Don't be afraid.'

Nerina drew in her breath sharply as she felt, rather than saw, Alcina's hands on her body. Part of her wanted to break off all contact, to withdraw from the path she saw opening before her, but she was held by those eyes, quite unable to do other than obey. It was the very first time anyone, man or woman had ever touched her body with clear sexual intent and it was a deeply moving experience for her. She shuddered as the full impact of Alcina's questing fingers on her nipples became apparent. For some reason, Leah's description of the way Count Michael had sucked on her nipples came into her mind and excited her, so that her knees began to tremble violently, her bare heels drumming on the tiled floor with the force of her shaking.

It was with mingled relief and disappointment that she felt Alcina's stroking stop and she was able to drop her own hands and look away from those eyes.

'Good,' Alcina said. 'You responded well and we can move on a little further. By that, I mean that we are ready to go to areas below the waist. Before we do that, it is important to understand precisely what you are dealing with. So many women know their own bodies only imperfectly and, as a result of that ignorance, neither obtain the maximum pleasure possible for themselves nor give as much as they could to others.' Alcina got up and extended a hand in invitation to Nerina, who rose also.

'Helga will help us,' Alcina said.

The fair-haired girl walked over to a vacant plinth and climbed nimbly on to it, lying down on her back with her hands under her head. She raised her knees and parted them, exposing her sex, then waited, smiling a little.

Alcina took Nerina over to stand beside the plinth, positioning her so that she had a perfect view of

Helga's crotch. 'I'm sorry that this has to be a little clinical,' she said. 'It will be less so when we start to put what you learn now into practice.'

Touching lightly with her hands here and there, she illustrated her lecture. 'Here we have the pubes, the *mons veneris* or Mound of Venus with its covering of hair; in this case very fair and small in quantity. Lower, and it becomes the vulva, the fleshy area around her sex, part of which is the outer labia, the fleshy lumps guarding either side of her division.' She placed her thumbs on each side of Helga's slit and pressed on them causing the pink slot to blossom like a flower. Helga stirred a little and Alcina shot her a quick smile.

'See within,' Alcina said. 'The outer labia were there to guard these secrets. Here are the inner labia, those narrow, crinkly lips.' She pulled those apart as well and Helga's buttocks tensed, raising her body a little way off the plinth. Alcina put her right forefinger gently between the parted lips and rubbed it up and down, then showed the finger to Nerina. 'See nature's lubrication gleaming. Helga is a young woman and easily aroused. Just the act of touching her in this way is sufficient to cause her to let down her healthy juices which alone make penetration pleasant and comfortable. For an older woman, it sometimes takes longer and something more stimulating. In this case, I know that I can penetrate her vagina, the canal leading up to her womb, without difficulty.'

Slowly and gently, Alcina pushed her forefinger into Helga until it disappeared up to the knuckle. Helga drew a sharp, hissing breath and her head moved rapidly from side to side. 'That creates a most pleasing sensation, particularly when I rub my finger against the underside of her pelvic bone, here. Isn't that right, Helga?' Helga nodded, her eyes closed and a rapturous expression on her face.

Alcina withdrew her finger again and looked at Nerina. 'What I have just done to Helga you must not allow anyone to do to you until your tryst with Prince Argan. You must not do it to yourself, however much you may be tempted in the near future. That is because you are a virgin and Helga is not. Only a little way inside your vagina is your hymen or maidenhead, a barrier made of stretched skin. Once break it and you lose your virgin status. Such a little thing, but kingdoms have been lost because of it.'

'But I have left the last and greatest treasure to the end,' she said. 'It lies buried here, right at the top part of her division, just above the inner labia and sometimes so well concealed by the outer labia being closed over it that the clumsy, the inexperienced and the over-eager fail to notice it, thereby depriving themselves of the joy of giving intense pleasure to the possessor of it. It is called the clitoris. See how, even when those fleshy lips are parted, it is still concealed beneath its own little hood of skin. Rubbing gently on that hood is sufficient to induce most enjoyable sensations.' She suited action to words, rubbing her forefinger in little circles on the place indicated. Helga moaned, her knees trembled and her hands opened and closed in grasping movements.

'As I rub, it grows harder and longer, just as does a man's penis. Now, when I retract the hood, you can see the little pointed scrap of pink flesh which is the true source of female rapture. In this exposed state, I need only touch it very gently, like this, to magnify all Helga has been feeling.' In witness of that fact, Helga's moans became louder and her head strained backwards so that her upper body was raised from the plinth, a movement reminiscent of those Nerina

72

had seen Gerda making when in the throes of coupling with Luther.

Alcina stepped back, her lecture complete. 'Now we can go back to your room for the next part,' she said. 'I must ask you to dress yourself. Helga and Mai will be otherwise occupied. It would be most unfair,' she added, 'if, having aroused Helga to such an extent, we left her in an unsatisfied state. Mai knows what to do about that.'

They dressed quickly, Nerina trying hard not to look at what was now going on between the two young women. She was very conscious of the fact that her own vagina had been lubricating for some time now and hoped, as had Leah, that this fact would not be betrayed by a damp patch on her flimsy knickers by the time they reached her room.

When they got to their destination, Nerina found herself shivering as though in the grip of some fever. There was now no doubt in her mind that she had been sexually aroused by all that had gone before. The odd, uneasy feeling inside her was stronger than it had ever been. At the same time, she was embarrassed and afraid of what was shortly to come. When Alcina followed her into her room and closed the door behind them, Nerina stood rooted to the spot, her knees almost knocking together despite her efforts to control them.

Alcina both saw and sensed her perturbation. She came to her and enfolded her in her arms, holding her as one holds a child, rocking her a little, stroking her back and making little crooning noises. 'There, there,' she said. 'There is nothing to be afraid of. Do you trust me?'

Nerina thought hard about this question before answering it and found that the answer was, on balance, in the affirmative. Although there was a tiny corner of her mind that still remembered the occasion on which she had been forcibly stripped by this woman, all that had happened since then had served to overlay that with a warm quilt of trust engendered by the care and concern she had been shown.

She nodded. 'I think I do.'

'Then there can be nothing to fear. Come, let's just get undressed and go to bed together.'

As in a dream, Nerina allowed Alcina to loosen her belt and draw off her dress over her head. She kicked off her slippers but Alcina made no attempt to remove her knickers, which relieved her a little. She stood impassively while Alcina removed her own dress. She, too, left her knickers on. Alcina pulled back the covers on the bed and held out her hand invitingly. 'Come,' she said.

Nerina climbed into the soft bed and lay down on her back. Alcina got in on her right side and pulled the covers up to their chins. 'There,' she said. 'All cosy. Isn't that nice?'

Nerina nodded again, unspeakably relieved that her semi-nudity was thus concealed.

'Now I'm going to touch you a little, just as I did before,' Alcina said. She reached across with her right hand and laid it on Nerina's left breast, her palm encompassing the nipple. Very softly and slowly, with the lightest of touches, she moved her hand in a small circle so that her soft skin dragged across Nerina's nipple. Nerina stirred, arching her back in an involuntary attempt to increase the pressure of that touch, but Alcina moved with her, maintaining a constant pressure.

'That feels so good,' Nerina murmured. 'Why does it feel so good?'

Alcina smiled down at her fondly. 'Because nature decreed it so. Your body was designed to give pleas-

74

ure, as well as receive it. To allow an infant to suckle at your breast gives that baby the greatest possible pleasure. In return for that, you are rewarded. This is what it feels like.' She raised herself on one elbow and pulled back the covers, exposing Nerina's breasts so that she could take her left nipple into her mouth, sucking hard and nibbling a little.

Nerina gave a great jump. 'Oh! Oh! What are you doing?'

Alcina took her mouth away. 'Exciting you,' she said. 'Making you want to be touched between the legs. Making you very wet down there.'

That was true. Nerina could feel the liquid leaking out of her. There could now be no doubt about the dampness of her knickers. Strangely, she found that she did not care. What Alcina was doing, and had done, to her breasts overwhelmed her with a want she could feel and yet not clearly identify: a longing for something as yet unknown. When she felt Alcina's right hand leave her breast and travel down the length of her body, it seemed a very right and natural thing to be happening. One finger paused at her navel, dipping a little into its hollow and she squirmed as she felt the muscles of her abdomen crawling and twitching in response. The hand went further, plucking at the waistband of her knickers and she waited in tense expectancy for the culmination of that move. When she felt it slide between the silk and her flesh, she cried out, threw back the covers and rolled herself towards Alcina, hugging and kissing her. 'Take them off,' she said in a hoarse whisper. 'Strip me! Make me naked, please!'

Alcina disengaged herself and pushed against Nerina's shoulders until she was again lying on her back. Kneeling up, she turned towards Nerina's lower half and inserted her thumbs into either side of the waistband of the knickers, urging them downwards. Staring at the bare back thus presented to her, Nerina was overcome by a sudden urge to see more. She reached out with her right hand and hooked her fingers into the waist of Alcina's knickers, yanking them down and exposing her beautiful buttocks.

Alcina turned and smiled at her. 'So!' she said and, with a swift rip, tore Nerina's knickers down to her knees, then pulled hard on them so that her knees came up in the air and her undergarment could be easily removed. Quite naked now, Nerina deliberately splayed her legs a little and watched as Alcina removed her own knickers before resuming her position beside her.

The touch of Alcina's hand in her pubic hair was now a blessing, rather than a threat and Nerina stretched her body like a stroked cat, rejoicing in the sensation. A questing finger sought and found the division of her sex and rubbed up and down in the soaking wet aperture between the crinkled lips of her inner labia.

Nerina groaned with joy. 'Oh, Alcina,' she gasped. 'That is such a wonderful feeling. I understand what you meant. There can be no greater joy.'

Alcina smiled at her innocence. 'Yes there can, my dear,' she said.

Nerina felt the finger slide upwards, still maintaining the separation of the lips. When it touched her clitoris, rubbing in gentle circles, she gave a great cry of rapture, her hips bumping and circling, almost of their own volition. 'Yes! Oh yes!' she gasped. 'Oh Alcina, what are you doing to me?'

'I am masturbating you,' Alcina said, calmly.

Nerina was panting now. 'Wonderful! Gorgeous! Please don't stop!'

'I won't.'

Nerina explored the sensations she was experiencing. It was like nothing she had ever felt before as though her veins were filled with warm treacle, instead of blood. She felt sleepy and happy, yet at the same time, her brain was razor-sharp, eager to miss no part of every touch and caress of Alcina's fingers. She felt a light perspiration break out over the whole of her body, cooling it and increasing the ability of every nerve ending to receive stimulation. When Alcina bent her head and again took her nipple into her mouth, her panting became a series of grunts.

Quite suddenly it seemed that the delightful sensation took on a more threatening aspect. Directly ahead of her appeared to loom a high and fearful precipice over which, unless she drew back, she must plunge. She pushed ineffectually at Alcina's shoulders. 'Stop! Please stop!' she cried. 'I can't stand any more!'

Alcina took not the slightest notice and now the pleasure became like a pain, sharp and with a wave-like motion that coursed up and down throughout her whole body, particularly in her stomach, causing the muscles there to ripple in time with it, sucking the flesh into great hollows. 'No more!' she screamed 'No more! I can't stand it! I can't ... Oh God! What's happening to me?' The pain exploded and fragmented into a firework display of unbearable tension which stiffened her whole body so that it rose from the bed, supported only by her head and heels. She ground her teeth and tried to hold out against it for as long as she could, but the end was inevitable. The wave of passion crested, broke and rolled over her, submerging and subordinating all thought into one huge sea of joy.

She flopped, her muscles liquefying and allowing her limbs to spread like softest butter on to the bed.

'Oh! Oh!' she gasped, trying to recover her breath. 'What was it? What happened?'

Alcina's movements slowed and stopped. 'It was a climax; a peak; an orgasm,' she said. 'Your reward for the pleasure you gave me in allowing me free access to your body. Remember that always. In the very act of giving, there is receiving. What we have done today should convince you that your body is just as normal as anyone else's and that you are capable of experiencing the joys of sex I, and others, can offer you. This first climax was very special and I consider it a privilege to have been here to give it to you and to see it. There will be others. As you grow in experience, they will become better and better, more intense and pleasurable, but this one will always remain in your mind, because it was the first.'

Nerina found it hard to believe that she could experience anything more intense than the orgasm she had just had, but subsequent events proved that to be the case. They no longer needed to go to the bath-house, but Alcina came to her every day and masturbated her to new heights of ecstasy each time until she came to long impatiently for such visits. After a while, even they ceased to be adequate to satisfy her new-found lust and she experimented with her own body, finding that she could induce orgasm herself by manipulating her clitoris with her fingers. This was very pleasant, but was somehow less satisfying than when Alcina did it. As she was quite certain that she could exactly duplicate what Alcina did, she concluded that there was an element to sexual gratification which increased the degree of pleasure if there was another person with whom to share it.

It came as something of a surprise to Nerina when, one day, instead of commencing their sex session in the usual way, Alcina said, 'I think you are ready to move on. It is time for the next stage.'

Nerina was puzzled. 'I don't understand. How can there be more than I have already felt?'

Alcina laughed. 'My dear little innocent. We have not even begun to scratch the surface.' She went to the door and opened it. Two young men came in carrying a large, wooden chest between them. Alcina directed them to put it down against one wall and they did so before leaving.

Nerina's curiosity was piqued. 'What's in there?'

Alcina knelt down in front of the chest and took a small key from the pocket of her dress. 'All the equipment necessary to introduce you to the joys of bondage,' she said. She opened the lid and Nerina, peering over her shoulder, gasped. The chest appeared to be filled almost to the brim with items of restraint, mostly made of leather. Near the top she could see cuffs and chains, ropes and straps. Also, more ominously, there were several canes of varying length and thickness, as well as a whip.

Nerina was filled with doubt. 'Do you plan to use those things on me? I don't think I like that idea.'

Alcina found what she was looking for and closed the lid of the trunk. She rose and faced Nerina, holding in her hands a length of broad red ribbon. 'This is all I will use to start with,' she said. 'The act will be symbolic, rather than anything else.' Nerina still looked doubtful, so she went on, 'Part of your training is to enable you to place yourself in the position of an underling; someone you hold in your power. Can you really say, now, that you fully understand how it feels to be totally dependent on someone else for everything, for food and gratification, for life itself?'

Nerina shook her head. 'No, I can't truthfully say that.'

'This exercise will help you to some small part of

79

that understanding. Only by placing yourself in a subservient role can you know what subservience truly means. Remember the rule of equal and opposite reactions. To give is to receive. Give your submission to me and I promise you that all you feel will be enhanced and improved.'

Nerina considered this. There was still a part of her that was doubtful, but she could also identify, deep within herself, an eager curiosity to see whether what Alcina claimed was true. She was already so addicted to the joy of orgasm that the slightest suggestion that this joy could be amplified in some way was sufficient to induce her to take a chance. Besides, apart from her first bad experience with Alcina, she had never received anything from her but the greatest consideration and a lot of pleasure. 'Very well,' she said. 'What must I do?'

'Very little. Just take off your dress and I will do the rest. Good. Now put out your hands with wrists together.' Alcina wound the red ribbon loosely round and round Nerina's wrists before tying it in a bow. 'For this first trial, I have tied you in this way quite deliberately. You can see that you could easily twist your hands out of the ribbon. If you found they got stuck for some reason, you could easily pull the bow with your teeth and get free that way. This points out to you very clearly that your bondage is completely voluntary. If you choose to remain in it, that will be because of your wish to please me and because your body tells you that it is a pleasurable thing. Pull against the ribbon. Try to force your hands apart. Do you feel anything?'

Nerina tugged at the slight constriction around her wrists. 'Yes,' she said. 'A strange feeling of helplessness.'

'Nice or nasty?'

'Nice, I think. I'm not sure.'

'I'm going to increase that feeling. I'm going to pull your knickers down and leave you naked.' She advanced on Nerina, holding her eyes with her own. Stooping, she pulled the silky knickers down to her knees, then left them there while she walked around her captive, staring at her.

The suddenness of the movement startled Nerina, but the jump she gave was only partly for that reason. She found herself sexually stirred by the situation in which she found herself. The fact that her knickers had not been taken completely off was, somehow, more humiliating and revealing than total nudity. She felt Alcina's eyes on her and squirmed uneasily, testing the security of her fastening.

'Stand still, slave!' Alcina commanded. 'Your body now belongs to me and not to you. I will do with it exactly as I wish.' She came close to Nerina, standing to her right. 'Do you wish to experience the bliss of orgasm?'

Nerina was quite certain about that. For some time now, she had been lubricating furiously and could feel the slippery fluid leaking from her. 'Please! Oh please!'

'I may choose to give you that and I may not,' Alcina said lightly. 'If you were polite, called me "Mistress" and acknowledged your subservience, I might be tempted.'

'Of course, Mistress! I am your slave! Please, though, please do it to me. I need it so badly!'

'Very well. Open your legs!'

Nerina blinked. 'Here? Standing up? I have never done it standing up.'

'You have never been a slave before. You will do it where I say you will do it, slave. And, if you fail to please me completely, I will spank your bare bottom for you. Now open your legs at once!'

Nerina found these words deeply moving, so that her stomach churned with emotion. Her erect nipples were tingling in a way she had never felt before. She set her legs apart and waited, breathing heavily. The touch of Alcina's finger on her clitoris was wildly stimulating and her hips began to move in a circular motion in time with the persistent rubbing.

'Keep still, slave!'

'I can't! I can't.'

'Then I must spank you.'

Hearing those sinful words again drove Nerina several notches up the scale of need. 'Yes! Oh yes!' she hissed, almost at her peak. When Alcina patted her bottom very lightly with her left hand, she was strangely disappointed. 'More!' she screamed. 'Spank me! Harder! Oh God! I'm coming! Agh!' She tugged furiously at the ribbon to reassure herself of its security before relaxing, her knees trembling with the effort of remaining upright.

Alcina put her arm around her waist to support her and kissed her cheek while she pulled at the bow to release her hands. 'What did you think of that?' she enquired.

'Incredible! It was so strong. I thought it would devour me.' Nerina panted, still trying to get her breath back.

'I told you, didn't I? To give is to receive.'

'You keep saying that, yet you have never allowed me to give to you.'

'The offer of your body is gift enough.'

'But I mean really give. To induce in your body those pleasures you cause in mine.'

To her surprise, Alcina drew her towards her and embraced her tenderly. 'I have waited for this moment,' she said. 'It is something I could not teach you. It had to come from your inner self. The desire

82

to give. I could have trained you to pleasure me, but I could not implant in you the seed which has matured today. There can be no true generosity of spirit in everyday things or in sex, without that heartfelt and genuine desire.'

'I have such a wish in my heart,' Nerina said. 'I feel it very strongly. How can I please you best?'

'Perhaps by allowing me to show you that stringent bondage is nothing to be afraid of, but most enjoyable. I can best do that by letting you play the part of my captor and mistress. Are you ready for that, yet?'

'I don't know,' said Nerina, doubtfully. 'Would you really like that?'

'I'd hardly suggest it if I didn't.'

'I suppose not.' Nerina was still uncertain. 'I wouldn't know how to do it, though.'

'Don't worry. I'll tell you and we'll muddle through. It's bound not to be perfect the first time.' Alcina went over to the chest and took out various items. 'Let's see. Silk scarves would be easier for you to understand, this time.' She rose with her arms full of light, semi-transparent material. 'Take these.' She took off her dress and her slippers. Wearing only her silk knickers, she went to the bed and lay down on it.

She offered her left wrist. 'Put a scarf round that. No, go round about three times, to make a wide band. That way it doesn't cut in. Now tie a knot. A tight one. No, tighter than that. Make me feel it. Now pass it around the bed-post and tie it off, so that my wrist is right near the post. That's right, good and tight. Now come around the other side and do the same with this hand.'

Nerina knotted a scarf around the proffered right wrist and passed it around the other bed-post.

'No, don't tie it off there. Pull really hard. Stretch me out tight. Agh! That's it. Now tie it off.'

'What now?' Nerina's heart was beginning to pound with the strangeness of what she was being asked to do.

'Just give me a minute. I like to feel it.' Alcina took a few deep breaths and bit her lip. Nerina could see, from the tensing of her shoulder and arm muscles, that she was pulling against the scarves, but the only movement possible was a wiggling of her fingers.

Now Alcina was panting slightly and her voice was a little unsteady. 'You'd better take off my knickers before they get too wet. Slowly. Very slowly at first, then suddenly pull them down and off. Agh! Yes!' Alcina grimaced, her lips drawing back from her teeth as her back arched off the bed and her breath was released in a long-drawn-out hiss of satisfaction.

Presently she recovered a little and laughed shakily. 'Exactly right. Now the ankles. A scarf around each, like the wrists. Now pull! Harder! Stretch me wide! Now tie off around the post! Now the other. Pull! Agh! Yes!' Now Alcina could not conceal the tremor in her voice. Her breasts rose and fell, spasmodically, with each panting breath. Nerina was in no better state. The thudding of her heart had increased dramatically. The sight of that beautiful body: bound, naked, helpless and vulnerable, stretched tightly like a great starfish, was madly stimulating. She felt herself lubricating furiously.

Alcina closed her eyes, dreamily. 'Now touch me. Put your hand between my legs and do it to me, the way I showed you.'

'Of course.'

Alcina's eyes shot open. 'No,' she said. 'That's quite wrong. You are the one in charge, remember. You have the power to tantalise and torment. Use it! Throw yourself into the part of heartless teaser. Make your victim beg. She will thank you for it.'

'I think I see what you mean.'

'Just remember that for the future. Now you may touch me.' Alcina closed her eyes again.

Greatly daring, Nerina said, 'No!' The sense of power and control that came to her with that monosyllable was exciting in the extreme. Before she uttered it, she was pretending to be in charge. Afterwards, there was no pretence about it and the fact that Alcina's eyes were open again and staring at her in disbelief fuelled her pleasure in her new-found mastery.

'What?'

'I said, "No!". I'm a fast learner, Alcina. I find I'm enjoying this far too much to rush. Anyway, I don't think you're nearly keen enough, yet. You'll get it when I'm ready, not before.'

'Little vixen,' said Alcina, wonderingly. 'What have I created?'

'Just for that, I think I'll do a little sewing and make you wait even longer. Half an hour? An hour? I might forget about you altogether until it's time for bed.'

'No! You couldn't.'

'I might, mightn't I? There's nothing you could do about it. Just remember that and be more polite, next time. Now, are you sorry for your rudeness, slave?'

'Yes, Mistress.'

'Very, very sorry?'

'Yes! Very, very sorry.'

'All right, I'll forgive you.' Nerina leant forward and clamped her lips around Alcina's stiffly erect right nipple, sucking hard.

Alcina gasped and wriggled as much as her bonds would allow, hissing, between clenched teeth, 'My God, you're good at this.'

'I am, aren't I?' Nerina was amazed at her

new-found power and confidence. 'Let's just see how long your nipples will get if I pull on them really hard.' She took a nipple between the finger and thumb of each hand and slowly extended them, pinching slightly and rolling at the same time.

Alcina went into paroxysms of pleasure. 'Yes! Oh yes! Do that! Just like that!'

Nerina moved her right hand away from the nipple and slid it gently down over the flat, smooth stomach to toy with the stretched navel, running her finger in circles around it and, occasionally, dipping into it as though into the sweetest of honey pots.

Alcina watched her hand, breathing heavily. 'Go on! Lower! Go lower, please! Touch me, please Nerina. I'm going mad.'

Nerina trailed her fingers down across the naked belly and gently tickled the extreme tips of the black curls. 'Here, do you mean?' she asked, innocently.

Alcina did her best to arch up towards the contact, but was prevented by her strained pose. 'Oh God! I can't wait. Do it! Please! Oh please!'

Nerina shifted her position to kneel between the spread legs. The view from there was overwhelming. She thought that she had never seen anything so erotic as the sight of the two great tendons at the top of those straining thighs, pointing the way towards Alcina's gaping sex. Nestling in their cosy bed of hair, the crinkly outer labial lips were parted so that Nerina could see right into her vagina. She observed, with satisfaction, that a bead of moisture was oozing from the lower part of that beautiful slit. Alcina was certainly ready now. Nerina put her forefinger into her mouth and moved it, seductively, in and out, then held it up for inspection.

'Do you think I ought to check you for virginity?'

'Yes! Oh yes! Put it in me. Do it now. Agh!'

Alcina's head thrashed from side to side and she moaned as Nerina inserted the finger and pushed it further.

'Now, where was that place you were talking about?' Nerina experimented. 'Here? Or here?'

'Oooh! Just a bit further . . . A little more . . . Now push upwards against the bone and . . . Uhh! Yes! Yes! Rub it like that!'

'My thumb's near your clitoris. Would you like me to do that at the same time?'

'Oh yes! In little circles, just like that. Oh God, I can't stand it!'

'Would you like me to stop?'

'No! Please no! Don't stop. For the love of God, don't stop. I'm so close. I'm right on the edge. Keep your finger in me and smack me with the other hand!'

'Smack? Where?'

'Right on my sex, over the clitoris. Spank me! Faster! Do it faster! Harder! Keep your finger rubbing. Don't stop. I'm coming. I'm coming!' Alcina's words degenerated into one long, sighing groan and she climaxed, rolling her head from side to side with an expression of agony on her face.

Nerina felt the contractions of the vagina gripping her finger ease off and gradually slowed her massage to coincide with Alcina's descent from the peak. She watched Alcina's face as it relaxed into an expression of deep peace. She lay for a long time, her breathing gradually returning to normal, then opened her eyes and smiled, brightly.

'Amazing! That was far more than I could have hoped for. I sought to teach you something, only to find that you already knew it, except that you were unaware of your knowledge. You can let me up now.'

Nerina released her and she sat up, rubbing at her wrists and ankles which bore the weals left by the scarves. 'I meant what I said. You are really good at that. You have a natural talent.'

Nerina was gratified. 'I wanted to please you, but found that I pleased myself in the process. Are you sure you're not hurt?'

'Oh, you mean these marks. They soon wear off. It's no good for me if it's not tight. You'll see. It'll be your turn soon.'

'Oh no! I don't think so ... You see, I ...'

Alcina smiled and patted her shoulder. 'We'll see when the time comes. We certainly won't rush anything. This has been an excellent learning session for both of us, but there's still more you have to know.'

Five

Alcina's gentle way of introducing her to mild bondage had a strange effect on Nerina. Already addicted to masturbation, the powerful feelings induced by this added stimulation meant that most of her waking thoughts centred around sexual gratification and the means of achieving it. At first hesitant, she became impatient at Alcina's refusal to go forward with new and more stringent methods of restraint. Each morning, on waking, she fantasised about being tightly bound in various positions. Sometimes, in her daydreams, it was Alcina who was her stern mistress, forcing her to orgasm; sometimes it was Prince Argan himself. Always, these phantoms in her mind aroused her to the point where she felt that she would burst if she did not masturbate. Always, this solitary, selfinduced orgasm was vaguely unsatisfactory, leaving her with a fresh hunger.

On the day that Alcina told her that it was time to move on again, she could not conceal her pleasure.

'Will you tie me down, this time?' she asked. 'Will you tie me as tightly as I tied you?'

Alcina shook her head. 'You are not ready for that, yet.'

'Oh, but I am!'

'No. To obtain full benefit of that, you have to learn other things first.'

'What other things?'

'How to deal with a spanking, for instance.'

Nerina tossed her head haughtily. 'Is that all? If you are saying that I have to be spanked before you will tie me, then get on and do it. I can take it.'

Alcina shook her head again. 'You see what I mean. There is still a trace of your old ways left in you. You have not truly learned how to be humble and contrite. As if that were not enough, you regard a spanking as something to be endured. It isn't. Properly taught and properly executed, a spanking can be a most blissful experience.'

'Teach me, then.'

Alcina bit her lip. 'When you adopt that imperious attitude and tone of voice, I am severely tempted to cut short your training period and proceed to a full-blooded slippering which, unprepared as you are, you would not enjoy one bit. I invite you to remember our first meeting, when it was just that sort of thing that brought about dire consequences.'

Nerina remembered the way she had been forcibly stripped. She wanted to do nothing which would encourage that sort of relationship to replace the close one she had established with this woman. 'I beg your pardon, Alcina,' she said. 'Of course it's good of you to take so much trouble with me. I get impatient sometimes. Forgive me.'

'I am pleased to see you showing such good sense. As a reward, I am prepared to go a small part of the way towards what you want. Perhaps today we can abandon the symbolic ribbon and move on to something from which you could not so easily free yourself? Would you like that?'

Nerina's stomach lurched. 'Yes, please!'

Alcina took the small key from her pocket and unlocked the wooden chest. From it, she took a pair of leather cuffs and brought them over to where Nerina was standing. 'See,' she said. 'They are lined with padded silk so as not to hurt your wrists. Take off your dress and I will put them on for you.'

Nerina discarded her dress, leaving her knickers on. Alcina put one of the cuffs around her wrist and fastened it with the buckle, careful not to pull the strap too tight. Nerina shivered, in spite of herself. The feel and weight of the thing was completely different from that of the ribbon. The dark leather added to the menace of the cuff and, for the first time, she had a sense of genuine captivity. She could feel her heartbeat increasing as Alcina buckled the other one about her other wrist.

'Shouldn't they be joined together?' Nerina asked.

'Patience,' Alcina replied and went again to the chest. She came back with a length of stout cord which she passed through a ring on the inside of one cuff, then through a similar ring on the other, leaving the ends dangling on the carpet. She fetched the stool from the dressing table, dragging it into the centre of the room. 'Come over here,' she said.

Nerina came to her obediently, trailing the cord behind her. Alcina stooped and gathered up the loose ends. Climbing on to the stool she reached up and, for the first time, Nerina noticed several large screw-eyes in the beam above her. Alcina passed one end of the cord through an eye, pulled the end down, then got off the stool. Adjusting the length carefully, she tied the ends of the cord together so that Nerina's hands were just a little above eye-level.

Hands on hips, she stepped back. 'There,' she said. 'That will do for our purposes, this time. You will see that you can still get your hands apart, if you wish; you could free yourself by reaching each of the buckles in turn. However, to do so you would have to raise your hands higher to give yourself slack and maybe stand on tip-toe as well. That means that your bondage is still voluntary, just a little more difficult. You are not yet ready for the full impact of total restraint.'

Nerina most vehemently disagreed with her, but kept her opinion to herself. She longed with all her soul for the sensation she was sure would come to her, as it had to Alcina, if she were properly secured. For the time being, this would have to do. 'Are you going to take my knickers off and masturbate me?' she asked, hopefully.

'Presently. First, you must be properly introduced to the ritual of spanking.'

There was that exciting word again. Nerina's stomach churned and her hips performed involuntary circles as her thighs rubbed themselves together, a movement which was not lost upon Alcina. She went to the chest again and came back with a circular object, about twenty centimetres across and fifty thick. From one edge a short handle protruded. 'This is a padded spanking paddle,' she explained, showing the thing to Nerina. 'It is pleasure and pain. See: it has thick fur on one side and leather on the other. The sensation of having your nipples stroked with the fur is quite exceptional.'

To demonstrate, she drew the fur side of the paddle across Nerina's breasts. She shuddered with pleasure, her nipples rapidly erecting themselves, and swayed forward towards the source of her enjoyment. Alcina transferred her attention to her naked back, dragging the fur slowly from top to bottom. Nerina rocked to and fro, mesmerised by the sensation. The fur moved all over her body, across her stomach and under her arms, even touching her face and neck from time to time. A pressure was building inside her. What was being done to her was extremely enjoyable, but slightly irritating. She knew that she wanted more and began to think about the other side of the paddle. She wanted to feel the cool leather against her skin as a contrast to the warm fur. The want grew and grew until she was groaning with it. Now her desire moved on. She did not want merely to be stroked with the leather. She wanted to be slapped with it. She wished, most of all, that Alcina would pull her knickers down and spank her bottom with it. Not hard, of course, but with enough force to make her realise that she was being chastised. She groaned again, unwilling to express her urge. If she did that, she would lose the feeling of being a captive and make her willing acquiescence apparent. She did not want to do that, so she clung on and endured the insidious intrusion of the fur on her skin. She could feel her vagina watering and longed to be touched in that place, to have her clitoris rubbed and to enjoy a glorious climax.

Still the stroking went on, but now every touch was torture. She was panting for breath and moaning, struggling weakly to pull her hands down to protect herself. Quite suddenly, she came to a peak. It was not the full-blooded orgasm she was used to and she was bitterly disappointed. It seemed to her that an opportunity had been wasted. She sagged, supporting her weight on her wrists.

Alcina stopped her stroking and came close to whisper in her ear, 'Want to feel the leather side now?'

Nerina jerked upright, all her sexual drive instantly restored. 'Yes, oh yes,' she breathed. 'Spank me!'

Alcina went behind her and pulled her knickers down. The draught of cool air on her bottom made Nerina almost faint with joy. 'Now. Yes, now!' she screamed.

The first light tap of the leather on her bare buttocks made her cry out; not in pain, but with long-suppressed lust. 'Harder. Do it harder! I want to feel it!'

The sound of the leather slapping on her skin, making her bottom wobble and dance, was music to her ears. The breadth of the paddle and the padding beneath the leather meant that it was quite impossible for Alcina, no matter how hard she spanked, to induce the stinging sensation that Nerina so ardently longed for. It was enough, nevertheless, to drive Nerina into a frenzy. She felt that the lightest touch anywhere between her legs would be sufficient to accomplish what she sought. It would not even have to be on her clitoris. Frantically, she pulled at her wrist-cuffs. 'I must have it! I must!' she babbled. 'I can't reach myself. Do me, Alcina! Rub me, for pity's sake, before I go mad.'

With huge relief, she felt Alcina's free hand intrude between her thighs and her fingers seek out her clitoris. In ecstasy, she strained her body forward, jiggling frantically to rub herself against the welcome invasion. Her body jerked into orgasm, all the more fulfilling because of her previous minor thrill. 'Thank you. Oh, thank you,' she sobbed.

Alcina did not stop rubbing or spanking. In fact, both those activities increased in pace. 'Another,' she hissed. 'Give me another!'

'I can't,' Nerina wailed, then, as the action of paddle and fingers got to her again, she surprised herself with a second orgasm, more powerful than the last. She jerked and wriggled in the throes of it for several seconds before slumping, exhausted.

'No more! No more!' she begged.

'Yes you will, slave!' Alcina commanded, remorselessly. 'Another! Come on. Obey! You must give me another.'

Nerina's mouth hung open slackly and saliva dribbled from one corner of her lips. Her eyes were glazed, staring unseeingly ahead of her. There was nothing in the world except her bondage, her humiliation and the overwhelming irritation of the fingers on her clitoris and the paddle on her bottom. She was being dragged unwillingly up the slope of lust towards the dizzy height of a peak such as she had never known. She was certain that she would die of pleasure if forced to yet another orgasm, yet that was clearly Alcina's intention. It was partly that dread of the violence of her emotions when she peaked that was fuelling her lust and driving her on. This time, her climax was like no other before it. The tension seemed to last and last until she thought the moment was never going to come. She hung on grimly, her stomach undulating in great waves and her breath coming in shouting gasps as she threw back her head and strained for air. When the moment did come, it was huge and spectacular, draining every ounce of her strength. Coloured lights whirled before her eyes and the room grew dark as she collapsed, to hang by her wrists, half fainting. She was only dimly aware of Alcina freeing her arms and half carrying, half dragging her to the bed.

For a long time she lay curled in a foetal ball, recovering herself and coming again to full consciousness. When she did, she rolled over on to her back, immediately exclaiming as her buttocks came into contact with the seeming roughness of the coverlet. She craned her neck over her shoulder, but could not see her own bottom.

'Don't worry,' Alcina said, observing the movement. 'It's nice and red. Look in the mirror if you don't believe me.'

Nerina got off the bed and padded over to the

dressing table. She examined the reflection of her back. On both cheeks of her bottom, red patches seemed to pulse and glow. This contrast with her pale skin was a forceful reminder of all she had gone through and she pushed both hands down over her stomach and through her pubic hair to caress the other part of her that had received such welcome attention.

Alcina, watching her, frowned a little. 'I hope you have not fallen into the habit of masturbating yourself when I am not with you.'

Nerina glanced up sharply, quickly removing her hands from her body. The very form of the question dictated the answer which would best please Alcina and Nerina gave it without adequate thought.

'No, of course not!'

'Good! It would upset the rhythm and pace of what I am trying to achieve.' She looked hard at Nerina. 'You are sure that is the truth?'

There was that in Alcina's voice which reminded Nerina very strongly of this woman's power over her. She shook her head vehemently, not trusting her voice to carry the proper conviction.

'Hmm,' Alcina said. 'On this occasion, I will take your word of honour that you will not masturbate alone in future.'

'I won't!'

The two women stared at one another for long moments, then Alcina said, 'Hmm,' again, a sound which was not even a word but which was sufficient to send shivers down Nerina's bare back and make her feel very small and childlike.

After another cool stare, Alcina said, 'Very well. I will see you again tomorrow afternoon and we will make further progress.'

That night, Nerina had great difficulty in getting

off to sleep. She had acquired the habit of masturbating before sleeping and, in spite of the fact that she had gone through three massive orgasms that day, not counting her routine, self-induced, morning climax, these had in no way quenched her appetite for another. She had given this sudden hunger for sexual satisfaction some thought since she first became aware of it. Sometimes she wondered whether the female body had been designed to experience a certain number of orgasms in a lifetime, so many per year, as it were. Perhaps, because she had deprived herself of a great number in the past, her body was merely struggling to catch up and would, at some unspecified time in the future, settle down to a more normal quota. At any rate, her itch to masturbate was certainly hard to control. Having given her word of honour, she felt obliged to restrain her impulse, though she did try to cheat a little by rubbing her thighs together. If she happened to come off inadvertently, surely that would not count as masturbation? She was disappointed to find that she could not achieve satisfaction in that way. Her movements only increased her intense frustration. Eventually, deeply dissatisfied, she fell asleep.

In the morning, her itch had not gone away but grown more intense with sleep and rest. Time and again, her hands stole to her crotch upon their habitual journey and, on every occasion, she snatched them away with an angry grunt of exasperation. She lay there, moody and irritable, hating Alcina, hating Paradon, hating Prince Argan but, most of all, hating herself for her weakness. Finally, she got up, stripped and went into the bathroom. She stood for a long time under the douche-bath, letting cold water pour over her until she was blue and shivering and could stand no more. That did little to calm her jangled nerves. All she had achieved was an even fuller erection of her nipples. The towelling to which she was obliged to subject her body to warm it up caused all the old feelings to well up again inside her until she thought she would explode with frustration.

Thus it was that when Leah came to bring her breakfast and to sit with her, as was her wont in the mornings, Nerina had already devised a cunning plan which would enable her to reach the goal she sought, thwart Alcina's intention, yet enable her to keep the strict letter of her word of honour.

'Leah,' she said, when they at last sat by the window together. 'When we were at the peephole together, I saw you doing something to yourself.'

Leah blushed a trifle and looked away, so as not to meet her eyes. 'Yes, Highness.'

Nerina touched her arm. 'Not "Highness", Leah. Not now. Now we are friends and equals. Now you call me "Nerina". So tell me as a friend, Leah, were you masturbating?'

Leah smiled shyly, meeting her eyes only with difficulty. 'Yes, Nerina. I was.'

Nerina gave the arm she was touching a reassuring squeeze. 'It's all right, Leah. I, too, have been taught how to masturbate and am aware of the intense pleasure to be had from it.'

Leah's smile became broader and much more frank. 'You have? I'm so glad. I used to think it was so sad that you were missing so much.'

'I agree with you completely. I did not realise what I was missing. Tell me though, do you do such a thing regularly?'

Leah's inhibitions were dropping from her rapidly. She giggled. 'I used to. Here at Prince Argan's home with its free and easy ways, it is hard to find the time. There is always Count Michael, of course. Sadly, he cannot visit as regularly as I would like but there are many eager young men who are only too willing to please me. I have had to institute a roster and keep as large an engagement book as any princess.'

Nerina's grip on Leah's arm tightened. 'Eager young men?' she enquired, meaningfully and with a heavy emphasis on the last word. 'What about eager young women? Have you had any experience of an approach from them?'

Leah's surprise was evident. 'Why no,' she said, wonderingly. 'Do you mean . . . ? Yes, you do mean . . . I don't know. I've never thought about it.'

'Think about it now, Leah. Suppose a young woman invited you to explore the joys of sex with her. Would you be disgusted and refuse, or would you find that proposition at all interesting?'

Leah was wise in the ways of the world and far from stupid. 'I would consider it, I suppose. It would depend on what the young woman looked like. Would she be fair or dark? Fat or thin?'

Nerina was deliberately casual. 'Let's say, for the sake of this hypothesis, that she is dark-haired and about my size and shape.'

'In that case,' Leah said, with equally careful artlessness, 'I suppose it would depend on what pleasures this woman could offer which my own hands could not.'

'Exactly what do you mean by that?'

Leah shrugged. 'Well, as a purely random example, I very much enjoy it when Count Michael kisses me between the legs and pleasures me with his lips and tongue.'

Nerina gulped and licked her lips. 'But perhaps this woman has no experience of such things and would not know how to go about it. What then?'

Leah shrugged again. 'That would not be

99

important. In fact it might be rather fun. I know everything there is to know and could instruct her in the art.'

Nerina swallowed nervously. Leah was demanding a high price of her. Then the aching tingle in her breasts returned and her vagina twitched, reminding her of her deep need. Whatever the price, she would have to pay it, or go without that which she earnestly desired. Still, she was most anxious to be absolutely sure what was being traded for before she clinched the bargain. 'But suppose,' she said, 'that for some reason this woman was unable to masturbate herself. You would not leave her unrelieved and in distress when you had got what you wanted?'

Leah stared straight into her eyes. 'Of course not, good friend, Nerina,' she said. 'That would be unthinkable. Although I have never yet done such a thing to another woman, this one, whoever she may be, would have not only my sympathy but the full benefit of all my many skills so that any satisfaction she gave to me would be returned in more than full measure.'

So there it was, Nerina thought. The deal was done. However, she was now completely at a loss as to how to proceed from that point. An awkward silence ensued, neither completely willing to break it or to meet the other's eyes until at last Leah yawned elaborately, putting her hand politely in front of her mouth. 'Forgive me, Nerina,' she said. 'I feel suddenly tired. Would you think it very rude of me if I asked whether I might lie down on your bed and rest for a while?'

Nerina was all concern. 'Of course you must lie down, dearest Leah,' she said. 'You have probably been overdoing things. In fact, I feel a little fatigued myself. Perhaps I should lie down, too.'

'By all means. But if you do, maybe you should take off your dress first, otherwise it will get creased.'

'Do you intend to take off your dress, too?'

'All in good time. First I must satisfy myself that you are completely comfortable. Take off your dress.'

Was Nerina mistaken, or was there the faintest hint of command in that solicitous request? She put the thought from her mind and took off her dress. She pulled back the covers and made to get into bed, but Leah said, 'I find it uncomfortable to keep my knickers on in bed, don't you?'

'No.'

'Surely you must. Anyway, they will get just as creased as your dress. Why don't you take them off?'

There could now be no doubt in anyone's mind, least of all Nerina's what Leah was up to. She was going to insist that her erstwhile mistress shame herself by stripping naked! That had not been part of the deal and Nerina felt cheated.

'I don't want to.'

Leah was not in the least put out. Her tone was infinitely servile. 'There is still enough of the maid in me to make me extremely concerned at the thought of my princess being less comfortable than she might be. I could not possibly lie down to rest with that on my mind, so I must insist that you take them off.'

That was it. The ultimatum. Nerina could accept or decline it. The fact that her clitoris was jumping like a hungry mouse inside the silk of her knickers and the thought that Leah was probably well aware of that fact was irritating in the extreme, but there was nothing she could do about it. She had to obey. She pulled her knickers down and stepped out of them. She made as though to get into bed, but Leah held out a hand to stop her.

'Just a minute. Turn round.' Nerina revolved, feeling Leah's eyes all over her body.

'You've been spanked.' Leah accused, seeing the red patches on her bottom which were only just beginning to fade.

'What of it?'

Leah grinned. 'Did you enjoy it?'

That was too much. Nerina jumped into bed and pulled the covers up to her chin. 'Never you mind!' she growled. 'Get undressed.'

Leah smiled and took off her dress with none of Nerina's embarrassment.

Nerina watched. 'Knickers, too.'

Observing Leah while she stripped did a little to restore Nerina's wounded pride. She had sometimes wondered what Leah would look like with no clothes on and now she was able to satisfy her curiosity. She was pleased with what she saw. The girl's breasts were definitely too big, she decided. They did not stand out as well as her own. In fact, there was just a hint of floppiness about them, evidenced by the way the flesh of each upper part was stretched and flattened by the weight of the orb it had to support. Her bottom was also just a bit too wide, while her thighs were decidedly chunky. She felt much better. Leah's brown pubic hair could not be faulted though, unless by virtue of the fact that there was too much of it. Its stiff curls extended all the way up her belly, almost to her navel and what she could see of the gap between her legs seemed to be equally profusely covered.

Leah pulled back the covers on her side of the bed and got in. They lay side by side for a while, not touching, staring at the ceiling until Nerina said, 'Before you go to sleep, there is something I am curious about.'

'What's that?'

'When you spoke of teaching this hypothetical girl to please you with her tongue, how would you set about doing that?'

'Oh, that is much too difficult to explain. I would have to show you.'

Nerina said, 'Well, show me, then.'

'You would have to get out of bed again.'

'All right.' Nerina got out of bed and stood beside it.

Leah threw back the covers and wriggled across towards her to sit on the edge, supporting herself with her hands behind her and her legs splayed. 'She would have to kneel down, between my knees.'

'You mean like this?' Nerina adopted the required position.

'Yes, that's right. To understand clearly what she has to do, she would have to examine me carefully.'

'How would she set about that?'

'She would put a thumb on either side of my sex and pull the lips apart.'

Nerina reached out, thrilling at the contact of her arms with Leah's spread thighs. 'Like this?' she enquired, opening Leah's labia to reveal pink inner surfaces already glistening with moisture.

Leah stirred uneasily, her bottom making circular patterns on the sheet. 'Do you know what a clitoris is?'

'Of course.'

'And where to find it?'

'Yes.'

'I would expect this girl you speak of, whoever she might be, to start by running her tongue very gently up and down between my lips, so as to get used to the taste.'

Nerina licked her lips nervously and steeled herself to what she knew she had to do. She moved her head forward, becoming aware for the first time of an odd scent. It was not unpleasant; faintly perfumed and musky. She jumped a little at the first contact of her tongue with Leah's wetness. She was pleased to notice that Leah's jump was greater than her own, evidence that she was not as fully in control of everything as she would like it to appear. Nerina withdrew her tongue into her mouth, rubbing it on her palate experimentally. The taste was not at all unpleasant. Slightly salty, it had a close association with the muskiness of the scent. Relieved, she put her tongue back between the lips and licked up and down.

Leah gasped, arching her back. 'This girl . . .' she panted, 'this girl would slide her hands up my body until she could pull my nipples.'

Nerina removed her hands from either side of Leah's sex, so that only her tongue kept the lips apart, then felt above her head. It was impossible to miss Leah's nipples, so long and hard had they become. She disengaged her mouth for a moment. 'How hard would she pull them?' she enquired, before returning her tongue to its task. She had to nuzzle a little to get it back into place and this did nothing to quiet Leah's rising sexual temperature.

'She would pull them hard until they were really long. Yes. Like that! Then she would twist and pinch. Harder than that! She would make me feel pain. Agh, yes! Perhaps not quite so hard. Still doing that, she would make her tongue really long and poke it right inside me. Oh! Oh! Yes! Can you feel me getting wet?'

That was an understatement. Nerina's lower face shone with Leah's lubricating juices and it was quite difficult to keep her plunging tongue in place, so wildly was Leah's bottom twitching and jumping.

'And – Oh! Oh! – just as I was on the brink of coming she would – Oh God! – she would move her tongue – Mm! Ooh! – move her tongue up to my clitoris and use it to push back the – Dear Lord save me! – to push back the hood so that she could suck and nibble me.' This last phrase was forced from her lips explosively, to be immediately followed by, 'Now! Yes! Do it now! Suck me! Bite me!' With a glad shriek, Leah clasped both hands behind Nerina's head, pulling it hard into her body to ensure that there could be no possible loss of contact at that vital moment.

Nerina sucked and gnawed at the tiny scrap of flesh between her lips until Leah's agitated squirming subsided and she was sure that her orgasm was complete before she withdrew her head, somewhat breathless. She dropped her hands from Leah's breasts and enquired innocently, 'And if this girl did all that, this would please you?'

Leah stroked her hair tenderly. 'Enormously.'

'Enough to make you remember your promise to her?'

'More than enough.'

'I am curious. Exactly how would you set about fulfilling your promise?'

Leah grinned. 'I would invite her to change places. She would sit here; I would kneel between her legs, then I would do to her exactly what she did to me, except that I would not rest until she had at least three climaxes.'

The prospect of that consummation of her lust was overwhelming. Scarcely trusting her voice, Nerina whispered, 'Show me.' She got up and took Leah's place on the bed. She felt firm hands on her knees stretching them even wider apart then Leah's had been so that a cooling breath of air told her that her sex lips were already gaping open. Her previous self-denial, plus the stimulation of what she had just done had created in her such a want that, at the very first touch of Leah's tongue, she jolted into immediate and obvious orgasm.

Leah paused for only a moment in her work to look up and smile. 'Never mind,' she said. 'We won't count that one.'

As in a dream, Leah leant back on her straight arms with her eyes closed, her body absorbing every morsel of the joy that was being meted out to it by Leah's questing tongue. When she felt hands sliding up her body, she knew their destination and wondered, for a moment, if she would like the treatment of her nipples which she knew was to follow. She did. The curious mixture of pain and delight so skilfully blended by Leah's experienced fingers, was a joy to her. She knew that Leah's tongue was not hard enough to put her maidenhead in any way at risk, so she thoroughly enjoyed the first ever contact of an object with the entrance to her vagina. She felt her peak approaching and cried out, 'I'm coming! I'm coming!'

To have her clitoris sucked and nibbled was an extraordinary experience which she thought would drive her insane. Just as Leah had done, she clutched the dark head to her and held it close, her knees trembling violently with the force of her emotions. At least part of what she felt was caused by the knowledge that it was about to begin all over again and she looked forward to that with all her heart.

Neither of them heard the bedroom door open. The first intimation they had that Alcina was in the room was when her voice cut like a knife into their concentration.

'Nerina! Leah! What do you think you are doing?'

Nerina jumped up so hastily that she sent Leah sprawling, so that she overbalanced backwards and sat down with a bump. Nerina grabbed at the bed sheet and tried to wrap it around herself. Leah, scrambling up, grabbed at the same sheet with the same intention, with the result that the pair of them confronted the angry Alcina like Siamese twins, jostling each other for a greater share of the sheet.

Alcina strode across the room with a face like thunder. 'Nerina! You have let me down. You gave me your solemn word of honour.'

'I promised not to do it alone,' Nerina protested, sulkily. 'Well, I kept my promise. I'm not alone.'

'That's no excuse. You know perfectly well that you have broken faith with the spirit of what you promised. As for you, Leah, for you to repay Prince Argan's kindness in this way is unforgivable. He shall hear of this.'

Swiftly, Nerina interceded on Leah's behalf. 'Whatever happened was not her fault. I asked her for information and instruction. She merely complied with my wishes.'

'That may be. It is not going to save her from the punishment she richly deserves.' Alcina went to the wooden chest and unlocked it. When she came back, she was carrying a slender, flexible riding whip. 'Get yourself over the end of the bed, Leah, and get your backside well up.'

Nerina gasped. 'Alcina! You can't. I won't let you.'

Alcina showed no sign of wavering. 'Ask Leah which she would prefer,' she said. 'Would she rather be beaten by me, or would she rather be reported to Prince Argan, forfeit all chance of employment here and be dismissed from the house, never to see Count Michael again?'

Nerina looked at Leah and saw by the expression on her face that the question was superfluous. 'I must,' Leah said. She dropped her part of the sheet and shuffled dejectedly to the foot of the bed. She reached forward over the footboard and rested her upper body on the coverlet. Her rounded bare buttocks, unnaturally strained by this position, twitched occasionally in anticipation of the treatment they were about to receive.

Nerina dropped the sheet and stepped forward protectively, placing herself between the two women. She stared defiantly at Alcina. 'If you're going to beat her, you'll have to beat me, too,' she said. 'I am more guilty than she is.'

'Very well. If that is what you want. Place yourself beside her.'

'And if I refuse?'

'I report to the prince that his experiment has failed. You are incorrigible and cannot be trained to rule. You will leave this house with Leah and you will fend for yourselves as best you can.'

Nerina gnawed at her lip, fuming at her helplessness. Whatever decision she made would not save Leah from a beating. The best she could hope for was to prevent her own training from being interrupted. If that meant accepting some pain, so be it. With as much dignity as she could muster, she joined Leah, draping her body over the footboard and offering her shapely buttocks for punishment. Leah reached for her hand and gripped it. This time, Nerina was in no mood to disdain any comfort she could get. She squeezed the proffered hand in as reassuring manner as she could.

Alcina stalked to and fro behind them. From that angle the view was extremely exciting. She had whipped many bottoms before, but to have two so enticingly presented at once was a little unusual. Leah's skin had a slightly darker tint than Nerina's.

That, and the breadth of her hips, made an interesting contrast with Nerina's very white skin and more slender shape. Alcina was going to enjoy this, she knew. Should she whip them one at a time, she wondered? Would the sight and sound of that be even greater punishment for the one who knew that it was her turn next? She visualised the tender flesh wobbling, dancing and reddening under her whip and wondered which of them would scream louder. She prolonged the agony of waiting and, thereby, her own sadistic pleasure.

'Get your legs apart, both of you!'

The two women hastened to obey, bumping knees in the process.

Alcina examined the fresh areas of their bodies thus exposed. With the extreme tip of her whip, she tapped lightly from beneath at the division of Nerina's sex making her start with surprise. 'That is the place that has got you into so much trouble,' she remarked, then slashed the whip through the air so that it whistled, being rewarded with the sight of the skin on Nerina's bottom actually crawling in anticipation.

Suddenly, she stopped and frowned. That tender skin was still a trifle red from yesterday's spanking. It would not take many strokes of her whip to break it or to cause some other serious damage. That would interrupt the training schedule which she knew Prince Argan was most anxious to maintain. She was to report to him at the party that very night and he would not be pleased to know what had happened. Not to use the whip on Nerina would cause her to lose face, yet now that the problem had come into her mind, she knew that she had to find an alternative.

To gain time, she tapped Leah's sex in the same way, only noticing her startled jerking with half her mind. Looking around the room, her gaze fell upon an ornamental statuette and the answer came to her in a flash of inspiration.

'Get up!' she said.

At first, Nerina and Leah simply looked at one another uncomprehendingly, then, as the full import of that order made its way into their brains, they scrambled to their feet, unable to believe their good fortune.

'A beating is too easy and over too quickly,' Alcina said. 'I have a different punishment in mind. One which you will not only remember for longer, but which will further Nerina's lessons in humility. As for you, Leah, it will teach you some of the necessary obedience you are so evidently lacking.'

'What are you going to do to us?' Nerina asked, suspiciously.

Alcina laughed. 'I am going to let you go to a party.'

'I don't understand. How is that punishment?'

Alcina was still smiling contentedly. 'You'll see. For all the other people there, it will be a normal party. For you two, it will be a fancy dress party.'

Nerina was still deeply suspicious. 'What sort of fancy dress?'

Alcina picked up the gilded statuette. It was in the shape of a naked young woman, holding a pitcher on her shoulder. 'The party takes place tonight. You will form part of the festive decorations. You will each stand on a plinth, holding a pitcher on your shoulder. You will remain as still as statues all evening. You will not move one single muscle, on pain of dismissal from this house. Do you agree, or would you rather get over the end of the bed again?'

Nerina and Leah looked at one another. Almost anything was preferable to the beating they had so narrowly escaped. After all, how bad could a little posing be? Nerina eyed the statuette more closely, observing its naked state. 'There will, of course, be some drapery allowed? Something to preserve our modesty?'

'No, of course not. There would be little humiliation in that. No, you shall both be as naked as this figure. And that brings me to another matter. You will observe that there is one significant difference between you and this statuette.'

Nerina stared harder. 'I don't see what you mean.'

'This statue has no pubic hair. You both have.'

Nerina's jaw dropped and she could see that Leah, although a trifle slower to understand, was equally stunned. It was impossible! Surely this woman must be mad? She couldn't intend anything so unthinkable?

'You mean . . . ?'

Alcina nodded. 'Precisely. I shall return at six o'clock sharp. At that time, you will both be here in this room, naked, having bathed thoroughly. I will bring with me the means to do what needs to be done before I prepare you for your duties at the party. That is all.' She turned to go, but stopped at the door. 'By the way,' she said, 'I need hardly add that any further masturbation will incur my most serious displeasure.' She swept out, leaving two flabbergasted and very apprehensive females to ponder on her words.

Six

Nerina took elaborate care with her toilet that evening. She and Leah had agreed that the best way to appease Alcina's wrath and, perhaps, dispose her to deal more leniently with them was to give an appearance of willing cooperation. Accordingly she had washed her body thoroughly under the douche bath and shaved her armpits. She had been glad to find one of the new safety razors in the bathroom when she arrived. At least Paradon was that advanced. It was not as good as her own, which had been imported especially, but adequate for the purpose, although the blade needed stropping every time she used it. On this occasion she stropped it carefully before she put it back in its wooden case. Alcina might just decide to use it on her and she knew all too well how painful a blunt blade could be.

Not for the first time she wondered how the woman would set about what she had threatened to do. Nerina had never shaved hair that long and had no idea what it would feel like. Standing naked in front of her dressing table, she stared at her dark pubic curls and tried to remember the distant past, before she had possessed them. It was impossible to imagine herself without them and she shuddered, instinctively pressing a protective palm over her crotch.

She sat down and pinned up her hair with care. She and Leah had studied the statuette and agreed that an upswept Grecian style would match it as closely as possible while pleasing Alcina best.

She was just putting the finishing touches to her work when there was a soft tap at the door and Leah came in. She was wearing a long robe and her face was well-scrubbed and pink. Her unfamiliar hairstyle made her seem quite a different person.

'It's nearly six o'clock,' she said.

Nerina got up from the dressing table. 'You'd better take off your robe,' she said. 'I didn't bother to put one on. We don't want to upset her.'

Leah removed her robe, revealing the fact that she was naked beneath it and that the rest of her body was as fresh and pink as her face. They sat down side by side on the edge of the bed, awkward with each other like naughty schoolchildren in detention. In spite of herself, Nerina found herself fascinated by Leah's pubic hair and kept stealing surreptitious glances at it. She observed that Leah was exhibiting the same interest in her own.

'I've been wondering what it will be like,' Nerina confessed.

'So have I. I've never had it done before. Do you think it will hurt?'

'I've no idea. I suppose it depends how careful she is. I thought about doing it myself, but I didn't see how I could.'

Leah nodded. 'That's funny, so did I, but I didn't for the same reason. Anyway, I wondered if she would really do it, after all. Perhaps she was just trying to scare us.'

Nerina entertained no such hope, knowing Alcina, but refrained from saying so. 'Perhaps you're right. We must hope so.'

At exactly six o'clock, Alcina came to them. They had both expected that. What they had not expected was that she would not be alone. Immediately behind her was the red-haired girl Nerina had seen in the garden. She was wearing the same white dress and carrying a very large tray. Nerina's heart sank as she saw that one of the items on it was a pair of barber's clippers. Her next emotion was one of embarrassment at being observed, naked, by a stranger. She tried to cover herself with her arms and, out of the corner of her eye, saw that Leah was attempting to do the same thing.

Such modesty was not something Alcina would readily tolerate. She stopped in the centre of the room. 'Get up and come here,' she ordered, pointing to a spot on the carpet just in front of her. The two naked women rose obediently and went to the appointed place.

'Put your hands behind your backs. You have both bathed?'

They nodded.

'And shaved well under your arms?'

Both blushed as they nodded again.

'Stretch your arms above your head while I check.' Alcina stroked the smooth skin of their armpits then stood between them and, dropping her hands, she grasped Nerina's pubic hair with her left and Leah's with her right, giving little tugs which were hard enough to rock the lower part of their bodies towards her. 'As for this, I will see to it adequately, I assure you. Now put your hands behind your backs again.'

Sheepishly, they did so, well aware that the red-haired girl was staring openly at their nudity and her interest seemed to be focused on their pubic region. She looked down at the articles on the tray, then back at them, before giving a half-smothered titter of amusement.

Alcina rounded on her. 'What are you laughing about, Zelda?'

Zelda stiffened to attention, her smirk erased. 'Nothing, Alcina.'

'Perhaps you would like to join them this evening? There is always room for another item of decoration.'

Zelda shook her head vigorously, her long red hair brushing her shoulders. 'Oh no, Alcina. I wouldn't like that.'

'You shall if I hear any more of that sort of thing. Your purpose here is to watch and learn how such preparations are made. Now put the tray on the dressing table and behave yourself with decorum.'

As Zelda brushed past them to obey, Nerina burst out. 'You don't mean that you're going to allow her to watch?'

'Of course. You are not the only one who is under training in this house. Suppose I am sick and cannot supervise these matters personally? Who would deputise for me if I had taught no one to do so?'

Nerina persisted. 'But to make a public display of me . . .'

'Oh? Of you? Why leave out Leah? Are her feelings less important than yours? I fear I see traces of your bad old ways returning. In any case, I would have thought you would be pleased to have a small audience now. It will introduce you more gently to what is to come later. How many eyes do you think will be on your body at the party?'

Nerina had been trying hard all afternoon not to think about that and to be so reminded was not helpful to her peace of mind.

'But time is wasting,' Alcina went on, briskly. 'We must get on. Who first? You, Leah, I think. On the bed, please.'

Leah's eyes filled with tears and she fell to her

knees, clasping Alcina's thighs and pressing her face against the material of her dress. 'Please! Please don't,' she begged.

Nerina realised for the first time that the silly girl had actually convinced herself that Alcina's threat had been merely a ruse to alarm them. She felt sorry for her, but vaguely contemptuous at the same time. When her turn came, she would not plead for mercy, she was sure.

'Oh, get up, girl.' Alcina's tone was impatient. 'Zelda, spread a towel so as to catch all that fluff. Now, Leah. Go over to the bed and sit down on the edge of it on the towel.'

She followed the sniffling Leah to the bed and watched her sit down, then stood in front of her. 'Lie back. Zelda, prop her head with a pillow so that she can see what's happening. You, Nerina, come over here and stand behind me so that you can see, too, but don't get in the way. Now spread your legs, Leah. No! Wider than that. Really wide. Zelda, the clippers, please.'

It was hard for Nerina to believe that this was really happening. What she was witnessing was like some bizarre nightmare. She watched with trance-like attention as Alcina knelt between Leah's spread thighs with the clippers in her right hand. She laid the flat of the cold steel blades on Leah's stomach just below her navel and, with rapid compressions of her strong fingers, clicked them across in a smooth pass which cut off a swathe of curls, leaving an ugly stubble behind. Leah looked down between her large breasts at what had been done to her and cried out in horror, then pressed her hands to her face and sobbed bitterly as Alcina expertly cut a second swathe just below the first. Soon she had shorn as far down Leah's belly as the beginning of her sex division. She leant forward to blow away some stray curls that were blocking her clear view, then altered the direction of her strokes, sliding the clippers first down one side of Leah's vulva between the chubby thighs, then the other.

Leah squirmed uneasily, her buttocks tensing and relaxing at this intimate touch and Nerina suddenly realised that what she was seeing was causing a reaction in her own body. Staring at Leah's private parts and witnessing this shaming violation of them was a source of erotic stimulation. She was deeply ashamed of herself and tried hard to force her mind not to accept what her body was telling it. She could not. There was no doubt that her nipples, clitoris and vagina were responding to the message from her eyes. With a slight shock, she understood that part of her excitement lay in the sure knowledge that before long she too would be spread-eagled on the bed and those clippers would move over her own skin, shearing away her dignity with her pubic curls.

Alcina's voice broke into her reverie. 'Knees up,' she said to Leah, then, 'That's right. Pull them right into your body and hold them there.'

Meekly, Leah doubled herself in two, thus exposing further hairy places. Alcina's clippers moved briskly about their business between the cheeks of her bottom.

'Down again!' Alcina snapped her fingers at Zelda, who brought her a morocco leather box from the tray. When Alcina opened it, Nerina could see that it contained a modern safety razor, like the one she had recently used herself, except that this set was obviously designed for a lady's use and of far better quality even than her own special set. Nestling in recesses in the doeskin lining were all the things necessary for shaving. The razor's frame, the strop, several blades and a stropping holder for them. There was a badger brush with an onyx handle and cylinder, the purpose of which eluded Nerina until Alcina unscrewed it to reveal a stick of scented soap.

Alcina snapped her fingers again. 'Zelda! A bowl of water.' While the girl was away, fetching the water from the bathroom, Alcina knelt at ease, absent-mindedly rubbing her fingers across Leah's shorn pubes as though she enjoyed the feel of the stubble. She looked up at Nerina, then nodded towards the shaving set. 'Seven blades,' she said. 'One for every day of the week. Plenty to do both of you without discomfort.' She turned to the sobbing Leah. 'For goodness' sake be quiet girl. You're getting on my nerves. Anyone would think I'd been plucking them out one by one.'

When Zelda came back, balancing a bowl of water, Alcina dipped the shaving brush in it and rubbed it on the soap to work up a creamy lather. Leah started as the brush touched her stomach, then Alcina was working the white foam all over her lower belly and down between her thighs. As she agitated the brush vigorously in small circles around Leah's labia and clitoris, the twitching and sighs showed that Leah was far from indifferent to the sensations those move-ments caused. Alcina laid down the brush and fitted the first blade into the razor's frame with care. Her first transverse stroke removed lather and hair com-pletely, leaving a trail of smooth white skin. The blade must have been stropped to a perfect keenness. Leah had stopped sobbing, unable to resist looking to see what was being done to her. As the razor moved lower about its work, Leah's face took on a more relaxed and dreamy expression. Several times she closed her eyes and sighed deeply.

'Knees up!' Again, Leah curled up to allow access

to her underparts. As Alcina lathered the gap between her bottom cheeks and around her anus,
Nerina thought she heard Leah stifle a giggle. Surely
she must be mistaken.

Alcina took a washcloth and wiped away the
remains of the lather.

'Am I done?' Leah asked.

'Not quite.' Alcina placed a finger on the natural
crease on either side of Leah's labia where the hair
was a little coarser than elsewhere and the clippers
had left it a trifle longer than the rest. 'These are
always difficult places. Scissors please, Zelda.'

While Zelda was on that errand, Alcina expertly
fitted a fresh blade in the frame. 'I'll just snip a bit,
then the razor won't get choked.'

When Zelda came back, Alcina took the scissors from
her. She inserted her forefinger between Leah's labia
and gripped one lip with her thumb, stretching it
away from her body until the crease was pulled flat
and the hairs stood out. 'Hold still now,' she cau-
tioned, then, with the extreme tip of the scissors, she
carefully reduced the hair to a shorter stubble. She
did the same on the other side, then put down the
scissors and picked up the brush again.

As Alcina dipped the brush and used it on the soap
to produce fresh lather, Nerina watched the eager
anticipation in Leah's eyes. There was now no doubt
in her mind that Leah, having accepted the inevitable,
was enjoying the novelty of what had been done to
her body and looking forward to the finishing
touches.

Alcina's application of the soapy brush this time
was even more vigorous than before. It went on far
longer than necessary and Leah began to squirm and
moan, her hands caressing her own breasts. Nerina,
looking on, found her hips revolving in sympathy. A

little shudder deep within her presaged the onset of spontaneous orgasm and she fought against it. Just in time, the lathering stopped. Leah opened her eyes and relaxed with what might have been a disappointed sigh, but now Nerina was in the grip of a horrifying lust. She knew for certain that what she most wanted to see was Leah's pubes and vulva emerging from that lather as smooth as an egg, with no detail concealed by even the finest stubble. She wanted to touch the place, feel its smoothness, even to lay her cheek against it.

Alcina repeated her stretching movement, pinching each labia in turn as she shaved the last residues of stubble. When she wiped off the lather, Nerina felt as though she were going to climax. There was an appealingly assailable appearance about Leah's shaven state that was wildly exciting.

If Alcina experienced anything similar, she did not show it. 'You're done, girl. Get up! A fresh towel and fresh water, Zelda.'

Leah rose and stood, fingering her bald places and moving her bottom experimentally. 'It feels funny.' She looked at Nerina. 'It's all right,' she said. 'It's quite nice, really.'

'I hope you'll say that in a few day's time when it starts to grow in again as bristles,' Alcina remarked, drily.

Zelda laid a fresh towel on the bed and Alcina jerked her thumb at Nerina. 'Very well, miss. Now you.'

Nerina arranged herself as Leah had done with as much dignity as she could muster. As she lay back and put her head on the pillow, there was one major problem uppermost in her mind. Before Leah's shaving had begun, she had been worried only about the humiliating nature of the procedure itself. Her new concern lay in the fact that she knew herself to be very close to orgasm. Surely, the wetness leaking from her vagina would reveal that fact to Alcina, who missed nothing. Nerina also had grave doubts about whether she could hold out against climax if Alcina put her fingers into her and manipulated the shaving brush at all briskly. To give way and so obviously display her enjoyment with three women watching her would quadruple the shame of it all.

She turned her eyes towards the ceiling and began to recite the twelve times table to herself, in order to calm her thudding heart and all the jangled nerve endings between her legs. She felt the coldness of the clippers on her pubes and it took all her will-power not to look. She was proud of the way she held out while the clippers came close to the slit of her sex and raised her knees, unasked, when it was time. The clippers did not linger long around her anus, so she deduced that she was not as hairy as Leah in that area.

There was a respite while Alcina lathered the brush and fitted a new blade in the razor's frame. Nerina steeled herself and concentrated hard on a compli-cated piece of mental long division. This lasted her through the ordeal of lathering, but when the scrap-ing rasp of the razor began, she made the mistake of looking down to see what was happening. From that moment, the battle was lost, had she known it. As more and more of the smooth skin of her lower belly and pubes came into view, her erotic mental image of Leah and her vulgar, hairless exposure overwhelmed her. She consoled herself with the prospect of a pause in the proceedings while Alcina used scissors, as she had done with Leah.

Unfortunately, Nerina's pubic hair was finer and the scissors were unnecessary. When Alcina's finger went between her labia and the razor's scrape followed immediately, Nerina came to a peak at once. By a supreme effort of will, she managed to conceal the evidence of it with a cough and a few uneasy movements. Thank God! It was over and she had not disgraced herself too badly. She waited with eyes closed and a happy smile for the touch of the wash cloth that would signal the end of her torment.

The smile vanished in a trice and her eyes shot open as she felt the lather brush on her again. She stared down at Alcina, kneeling between her thighs. What she saw there confirmed her worst fears. Alcina had not been in the least deceived. There was a look of evil glee in her eyes as she twirled and manipulated the brush so that it parted Nerina's sex and rubbed up and down over her clitoris. Nerina put a knuckle in her mouth and gnawed on it, hoping that the pain would distract her. Surely she could hold out?

Alcina looked at the audience behind her. 'Look, girls. I do believe she's going to come.'

That was the last straw. Nerina took her knuckle out of her mouth and seized her breasts with both hands, grinding and squeezing them against her torso. As the remorseless torture of her sex went on, her head strained back and she grunted as though lifting some heavy weight. Then the storm broke. She jerked into a series of orgasms that racked her body, tossing it about against her conscious volition. Through it all, she was aware enough to know that three pairs of eyes were witnessing her shame.

When it was over, Alcina's look of triumph was hard to bear as she wiped her clean. Nerina got up, touching herself as Leah had done. The bare places felt so strange. She wanted very badly to look at herself in the mirror, but before she could find an excuse to pass the dressing table, Alcina was shepherding them towards the centre of the room again.

'There remains the finishing touch,' she said.

Nerina and Leah stared at one another blankly. Neither could imagine what else remained to be done.

Alcina picked up the statuette again and turned it in her hands. 'There is still one more difference between this and you two.'

Nerina looked at the object. Try as she might, she could not see what Alcina was getting at. The statuette's hair style matched their own; she was naked and had no pubic hair. What else was left? She shook her head in bewilderment.

Alcina tossed the figure in the air and caught it deftly. 'This is gilded. You are not.'

Leah said, 'Gilded? How can we be?'

'Like this,' Alcina replied. She gestured to Zelda, who came to her holding a fairly large cardboard drum. Alcina took off the lid to reveal a huge powder-puff. When she took it out and shook it, a rain of golden dust showered from it and drifted to the carpet. 'You,' she said, pointing at Leah. 'Turn round!' She dipped the puff into the box and patted it onto Leah's naked back. The gold powder stuck to her skin, leaving it with an attractive, slightly matt, gilded surface.

Leah twisted her neck, trying to see what was being done to her. 'You're not going to go all over with that, are you?' she asked.

'All over. Everywhere!' Alcina finished Leah's back and covered her broad bottom, then knelt to deal with the backs of her legs. 'Bend over. Legs apart.' Alcina patted and rubbed at Leah's bald vulva and anus. Nerina, looking on, became aroused all over again. Those areas, shining and golden, were irresistibly attractive. The division of Leah's sex was now even more clearly delineated. Even the extreme tips of her protruding labial lips were gilded, while every wrinkle and pucker around her anus stood out in sharp relief.

'Turn around. Arms up.' Now Leah's armpits were receiving attention. Smearing and patting, Alcina worked her way all over the front of the naked Leah, paying particular attention to her navel and lifting each breast in turn, by the nipple, so as to be able to get the puff into the creases below them.

Alcina took Leah's chin and pushed it upwards, tilting her head back. 'Stay like that,' she commanded. 'Close your eyes.'

'Oh no, not my face. Please don't put it on my face,' Leah begged.

It was as if she had not spoken. 'You'd better hold your breath, too,' Alcina said. 'Otherwise you'll be sneezing all night. No! Don't screw your face up like that, or I won't be able to get into all the creases. Relax. Yes, hold that.' Deftly she puffed and dusted at the upturned face until every part of it was covered, even the closed eyelids.

Nerina had watched the other parts of Leah's body being gilded, finding sexual excitement in the procedure, particularly when breasts, navel and vulva had received attention. Now that it was Leah's face that was being covered, she was surprised to find that even more stimulating. Her face was the very essence of Leah's personality and femininity. To watch it being shamed, possessed and subjugated to Alcina's will, as expressed by the powder, was a most moving experience and Nerina found her own body trembling with suppressed emotion.

When Alcina had given each of Leah's ears careful attention and dusted her hair as well, she walked all around her, inspecting her work before giving a satisfied nod. 'You'll do,' she said. 'Just stand still and don't move about too much. I don't want perspiration to spoil the finish.'

Nerina stared at Leah, no longer recognising her. Apart from the fullness of her figure, she was the very image of the statuette and, somehow, no longer human, in spite of the fact that she visibly breathed and blinked. She was now something to be aesthetically admired, not warm, desirable flesh. The sudden transformation was astonishing.

There was no more time for such philosophical reflections. Already Alcina was pointing at her. Nerina resignedly turned her back and stooped slightly so as to make application of the powder simpler. The feeling, she decided after the first few pats and strokes, was not at all unpleasant. The powder had a slightly greasy, slippery feel that was vaguely erotic. She looked down at her breasts and noticed that her nipples were already erecting themselves, so that she was glad when the order came to bend over. That way, her sexual agitation would not be so apparent. The feel of the puff between her legs did nothing to quiet her rising passion, while Alcina's fingers on her nipples, when their turn came, increased her tension even more.

It was with a sense almost of eagerness that she closed her eyes and held up her face to be treated. She felt the golden powder on her eyelids, submerging and then expunging her personality. She had a sudden surge of irresistible curiosity and could hardly wait for Alcina to step back and declare her finished.

'Please! Please! May I look in the mirror?'

Alcina smiled indulgently. 'Certainly, if you can bear to do so, knowing that you are to be on exhibition like that all evening in front of dozens of pairs of eyes.'

Nerina hurried to the mirror and stared into it,

twisting and turning to see as much of her body as she could. It was true! She was no longer herself! Nerina had vanished, leaving in her stead this statue. Moreover, it was a beautiful statue. She was able to admire it in a purely detached way: the narrow waist with elongated navel dipping into the soft curve of her golden belly; the elegant line of hip and thigh, tapering to shapely calves and ankles; the long, slim arms and fingers; the high, firm, golden breasts with their attractive golden nipples. The face was best of all. Serene and exquisite, the metallic countenance that stared back at her was inanimate, incapable of human emotions such as shame or embarrassment.

Triumphantly, she turned back to Alcina. 'At last, you have made an error of judgement,' she declared. 'You sought to humiliate me. I can tell you now that, adorned like this, I am beautiful and I know it. Pah! Dozens? Let a hundred people come, if they wish. I will be the best decoration you have ever known. Let them all see me and envy my beauty!'

She was delighted to see her would-be tormentor bite her lower lip in chagrin. 'It's too late to start again, now,' Alcina muttered, almost to herself. Perhaps because of her mistake, she was a little sharper than strictly necessary when instructing them how they should pose when they got downstairs. Supporting a gilded pitcher on one shoulder, they would bend one knee slightly forward so as to extend the ankle into a graceful arc while the thigh made a slight support for the free arm and hand, the latter turned outwards in a gesture of offer. Satisfied with her rehearsals at last, she herded them from the room.

It was a tribute to Nerina's new-found confidence that she did not in the least mind walking through the house stark naked. It was as if the golden coating all over her body, while physically concealing nothing,

126

was shielding her inner self from all approaches from the outside world. She felt happy and comfortable, rejoicing in the knowledge that she had beaten Alcina at her own game. It was true that she looked forward to the evening being over, but only so that she could be alone in bed with her triumph, remembering over and over again that look of vexation on Alcina's face when she realised that her plan had backfired.

It was apparent that the powder had not had the same effect on Leah, who showed evident signs of distress when they passed other people on their way downstairs. She responded to the giggling and pointing by crouching a little and had to be reprimanded for that by Alcina. When they got into the large assembly room which was their destination and had to climb on to their low plinths, Nerina did so with sublime indifference, immediately assuming the correct pose. Opposite her, she could see Leah having immense difficulty and being scolded because of it.

Before leaving, Alcina addressed both of them sternly. 'Remember,' she said, 'absolutely no movement at all, no matter what.' Nerina did not deign to reply. Leah just wobbled piteously.

When the first couples began to arrive, Leah trembled violently and crouched perceptibly before she got used to the idea and steadied herself. Nerina was rock-steady from the first, rejoicing in the opportunity to show off her perfect body. A man and woman she did not recognise paused in front of her and looked her up and down.

'Beautiful. Quite beautiful,' the man said.

His companion stared into Nerina's face. 'Exquisite,' she agreed and Nerina's heart almost burst with pride.

The woman's gaze travelled down the gilded body before her, then paused. She raised her fan in front of her face and muttered something inaudible to her friend. He looked down and had obvious difficulty in concealing a smile. They moved off, leaving Nerina very puzzled.

Thinking they were out of earshot, the couple paused. 'Quite beautiful, as you remarked,' the woman said. 'But my dear! Those feet!' They laughed openly before mingling with the crowd.

Nerina was nonplussed. Her feet? What could be the matter with her feet? They were as beautiful as the rest of her, weren't they? She tried to look down her body without moving her head, but her protruding breasts got in the way and she could not see her feet. Stupid woman! What did she know? Her eyesight must be defective.

The room was filling up. A young, well-dressed woman accompanied by an older one who might have been her mother, stopped to inspect Nerina. She watched them carefully, seeing their eyes travelling down her body. Suddenly, the young woman's eyes widened and her jaw dropped. She clutched her companion's arm. 'Oh mother,' she hissed, breaking into giggles. 'Have you ever seen anything as funny as those feet?'

'Hush, daughter,' the older woman reproved. To Nerina, she said, 'I'm so sorry. My daughter lacks manners. I'm sure your feet are ...' She looked down. 'Er ... You must excuse us, my dear.' She dragged her daughter away, she still helpless with giggles and leaning her face against her mother's shoulder.

Nerina's mind was in a turmoil. What on earth was it about her feet that made them so different from anyone else's? She had not paid them more than routine attention in the past, considering them just part of a gorgeous whole. Why had no one ever commented on them before? Suddenly the answer occurred to her. How stupid she was not to have thought of it. Of course! No one would criticise a princess' feet. They would be unfailingly polite about them, no matter how ridiculous they were. All her life, people must have been refraining from comment while making secret jokes behind her back. That was a hideous realisation. What was her shoe-size? She couldn't remember ever having heard it. All her shoes had been made specially for her, so she had never had need to know their measurements herself.

She watched the crowd with nervous apprehension now, praying that no one else would come close enough to her to see those gigantic monstrosities on the ends of her legs. With their lumpy, buckled toes and huge dimensions, they could only provoke further mirth. She closed her eyes as if that might conceal her and prayed fervently that some over-heated gentleman might remove his coat and drape it on her plinth, so as to conceal her shameful extremities from view.

A familiar voice jerked her eyes open. Oh God! Oh no! The worst fate imaginable. It was Count Michael. Worse than that, Prince Argan was at his side: tall, blond and devastatingly attractive. Let her die now!

His white uniform immaculate as before, Count Michael met her eyes boldly, clicked his heels and nodded a bow. 'Highness,' he said. 'We meet again.' He folded his arms and took his weight on one foot, fondling his chin as he perused her body. His gaze rested pointedly on her bare, gilded breasts, then dropped lower.

She badly wanted to squirm as she felt his eyes on her pubic area, well aware that the slit of her sex was prominent and in no way concealed. She offered up a short prayer that this interesting object would detain

129

him so that his inspection went no further. No such luck. His eyes were already travelling downwards and she knew what he was staring at with such fascination.

His hand moved up from his chin to conceal the amusement which would otherwise have been evident in his smile. 'Hmm,' he said. 'Such a pity that Isingore is land-locked, otherwise you might have created a fine fleet of gunboats from your cast-off shoes.'

Her humiliation was complete. There was just a chance that the Prince would not have noticed her feet. He had not appeared to look at the rest of her body. She had not thought it possible to hate Michael any more than she already did, but now found it easy. Now that he had drawn attention to her deformity in such an insulting way, how could the Prince bear to look at her ever again? Even after they had gone, Nerina continued to tremble with despair and shame. A tiny tear escaped from one corner of her eye, leaving a small trace in the gilt powder on her cheek. She could not even mop at it. She could only stand there, naked and mortified, while every single person in the whole world came and stared in amazement at her incredibly ugly, huge and knobbly feet. Her arm, where it supported the pitcher, ached abominably and her fingers on the rim of it had gone to sleep long ago. Her legs and her head ached, too, and she wished with all her heart for the evening to be at an end, so that she might be released from her purgatory.

It seemed like several days before the last of the guests left and Alcina came to inform them that their ordeal was over. Nerina did not wait to be conducted upstairs. She dropped her pitcher with a crash, so that it shattered into a thousand pieces, jumped down from the plinth and rushed directly to her room.

Under the douche bath, she scrubbed and scrubbed at herself until every last trace of the hated gold powder was gone then ran, still wet, back into the bedroom and threw herself face-down on the counterpane, sobbing heart-brokenly.

She was roused by a touch on her bare shoulder. 'What's the matter?' Alcina enquired.

Nerina sat up, shoving straight legs in front of her and pointing at her feet. 'You ask me what's the matter? Just look at them. Why didn't someone tell me?'

'Tell you what?'

'Can't you see? My feet! They are so ugly.'

Alcina patted her wet hair. 'No, they're not. They are perfectly ordinary feet. Quite pretty, in fact.'

'Oh? Then why did everyone at the party laugh at me?'

'Because I told them to.'

'You? You told them to? Why?'

'My task is to train you to be humble. You weren't. You were the haughty Princess Nerina again. It was important that the evening should be a humiliating experience and your attitude would have made it quite the opposite.'

Nerina experienced a distinct dichotomy of emotions. Part of her was furious at the deceitful trick Alcina had played. Another very feminine part was vastly reassured to find that she would not have to go through life as a freak.

'You're not just saying that, are you? My feet really aren't huge and ugly? I looked at them in the bathroom and they were enormous.'

Alcina kicked off one slipper and put her foot up on the bed alongside Nerina's. 'See,' she said. 'Smaller than mine and prettier, too. Let that be another lesson to you. Your brain can play tricks on you.

131

Don't believe everything you're told. Make your own assessment of a problem and get all the information you can before you jump to conclusions and get worked up about it. That advice will serve you particularly well when you have a country to run.'

'So Prince Argan knows that what was said about my feet is untrue?'

Alcina smiled. 'Of course. He has eyes. I am permitted to tell you that he was upset about your evident distress this evening. He is a kind man, as I told you, and would not knowingly conspire to hurt your feelings were it not so vitally necessary for your own good in this case.'

Nerina thought about this. 'It's true that he did not say anything. Nor did he stare at my body. He must be a saint. Unless, of course, he found it uninteresting.'

Alcina's smile turned into an overt laugh. 'I was watching you at the time. I can assure you that Prince Argan is not as much of a saint as all that. The fact that he was considerate enough not to appear to stare does not mean that his eyes did not drink their fill of everything you had on display.'

Nerina coloured, crossing her arms over her breasts, then turned that gesture into a little self-hug. 'Oh,' she said, pleased beyond words.

Seven

Nerina leant on the sill in her room and watched the happy games in the garden below. She longed to join in, but Alcina advised against it, warning that she was still not yet sufficiently trained. It was hard to see what else there was to learn. She had begged Alcina to proceed more quickly, but she had refused. In particular, Nerina was intensely curious about the severe bondage which Alcina had appeared to enjoy so much but which she still denied to her pupil, however much she pleaded. Admittedly, what they did together was very pleasant. The leather cuffs, the masturbation and the gentle spankings were very stimulating, but Nerina felt that they ought to have been making better progress. Every night in bed, she fantasised about being confined so tightly that there was absolutely no possibility of escape while various people did abominable things to her body, particularly her newly-shaven sex. Always, despite Alcina's prohibition, those fantasies led to masturbation. Sometimes her assailant was Alcina; sometimes Leah. Occasionally, Prince Argan figured in her daydreaming. Strangely enough, it was when she cast Count Michael in the role of captor and tormentor that the force of her subsequent orgasm reached its greatest height. Afterwards, she felt deeply ashamed of this particular version and tried to pretend that it hadn't happened. A few days would go by during which she deliberately refrained from including him, then the lust for greater satisfaction would overwhelm her and he would figure in her sexual concoction again.

Because of Leah's infatuation with the Count, Nerina did not feel able to talk to her about her own, somewhat different, obsession, but she could and did discuss bondage in an effort to discover whether Leah might be interested in assisting her by subjecting her to the strict restraint she hankered after. Leah was quite emphatic in her refusal. Unlike Nerina, she had never experienced the phenomenon and was unwilling to experiment, however much Nerina coaxed or bullied.

'Well you could at least help me to do it myself,' Nerina said one day when they were sitting together.

Leah, somewhat tired of the constant pressure on her and hopeful of an end to it, said cautiously, 'In what way?'

'There's everything I need in that chest over there, but Nerina keeps the key. If I could get into it, I could fix myself up, I'm sure. You wouldn't even have to be here when I did it.'

Leah was mystified. 'What fun could there be in that?'

Nerina was irritated, mostly because she was not entirely sure herself. All she knew was that she wanted that feeling of helplessness which she was sure would stimulate her to spontaneous orgasm, if only it could be carried further than the milksop treatment she was currently getting from Alcina. 'Never mind about that!' she snapped. 'Are you going to help me or not?'

'I don't see how I can.'

'I need Alcina's key. Can't you think of a way of getting it for me?'

'I could steal it, I suppose,' Leah said, doubtfully.

'Will you?'

Leah shook her head in a definitive negative. 'As soon as she finds it's gone, there will be fearful trouble. I'm just making real progress with Count Michael and I'm not going to risk spoiling it, even to help you.'

Nerina's mind drifted away from the problem at hand for a moment. 'You're really getting on with him, then?'

'Mm. Rather,' Leah tittered. 'Particularly since my shave. He loves it. Says it drives him wild. I'm going to keep on shaving, aren't you?'

'No,' Nerina said, rather absently. Her mind was filled with images of Count Michael and Leah's bald sex. She dragged herself back from that with an effort. 'I don't know what I'm going to do,' she said despondently.

Leah took pity on her. 'I suppose there is a way . . .'

'Yes, go on. What way?'

'We wouldn't steal the key itself, just an impression of it.'

'I don't understand.'

Leah elaborated. 'You press the key into some wax or a bar of soap or something, then you get someone to cut another key in the same shape.'

'Who would do that?'

'Johann, the estate's blacksmith. He has been giving me the eye, but I haven't allowed him more than a kiss or two. If I'm nicer to him, I'm sure he would cut the key for you.'

'All right, how do we get the impression?'

'We don't. You do. I want nothing to do with that part of it. You get the impression and I'll get the key cut. I think the whole idea's mad anyway, and I'm not prepared to do any more than that.'

Getting an impression of the key proved to be a great deal easier than Nerina had expected. That very afternoon, after the training session, Alcina went into the bathroom to wash, leaving the key still in the lock of the chest. It was simple for Nerina to take from beneath her pillow the bar of soap she had soaked in preparation and press the key into its softened surface. She had all the time in the world to put the key back in the lock and hide the soap under the pillow again before Alcina came back.

'Same time tomorrow,' Alcina said as she walked towards the bedroom door, then she paused and directed a searching stare at Nerina, who was putting on her dress. 'There is something different about you today.'

Nerina pretended that any confusion she felt was occasioned by her difficulty in finding the armhole in the folds of material. 'Oh? In what way?'

'I don't know. A sort of resignation ... I know! This is the first time in days that you haven't begged me to move towards more stringent methods of tying.'

Nerina cursed herself for her stupidity in not remembering to behave exactly as before. 'Oh, that?' she said, lightly. 'I talked it over with Leah and she convinced me that it was better to accept the pace you set as being the very best for the progress of my training.'

Alcina nodded, apparently content. 'Leah is a good girl. She will do well here. Everyone on the estate likes her.'

Particularly the men, Nerina thought, but did not say so.

Within the hour, Leah had taken the bar of soap and gone off on her errand. Time passed slowly for Nerina and she sat staring out of the window, watching dusk turn to night. Frequently, she consoled herself with the thought that she knew nothing of the work involved and that it probably took quite a while to cut a key. That did not prevent her from growing annoyed at the delay and venting her anger on Leah when at last she did return.

'Where have you been?' she demanded. 'Did you see Johann?'

'Of course.'

'Well? What took you so long?'

Leah smiled, slyly. 'He is a blacksmith. I had to be nice to him. It takes time to be adequately nice to such a powerful young man.'

'Nice? What did you ... No, never mind. I don't think I want to know. Anyway, you have the key?'

'No.'

'Perhaps you weren't as nice as you thought?' Nerina said, sarcastically.

Leah shrugged, refusing to be put out. 'He did not complain. He simply demands a higher price.'

'What higher price could there be than the use of your body for his pleasure?'

'And mine,' Leah reminded her. 'No, the price he asks is the use of yours, too.'

Nerina was stunned. 'Mine?'

'Yes. Apparently, exaggerated tales are going around the estate of your appearance at the party. Many men are anxious to boast that they have tried you out, so to speak. Johann just wants the kudos of being the first.'

'How dare he? My virginity is not some sporting trophy to be hung on the wall of a blacksmith's shop!'

'Now, now,' Leah soothed. 'Johann is well aware that the particular trophy you speak of is destined for the wall of Prince Argan's bedroom.'

For Nerina, this was shocking information. 'Does everyone on the estate know that?'

'Of course. It is common knowledge. There are even bets as to the date on which it will happen. Johann would not dream of interfering with that. It will be sufficient for you to serve him in a different way.'

'How?'

Leah hesitated, uncertain as to how to proceed in broaching an extremely delicate subject. 'You remember the peep-hole,' she said, 'and what that couple did?'

'Of course. Do you mean that he wants me to tie him to a pillar?'

'No, no! Johann doesn't care for that sort of thing. You remember what the woman did to the man?'

'Yes. She backed on to him and embraced him with her ... with her ... embraced him,' Nerina concluded, rather lamely.

Leah sighed, but pressed on bravely. 'But before that! Can you remember what she did before that?'

'Yes, she ... she ... Oh my God!' Nerina jumped to her feet in her agitation. 'You're not saying that Johann wants ... that he wants ... Me! I should do that? I, a princess in her own right!'

Leah shrugged again. 'Why not? It's nothing, really. I've done it hundreds of times. And it's not as if you are really a princess any more, is it? Look,' she wheedled, 'Johann does not know why you want the key, but he does know that you want it very badly. It's a matter of supply and demand. He has something you want and you have something he wants. Can you not look upon it as a simple trading transaction?'

'I suppose if you put it like that ...' Nerina said, doubtfully. 'But I have never done anything like that. I wouldn't know how to begin.'

Leah grinned broadly. 'That's no problem. I will be

there; that's part of the bargain. I will show you exactly how to set about it.'

Nerina thought about it. She was only now beginning to understand the extent of her addiction to the bizarre practices to which she had been introduced in that house. Something deep within her longed for the past, for the days of childlike innocence when problems such as that which now confronted her would have been unthinkable. A much larger part, however, was driving her on, urging her to greater and greater heights of insane and immoral conduct in pursuit of the elusive Grail which was the ultimate, consummate, most perfect of orgasms. This mental debate was superfluous. Even before she began it, she knew in her heart what the outcome would be. She had to have that key, no matter what. The fact that Leah would be there was a relief and a comfort but she knew that even if she had been obliged to face the ordeal alone she would have done so.

'All right,' she said. 'When and where?'

The forge was an isolated building set apart from other barns and cottages. Leah and Nerina, with dark cloaks over their white dresses to render them less conspicuous in the darkness, stole towards it. Nerina had expected to hear the roaring of the fire and the ringing of hammer on anvil, but all was deathly quiet; only the occasional hoot of an owl or a sheep's cough disturbed the night's stillness. Leah pushed at one of the large heavy oak doors to reveal the interior. A curious smell assailed Nerina's nostrils. It seemed to be composed of horse and leather, earth, rust and coke-fumes. A few lanterns hanging on nails provided a subdued light, only a little increased by the dull glow from the forge itself, which dominated the centre of the building. All around the walls assorted tools and specialised instruments were arranged neatly in rows. Nerina had no idea of their purpose. In her agitated state the place seemed sinister, more like an alchemist's kitchen than anything else.

Johann, the smith, came towards them out of the gloom of the inner recesses, startling Nerina. His brown shirt, brown hair and brown leather apron had blended so well with the earthy brown of the walls and the rust that she had not seen him on her first inspection.

He held out both hands to Leah and she took them. 'My little sausage!' he said, and kissed her soundly on the lips. He turned towards Nerina, clicked his heels and bowed. 'Highness,' he said. 'You do my humble forge great honour.'

In spite of herself, Nerina bobbed a tiny curtsey in response and held out her hand. She could feel her misgivings taking flight, vanishing like the morning dew in the sunbeams of his courtly deference. Added to that, this Johann fellow was not the uncouth, ugly lump of a thing she had feared to find. He was young, she assessed, eyeing him covertly, probably not much more than twenty-five. His shock of unruly, brown curls framed a face that was tanned, open and friendly. His smile reached deep into his eyes, too. His clothes were not those of a courtier, of course, but they were clean. His shoulders were broad and his forearms showed evidence of his occupation in their well-muscled strength. Perhaps, too, there was something rather masculine and sexy about his leather apron. Altogether, he was not bad at all, she decided If she had to do this awful thing with anyone, she might have searched long to find someone more to her taste. She extended her hand to be kissed.

'*Gnadig frau*!' he murmured, stooping over it. Still holding her hand he straightened, meeting her eyes boldly. 'I had heard tales of your beauty. Now that you are here in person, it is apparent to me that no mere mortal tongue is capable of doing it justice.' He turned to Leah. 'In future, see to it that only angels are allowed to make these reports.'

His hand was big and warm, inspiring confidence. His smile dazzled her and Nerina felt a longing deep inside her. Suddenly, she found herself wishing that she did not still have the virginity which was destined to keep her so far apart from him. Fortunately, the slight colour that came into her cheeks could easily be mistaken for her pleasure at his compliment. Perhaps, though, her embarrassment at the images passing through her mind made her next statement sound more brisk and businesslike than she intended. 'I have come to collect a key. I understand from Leah that there is a certain price to pay.'

He laid his hand on his heart. 'Forgive me, Highness. I am only a man and was led away by a man's passion. It is true that I bargained in this way with Leah, but that was before I met you. Now that I have seen your grace, your beauty and your obvious breeding, how could I persist in such an uncouth design. Princess, I realise now that I, a humble smith, could never aspire to such a privilege, so I release you from any bargain and offer my most contrite apologies.'

Nerina experienced a flood of relief, mingled with a real appreciation of this further compliment. Instantly following on the heels of those emotions came another and it felt to her suspiciously like regret. 'Hold hard,' she said. 'It is important that bargains be kept when made.'

He held up both hands in a gesture of protest. 'No, no,' he said. 'I could not ask it of you. You must take the key without obligation.'

Nerina chose her words with great care, woman

enough to wish to conceal her mounting curiosity and lust. 'I must insist! I asked you to make the key and I agreed the price.' She sighed and cast her eyes down. 'However distasteful it may be to me, it would be dishonourable not to pay in full.' She looked about her. 'This will not be the place for payment, I assume?'

'No, Princess. My living accommodation backs on to the forge. It is much more comfortable. If your Highness will be kind enough to give me a moment, I will wash up and put the fire to bed.'

He went over to the forge and damped it down with a few shovelfuls of wet coke, then removed his leather apron and shirt before plunging his head and arms into a tub of water. He stood up, rubbing at his streaming body with his shirt and Nerina gulped. His chest, except for its light covering of brown hair, reminded her of the classic Greek statues she had seen in books. It tapered down to a flat stomach ridged with hard, transverse muscles. Below that, a broad leather belt with a huge brass buckle divided his naked from his clothed state. When that belt was undone, Nerina thought, and when those breeches came off . . . She found her heart bumping against her ribs and her breathing becoming ragged. Leah was looking at her with an expression which was too knowing for her liking, so she hastily turned her mind away from such thoughts.

'Please follow me,' he said, and led the way through the doorway to his private quarters. Nerina, directly behind him, now had a view of his bare back and found it just as desirable as the front. She also had the full benefit of his buttocks which were tight and slim, moving enticingly beneath the covering breeches. The room to which he took them was attractive, in its own rustic way. A bright fire burned in the grate so that the air was pleasantly warm. He turned up the wick of the lamp on the small table and the cheerful glow illuminated the neat surroundings. Nerina's eyes flew to one corner, in which there was a small cot, large enough only for one.

He followed the direction of her eyes. 'I could pull the mattress on to the floor?' he suggested.

Leah chipped in. 'Not yet. Let's see how it goes. I told you that I would have to help Nerina. Why don't you take those silly breeches off now and have done with it.'

'You want me to undress?'

'Of course!' Leah said. Encouragingly, she enticed him, 'If you take yours off, we'll take ours off, won't we, Nerina?'

Nerina blinked and thought, We will? Well, Leah knew what to do and she didn't. She had better follow her lead. 'Yes, we will,' she said, aloud.

Johann unbuckled his belt and removed his breeches, shoes and stockings. Nerina was pleased to notice that he did so with some embarrassment, turning his back to them while he disrobed.

Leah watched him. 'Come on, Johann. You weren't so shy last night. Turn around and let's have a look. No, take your hands away. Nerina wants to see what she's got to deal with.'

And that, at least, was completely true. Nerina knew it. The way her vagina was twitching and watering told her so, even before Johann turned round. When he did, the involuntary movements in her stomach increased enormously. She had little with which to make comparisons, since this was only the second penis she had seen in her whole life. It seemed to her to be enormous. Stiff, thick and straight, it jutted from an aggressive patch of curly hair and the single eye in its head seemed to be staring straight at her.

143

'Sit down and watch the show,' Leah said, throwing off her cloak and unfastening her belt. She nudged Nerina. 'Come on. You too.'

Nerina started, then copied her, removing her own cloak and fumbling with her dress. She was preoccupied with that massive penis. Johann was lying back on some pillows and caressing himself; maintaining his erection while he watched them undress. Leah was naked now and watching Nerina's progress with hands on hips. When Nerina paused while wearing only her knickers, Leah became impatient. Going behind her companion, she grabbed her knickers and dragged them down to the floor. 'Those too,' she said.

Nerina covered herself with her hands, but Johann said, 'Please won't you let me look at you?'

Nerina knew then that there was nothing she wanted more than for this naked giant to see and admire her. She dropped her hands to her sides and stood still, amazed at her own calmness under such a scrutiny. Had they been alone, they might have remained thus all night, several feet apart, worshipping each other from a distance.

Leah had other ideas. Taking Nerina's hand, she dragged her forward. 'I'll show you what to do.' She fell on her knees at the bedside, bringing her head to a level only a little above Johann's groin. 'Take your hands away!' she commanded. As he removed his hand from his penis, she reached out and grasped it firmly, encircling it just below the glans with her right thumb and forefinger. His body jerked in response and he sighed.

'Silly!' Leah looked up sharply into his face. 'I haven't even started yet.' She put her head forward and extended her tongue. With an exaggerated gesture, she licked right across the tip of his engorged organ, then turned to look up at Nerina. 'Kneel down the other side,' she said. 'That's right. Now you do what I've just done.'

Nerina licked her lips, nervously. As Leah released Johann's penis, she took hold of it with her right hand, copying Leah's grip exactly. She sensed, rather than saw, Johann's muscles tighten at her touch. She paused for several seconds, getting used to this, her first experience of the male organ. It had a strange sort of hardness, rather as though it were made of green wood with a soft leather covering. It was most certainly not wood, though. This was a living thing, with hot blood pounding through it. The heat of it aroused her all over again and she could feel the entrance to her vagina quivering between her thighs as she knelt there on the hard wooden floor. She leant forward and licked the head. Remembering her experience with Leah, she tested her tongue on her palate. There was no taste at all, which was a little disappointing.

Leah reached across and pushed her hand away, regaining her own grip. She slid her hand down the length of flesh, right to the root of it, just above Johann's testicles, then bent forward again. This time, she put all her mouth right over his penis and slowly took more and more of it inside. Suddenly, she coughed a little and pulled her head back. 'Here,' she said. 'Try that. You won't be able to do it as much as that at first, because it will make you choke when it hits the back of your throat. Just keep trying, though, and you'll get used to it.'

At her first attempt, Nerina gagged violently. However, the feel of this thick instrument in her mouth, pushing against her tongue and the roof of her mouth was fascinating. After a little while, she found that what Leah had said was true. There was an extent to which she could allow it to touch the back of her throat without discomfort. She was pleased with this discovery and moved her head up and down, sucking a little at each withdrawal. She could hear Johann groaning and the thought that she was the cause of his sexual excitement was stimulating for her, too.

Suddenly, she felt a new stickiness and tasted something different. She removed her mouth, allowing his wet red penis to slide out. 'I tasted something!'

Leah nodded, 'That's normal. It's a little leak. It means he's close to coming. Do you like the taste?'

Nerina moved her tongue against her palate. 'It tastes a bit like you, sort of musky and salty.'

'You'll taste a lot more when he comes in your mouth.'

'What? In my mouth? Oh, no! I don't think I could.'

Leah smiled. 'We'll see,' she said. 'Let me show you another trick.' She grasped Johann's penis as before, but this time, she used only her tongue, swirling it rapidly around the thickness of it. Handing it back to Nerina, she said, 'Now you do that, but keep him inside your mouth and rub up and down with your hand at the same time.'

Nerina experimented with this new technique. Johann's moans became staccato grunts and his body heaved in time with her movements. That was exciting enough for Nerina, but when she felt Leah's hand slide between her legs from the rear and a finger begin to massage her clitoris, her lust mounted quickly to a crescendo. Her own groans of pleasure were muffled but unmistakable. She could feel herself climbing towards a peak and, from the noises he was making, guessed that Johann would climax soon, too. She would have to be ready to take her mouth off him when that moment came.

146

She heard Leah's voice beside her. 'I'll only keep doing you as long as you keep him in your mouth. If you let him go, I'll stop.'

Such noises as Nerina could make became frantic, pleading sounds. She was in desperate need of orgasm. With her free hand, she groped down towards her clitoris, only to find her wrist grasped and held firmly. 'Oh, no you don't,' Leah said. 'You do him and I'll do you.'

Nerina was in an agony of indecision. She needed that orgasm, but would it come before Johann's? His body movements and the way his hands were stroking her head and back told her that an explosion was imminent, but so was her own. Just then, Leah's movements slowed and almost stopped. Nerina was in a frenzy. With agitated, pleading noises, she rubbed and sucked at Johann with renewed vigour so as to be rewarded by an increase in Leah's masturbation. Johann's organ began to pulse in her hand and she guessed that to be a sign of imminent ejaculation. She wriggled her hips desperately, but she was still not quite there. She must keep him in her mouth just a little longer if she wanted an orgasm herself.

Suddenly, Johann gave a loud shout and a gush of hot liquid shot into Nerina's mouth. She jerked in reaction, but managed to keep her mouth in place.

Leah slowed her rubbing again. 'Swallow it,' she hissed 'Swallow all of it!'

Frantically, Nerina swallowed, trying to nod and make her gulps obvious at the same time. The salty cream slid down her throat. It was not so bad, after all. Better though, was what Leah was doing to her now, masturbating her clitoris in a most expert fashion. Gratefully, Nerina jerked into orgasm, finding extra satisfaction in sucking the last drops of sperm from Johann's softening penis and swallowing them.

For several minutes afterwards, Nerina found herself incapable of moving away. She had slumped from her knees to sit on the floor on one haunch, her cheek resting against Johann's stomach while she played idly with his now flaccid penis, reluctant to part with this intriguing new toy. He lay still, content to let her do what she would, only occasionally caressing her dark hair with one gentle hand. Neither spoke. While there was intimacy in the position of their bodies, there was a certain awkwardness in both their minds. After that experience, it was very difficult to know what to say.

In the end, it was Leah who broke the spell. 'Come on, Nerina,' she said. 'If we don't get back soon, we'll be missed.'

Nerina got up and, with a final caress, relinquished her possession of that part of Johann which had pleased her so much. While she dressed, he put on his breeches and buckled his belt. In silence, the three of them went back into the forge.

It was time for farewells. Just what did one say to the man whose sperm had so recently erupted into one's mouth, Nerina wondered. Feeling faintly ridiculous, she held out her hand. 'Goodbye, Johann.'

He bent to kiss it. 'Goodbye, Princess.'

There! The thing was done. Nerina pushed Leah towards the door. They were just about to go out, when Johann called her back. 'Highness!'

Nerina turned back. Was he about to make some further demand? He certainly looked handsome in the half-light. Handsome enough to make a refusal unconvincing.

He held out a small, gleaming piece of metal. 'Your key.'

Nerina blushed. How obvious it must be to him that what had passed between them had been enjoy-

148

able enough to drive all thought of her original purpose from her mind. She hurried back to him. 'Thank you, Johann.'

As she reached out her hand for the key, he caught her wrist and detained her. 'No, it is I who thank you, Highness. Leah may have told you that I made the bargain in the hope of being able to boast of being the first man on the estate to be with you.'

Nerina nodded. 'She did tell me that.'

He squeezed her hand. 'I swear to you, Highness, that no word of what happened here tonight shall pass my lips, no matter what the temptation.'

She squeezed back. 'Thank you Johann, that means a lot to me.' On a sudden impulse she kissed his cheek, reaching up on tip-toe to do so. Then she turned and fled back to the door, pushing an open-mouthed Leah out of the way in her haste to get out into the concealing darkness. She had surprised herself again. Princess Nerina of Isingore, of her own free will, had kissed a common blacksmith in front of a witness! Why, she was no better than Leah herself! She touched her lips in the dark. His cheek had felt nice, though. She smiled to herself a little as she hurried on her way.

Safely back in her room, she could hardly wait to try her new treasure. With Leah behind her looking on, she knelt and fitted the key into the wooden chest's lock. For a moment, it did not seem as though it would turn, then it did. She lifted the lid and sat back on her heels. She had never been able to make a careful examination of the chest's contents. Leah, of course, had not even seen the few items visible near the top.

She lifted things out one by one. Near the top, as she had expected, were the articles she had already used: the ribbon, the wrist-cuffs and the padded paddle. Beneath them was a curious gadget. A metal bar about half a metre long had a leather cuff attached to each end.

'Whatever can that be for?' she said to Leah, turning the thing over and over in her hands. 'See, the cuffs are too big for anyone's wrists. They are even too big for ankles.'

'Knees, perhaps?' Leah ventured.

'Knees? I don't know. Do people do that?'

'I have spent more time at the peep-hole than you, Highness. Believe me when I say that they do.'

'I see.' Nerina found that information wildly exciting. Anyone wearing this thing just above their knees would be completely unable to close their legs; unable to prevent unspeakable things being done to her helpless body. She wriggled her hips uncomfortably and set the implement aside.

The next article was obviously a gag. A short metal bar through a black rubber ball had straps at either end to buckle behind the head. Anyone wearing that would have their jaws forced apart. She would be unable to cry out, no matter what dreadful torments were inflicted upon her. In addition to that, its likeness to a horse's bit reeked of the power and control her captor would have over her. That was infinitely exciting, she found, and her hip movements became more pronounced. A blindfold came next. Made of padded, shaped, black velvet, it was intended to be fastened in place with an elastic strap. Experimentally, Nerina slipped it over her head and pulled it into place. It shut out the light completely. No matter how she turned her head, no glimmer penetrated the material or leaked in around the edges. She took it off again and rummaged further down. She brought out a whip with many short leather thongs for tails. Tentatively, she tapped it on her forearm. Even that light touch was sufficient to sting like a swarm of wasps, and she shivered a little as she set that aside, too. That was almost all there was in the chest. She took out a few canes, several long goose-feathers and some chains of various lengths. That left only a few padlocks made of brass: small, but sturdy.

She looked up at Leah. 'Aren't they marvellous?' she breathed.

Leah shook her head in bafflement. 'You're demented.'

Nerina laughed. 'You only say that because you've never tried it. Are you sure you wouldn't like me to use some of these on you so you could see how nice it is?'

'No fear! You keep well away from me with those things.'

Nerina was fingering her trophies again. 'I can't wait to use them.'

'Well, you'll have to. It's far too late tonight. I have to be back in my room.'

Nerina frowned. 'Tomorrow morning, then. Alcina doesn't come until the afternoon. Will you help me then?'

Leah shook her head vehemently. 'I've told you I won't tie you up.'

'I know! But if you came into my room and found that I couldn't get out of these things by myself, you'd help me then, wouldn't you?' With great reluctance, Leah said, 'I suppose so.'

'That's all right then. Just make sure you come in at exactly ten o'clock. Not a moment sooner and not a moment later. Will you promise to do that?'

Leah stared at her. 'You're mad!' she said, then, seeing the pleading in Nerina's eyes, relented. 'Oh, all right,' she said. 'Ten o'clock.'

Eight

It was too bad of Leah to refuse to help her, Nerina decided. Last night, what she intended had appeared simple. She had run over it in her mind several times and had thought that there would be no problems. She had rejected her original idea of strapping herself to the bed. She particularly wanted to be stretched as Alcina had been and, as far as she could see, the only way to do that would be to use the hooks in the beam so that her own weight would provide the necessary strain. She had put the dressing table stool in position before strapping the cuffs of the knee-spreader around her lower thighs. Now she found it quite impossible to climb on to the stool.

Exasperated, she stooped to unbuckle one cuff, then held the bar out of the way while she got up. The stool was only just wide enough to stand on when she parted her legs to readjust the loose cuff. She wobbled precariously for a moment. The sooner she received some support from above, the better. She had already donned the wrist-cuffs with which she was familiar. The blindfold was in position on her forehead, ready to be pulled down, and she had buckled the strap of the gag loosely about her neck. To give her wrists the necessary room for manoeuvre, she had padlocked short lengths of chain to the rings on the cuffs, hooking the hasp of another, open padlock to the end of each.

She glanced again at the clock on the dressing table. Ten minutes past nine. She had planned an hour for herself in total restraint, but the errors she had made had delayed her. Never mind. Fifty minutes would have to do. She pulled the gag up and settled the rubber ball in her mouth. As she had anticipated, it stretched her jaw and she was careful not to pull the strap too tight before securing it, merely satisfying herself that she could not possibly eject the thing. She craned back and reached up with her left hand, holding the padlock on the end of that cuff's chain. It was easy to hook the hasp through a screw-eye and click it shut. The sound seemed to echo through the still room and she shivered a little, not quite certain whether it was excitement or apprehension she felt.

Her left wrist was fixed to the beam. Even now, she thought, it was still not too late to turn back. She could reach across with her free hand and unbuckle the left cuff to release herself. For a moment, she seriously considered doing just that. Perhaps Leah was right and she really was insane? Then the demon inside her rose up again and drove her on. The uneasy itch between her legs and in her lower stomach was demanding experience of this unknown sexual adventure. The image of Alcina's stretched pose flashed into her mind and she knew that she would be curious and unsatisfied until she had duplicated that as best she could.

She took a deep breath and drew the blindfold down over her eyes, adjusting it so that it was comfortable yet permitted her to see absolutely nothing. Holding the open padlock, she raised her right hand and groped along the beam above her head, feeling for the screw-eye which she had determined would give her arms exactly the right amount of separation. It took her a while to find it and a little fumbling to put the hasp of the padlock through it. Doubt assailed her again at that point and she stopped. Once she clicked that padlock shut she would not be able to change her mind. She found her heart beating faster and noticed that her knees were trembling, despite the support of the cuffs. Was she mad?

She clicked the padlock shut.

Immediately, she was overwhelmed by panic. What had she done? With her own hands and in her stupid desire to use as much of the equipment as she could, she had deprived herself of the ability to call for help. Now her only hope of release lay in Leah's promise to come to her at ten o'clock. Suppose she overslept? Suppose she had died in the night? What time was it now? How long had it taken her to fix her wrists to the ceiling? She cursed herself for not looking at the clock again before pulling the blindfold down. She tried to bend her wrists far enough to reach the cuffs' buckles, in spite of the fact that she already knew she would not be able to do that. She tried to calm herself. At any rate, she need not proceed to the next stage. She had planned to kick the stool away and leave herself dangling helplessly with her full weight on her wrists. Better not to do that, now that she had experienced the terrible sensation of helpless uncertainty that had overwhelmed her as soon as she closed that last lock. Now she realised that Alcina had been completely right. She wasn't ready for this.

Because of the narrowness of the stool, she was obliged to keep her widely parted knees slightly bent. Her calves were beginning to ache and tremble and she tried to take some of her weight on her wrists. Already, she seemed to have been stuck like this for hours. How long had it really been? She had lost all sense of time. Alternately shifting her weight from legs to arms, she waited with as much patience as she could muster.

The sense of relief that flooded through her when she heard the bedroom door open was enormous. That fifty minutes had seemed much longer, but now it was over and Leah would climb up, unbuckle the cuffs and get her down. There was the sound of soft footsteps on the carpet. It was odd that Leah had said nothing. She grew increasingly uneasy. Had her fevered imagination provided those sounds? No; there was the sound of footsteps again. She had not imagined them. Why was she not getting her down? She longed for the power of speech that would enable her to interrogate Leah, but could manage only a few snorts and whistling breaths through her nose. Surely that would attract Leah's attention to her predicament.

Suddenly, her skin prickled and an icy chill ran down her back. The stool on which she stood had moved a fraction backwards, yet she had not felt anything resembling Leah climbing up beside her. Why was she moving the stool? She froze as a dreadful thought crossed her mind.

Suppose it was not Leah?

The stool moved again, more distinctly, this time, so that she was obliged to shuffle forward a little to keep her balance. Now she was convinced. The person in the room with her was not Leah! Furthermore, whoever it was did not have her welfare at heart, otherwise they would have released her at once. Someone, male or female, had her completely in their power. Her pinioned nudity was available for them to toy with or to torture as they wished. She pictured herself as they would see her: naked, with arms stretched wide and high, her bald vulva fully exposed

155

by the knee-spreader and her labia gaping open. That image both distressed her and, at the same time, caused her vagina to twinge and water. The stool was dragged backwards again and this time her compensating forward shuffle brought her to the front edge so that she could feel vacant space beneath her toes. Leaning far forward, she could just manage to keep some weight on her feet. One more tug like that and she would be left without the support of her legs, hanging by her wrists alone.

That tug came and the stool was gone. She swung forward into space, her legs pedalling frantically within the limits prescribed by the spreader, her toes stretched vainly downwards, feeling for a support that was not there and would not be there until her tormentor relented. Who could this monster be? Alcina? Prince Argan? Oh God! Suppose it was Count Michael! Suppose her bedtime fantasy had become all too cruel reality? That would be a judgement on her. A punishment she richly deserved in return for her disobedience and insane urges. The more she thought about it, the more certain she became that it was he. She pictured him in all his loathsome arrogance, standing with his hip stuck out and his arms folded as he had stood before her at the party, stroking his chin and staring at her with that idiotic half-smile of his.

Why did he not speak? Even the sound of gloating in his voice would be better than this unnerving silence. She stopped struggling and grunting so as to be able to use the main sense left to her: her hearing.

He was on the far side of the room now. That was where the chest was. She distinctly heard her key turn in the lock and the lid open. He was taking something out. Oh God! The whip! Even now, he was coming back towards her with that vicious tool in his powerful hand. He was going to lash her naked body with those leather thongs, thongs that stung and burned, even when delicately applied. Now he was standing on her right side. She could hear faint breathing. She braced herself for the unbearable pain of the first slash. A touch on her left armpit made her leap mightily and scream into the gag. It came again and she tried to cringe away from it. Now it was running lightly up and down the tender skin in that area. What was it? It was certainly not the whip and it did not feel like a hand or finger. It was dreadfully tickly and she suddenly realised that she was being touched by one of the goose-feathers from the bottom of the chest. She squirmed, trying to wriggle her body away from that insidious touch, but the contact was maintained. Now the irritation was serious. Even as a child she had been ticklish and this torture, applied to her body when it was suspended and totally helpless, was impossible to bear. The laughter forced from her could not escape by the usual passage and was obliged to emerge through her nose as undignified snorts.

The feather moved around to the front of her body, touching and circling her breasts. Not my nipples, she prayed. Please not my nipples! The tormenting feather touched first one, then the other. Although she could not see them, she knew that her nipples were hugely erect, responding not only to the tickling but to the way she was sexually excited by what was being done to her. Again and again, she tried to scream her protests, but all that came out were muffled, unintelligible moans and grunts.

The feather moved again. This time it went down over her stomach and probed her navel. Her whole body tensed, every muscle stiff as a board. She knew where the feather was going! Her sex was gaping open in clear invitation. She held her breath as she felt light touches on her pubes. Time and again, it dipped downwards and she tensed her thighs instinctively in an attempt to bring them together and shield her private parts, even though she knew the spreader most effectively prevented that.

To her great relief, the touching stopped altogether. She relaxed, swinging gently, and listened. She could hear nothing. What was he doing? Was he in front of her or behind her? When the feather stabbed directly on to her clitoris, jiggling and circling, it was a huge surprise that set her whole body leaping and dancing. This was a nightmare. Count Michael was no longer a product of her own bondage fantasy. He was here and very real. She felt the familiar signs within her lower stomach and knew that if he did not stop what he was doing at once she would suffer the supreme humiliation of allowing him to see her climax.

He did not stop. Occasionally, the feather left her clitoris, but only to probe between her labia, softly rubbing up and down before returning to the focal point of his attention. She stopped trying to laugh. This was not tickling. This was purest heaven. Now she no longer cared if a thousand Count Michaels were there to see it. This time, surely, she was going to find her Grail, the perfect orgasm.

Her breath was hissing through her nose in delirious puffs of pleasure. All her muscles liquefied and ceased to obey the commands of her brain as her whole attention centred itself upon the inflamed nerves of her vagina and clitoris. A silent voice within her prayed, 'Don't stop! Don't stop!'. She was on the brink, hovering in that limbo of suspense and tension which was at once frightening and intensely enjoyable. She struggled to prolong the moment, to tease herself into greater pleasure by delaying that for which she most longed. She knew that it was a battle she could not win. Indeed it was one she ardently looked forward to losing. When the final moment of capitulation came, it was all she had hoped for and more. With a long moan, she jerked and wiggled into a stupendous orgasm which drained every ounce of sense from her brain. It went on and on, while she floated on a cloud of sheer bliss. When it was over, she hung by her wrists, completely drained, only twitching a little now and again with the after-shocks.

As she recovered a little and her heart regained a more normal rhythm, she became aware of the fact that she was becoming uncomfortable. Her arms were aching and it felt as though her shoulder joints were being dislocated by her own weight. She bent her elbows and hoisted herself up in an effort to relieve the discomfort. The strain was now on her biceps and she knew she could not sustain that for long. Eventually, she had to subside into her former position, but she had, at least, made a temporary respite for her shoulders. She listened intently. Had Michael finished with her? Perhaps he had left the room while she was too confused by her recent experience to notice the sound of the door opening and closing?

No! There was that soft breathing on her left again. She tensed herself for further assaults with the feather. The first smack on her bare bottom took her completely by surprise, so that she flexed her knees and hauled herself up with her arms. Another smack and she quickly realised that no matter what she did, she would not be able to prevent the blows from landing precisely on such an exposed target. She tried to keep still, to spare her aching arms while the spanking went on, but couldn't. Her body insisted on jolting at each stroke, despite her best efforts. She could not make out what it was that was being used. She knew it wasn't a hand. The sound and feel were wrong. It certainly wasn't the padded paddle she had grown used to. This had a sharper sting and a different sound. Then she guessed what it was. She was being spanked with one of her own light slippers and it was the leather sole she could feel making sharp contact with the white flesh of her bottom.

For some strange reason, that was exciting. What she was undergoing was what was done to naughty children. That increased her sense of weakness and subservience. She had already had a massive orgasm, but could feel certain forces building within her again. She tried to think of other things, but the erotic masturbation fantasies of her daydreams pushed through relentlessly. She was suspended: a naked, blind, dumb captive. Every part of her body was available for abuse and her bare bottom was being most comprehensively slippered. As if that were not enough, it was the despised Michael who had her in his power and was doing the slippering! She whimpered through her nose, but the sound was not entirely one of humiliation and pain. What was happening to her buttocks was lighting powerful fires within her and now her movements were not designed as a defence, but as an effort to rub her thighs together. If only he would touch her clitoris again!

Her buttocks were warm and glowing and she felt close to spontaneous orgasm. That voice inside her head spoke again. 'Harder! Make it really sting!'

The spanking stopped and a wave of disappointment swept over her. Surely that could not be all? She listened again. Now he was at the dressing table, opening a drawer. In a fever of anticipation, she hung by her wrists, awaiting whatever new torment he planned. Another touch on her bottom made her wriggle anew. This time it was not spanking. A finger was running up and down between her buttock cheeks and it felt greasy and cold, as though loaded with some sort of cream. It passed to and fro over her anus, then centred itself there. She froze. Surely he could not intend to ...

The finger pushed insistently at her tight sphincter. She heaved herself up, frantically trying to escape the pressure being exerted. The finger merely followed her movement so that when she let herself down again, it was to assist ingress by impaling herself. She felt her sphincter muscles give way and admit a tiny portion of the finger. That was disgusting! She groaned in impotent rage and shame. The finger moved a trifle further then stopped. She held her breath, not daring to move. The finger moved in tiny circles, making minute up and down movements at the same time.

That was terrible! Not because of pain or discomfort but because the intrusive finger was no longer disgusting, It was delightful and sent most lively tingles into her vagina. She groaned in shame and self-loathing. How could she be enjoying such a deviant abuse of her private place? The potential orgasm that had receded when her spanking stopped reared its head again, demanding to be squarely faced and dealt with. She fought successfully against it for a while until she felt the slipper slap against her vulva. With his finger still irritating her anus, he was smacking lightly at the area right over her clitoris and she felt it bounce at every tap. Now she must look as Alcina had looked when she was having her clitoris spanked and Nerina understood for the first time what a powerful aphrodisiac that must have been for her. In her own case it was worse, for she had no protective pubic hair as Alcina had. The slaps were landing on shaven skin and producing a sound which served to drive Nerina even further up the scale of tension.

Now her struggles had a different purpose. She tried hard to impale herself further on the finger, to feel it thrusting into her right up to the knuckle, as far as it would go. The fact that it maintained exactly the same small insertion and movement was frustrating in the extreme and piled on even more sexual pressure. She could hold out no longer. She plunged into a chasm of orgasm even deeper than the previous one, which she had thought could not be surpassed. She did not notice the withdrawal of the finger. Her head was in a whirl of confusion and the tears which trickled into her blindfold and became trapped there were of rapture, relief and shame, coupled with pain, as she slowly became aware of the burning sensation in her buttocks and vulva.

Coming back to her senses a little, she tried to control her breathing and listen again. The pain in her shoulders was now very real and urgent. In spite of the padding and the width of her wrist-cuffs, her fingers were quite numb. Surely he had finished his torture now. To her great joy, she heard the door open and close. He had gone!

Leah's voice startled her. 'Oh my! Whatever have you done to yourself?'

She felt the stool beneath her extended toes and the bliss that came from being able to take her weight on her feet again was inexpressible. Her knee-cuffs were unfastened, then she could feel Leah clinging to her body for balance as she, too, climbed on to the stool. With the last part of her strength, Nerina raised one arm after the other to allow slack for Leah to unfasten the buckles of the wrist-cuffs. With clumsy, numb fingers, she pushed up the blindfold and tore it off, then, unable to stand the pain of returning circulation any more, she dropped her arms limply to her sides. Together, she and Leah half-stepped, half-fell from the stool and Nerina, quite unable to stand, sank to her hands and knees on the carpet. She felt Leah's fingers behind her head, then the hated gag was free and she could eject it from her mouth. She worked her aching jaw back and forth, inhaling great gasps of air.

She stayed there for several minutes, naked and trembling, before Leah helped her up and half-carried her to the bed. She sat down on the edge of it, wincing at the contact of the coverlet with her burning behind.

Leah was distraught. 'It's all my fault!' she said, over and over again. 'If only I hadn't been late! I'll never forgive myself.'

'Late?' Nerina raised her eyes wearily and focused on the clock on the dressing table. It was twenty minutes past ten. 'You were late,' she said, dully.

Leah wrung her hands. 'Forgive me, Highness. Count Michael . . .'

'Aha!' Interest returned to Nerina's eyes. 'You saw him then?'

'Of course.'

'Where and when?'

Leah's puzzlement was clear on her face. 'Why, when he came to me in my room at dawn. It was so romantic. I could refuse him nothing. Our love-making was so sweet that I quite lost track of the time.'

'But when did he leave?'

'Just a few moments ago. I came straight here after he had gone.'

Nerina blinked, her head spinning. 'Are you telling me that Count Michael has been with you in your room from dawn until a few moments ago?'

'Naturally. Why do you ask?'

Nerina fingered the sore places between her legs. 'Oh, no reason,' she said. She got up and went over to the dressing table. Turning her back, she studied her reflection over her shoulder. On both cheeks of her bottom were circular patches of vivid red that seemed to glow and pulsate. Rotating, she observed that her pubis was hardly less bright.

Leah came over to her. 'How on earth did you manage to do that to yourself?'

'It's a secret,' Nerina replied, shortly.

That afternoon, she awaited Alcina's daily visit with considerable trepidation. She had put the bondage implements she had used back in the chest, copying their original positions with what she thought was precision. Using face-powder, she dusted over the reddened areas of her body until they looked almost normal. Over all her thoughts, however, there loomed one enormous question. If not Count Michael, who was it who had come into the room while she was suspended? Who had examined every nook and crevice of her nudity and amused themselves by abusing her so cruelly? Not knowing the answer to that question made the morning's events somehow even more frightening and sinister, if that were possible. Still, if it had been Alcina, she felt that she would soon find out about it and it was the form Alcina's wrath would take which caused her so much anxiety.

When Alcina came into her room, she concealed that anxiety as best she could, but some sixth sense made Alcina keep darting sharp glances at her as they stripped to their knickers for their routine training session. Alcina unlocked the chest and brought out the usual items. Nerina held her breath, but the older woman appeared to notice nothing untoward. No longer needing to be told, Nerina held out her wrists for the cuffs to be put on. Alcina made as if to do so, then stopped. She grabbed Nerina's hand, rotating it so as to turn the inner side of her wrist uppermost. She rubbed with her thumb at the slight bruising and indentation there.

'What's this?'

Nerina had been quite unable to concoct any story that sounded remotely plausible, so she could make only incoherent, embarrassed noises.

Alcina grabbed the other wrist and examined that with equal intensity. Dropping it, she stood back and allowed her eyes to rove all over Nerina. Noticing some small detail, she stooped and made a careful examination of her knees, feeling and prodding.

She stood up again. 'Pull your knickers down,' she ordered.

Nerina obeyed, easing them down to mid-thigh, then standing there, acutely embarrassed and praying to be snatched up to Heaven. Even the Other Place would do, she thought. Anywhere, so long as it was away from the detailed scrutiny of this woman's eagle eyes.

'Turn round.'

Nerina rotated obediently. Alcina wet her finger in her mouth and rubbed it against Nerina's bottom.

Nerina winced and jumped. 'Ow!'

'Turn round again. Wait there.'

With sinking heart, knowing that the game was up, Nerina watched her go to the chest again and stoop over it. She sorted through the contents for only a moment, then stalked back to Nerina, who was still standing where she had been told. Her head was hanging in shame and her face blazed a message of guilt for all the world to see.

'So! Look at me when I speak to you.'

165

Nerina forced herself to meet those terrible, vengeful eyes, but could not sustain her gaze. She looked away again.

'Where is it?' Alcina was standing with hand outstretched.

Nerina pretended innocence. 'Where's what?'

'The key, of course!'

This was terrible, but Nerina determined to play the charade out to the end. 'I don't know what you mean. There is no key,' she mumbled.

Alcina pursed her lips. 'I knew that you were anxious to make more rapid progress with your training. Congratulations! You have achieved your end.' She turned away and went back to the chest. When she got up, she was holding in her hand the short whip with its deadly leather tails. A whip that would sting and burn like fire at every slash, that would quickly tear its way into already tenderised flesh!

Every drop of blood drained from Nerina's face as she stared at that fearsome instrument of torture, already feeling it cutting into her back.

'Get yourself over the end of the bed.'

Nerina backed away, consumed by terror. 'No, no!' she pleaded, in a voice made squeaky with horror. 'Please don't!'

There was no hint of compassion on Alcina's face. She pointed with the whip. 'Over the end of the bed.' she repeated.

Whimpering, Nerina complied, draping herself face-down in the required position. Out of the corner of her eye, she could see Alcina behind her, striding back and forth. Every now and again, she slashed the whip through the air so that it whistled and cracked. 'Liars have to be beaten,' she said.

'The key's in the dressing table drawer,' Nerina sobbed.

Alcina stopped her pacing. 'What key?'

'The key to the chest.'

Alcina shook her head decisively. 'Impossible! You said there was no key.'

Desperate now, Nerina screamed, 'I lied! It is in my box of hairpins.'

'I've warned you that liars have to be beaten. Now you tell me that you are a liar, which means that I am definitely obliged to whip you.'

Half mad with fear, Nerina moaned, 'No, no! Mercy! Don't whip me, please. I apologise for lying to you. I'll never do it again.'

There was a short silence. Nerina heard Alcina go to the dressing table, then the sound of pins being emptied on to its glass surface. When Alcina came into view again, she was holding the key between finger and thumb. 'You may yet save yourself from a thrashing,' she said. 'Just tell me where you got this.'

Nerina bit her lip hard. The temptation to save herself from intense pain was insidiously attractive. Then the image of Leah came into her mind. She would be torn bodily from the arms of the man she loved dearly, and all because she had helped a friend in need. Then there was Johann: gentle, handsome, courteous Johann, who had stroked her hair so tenderly, whose cheek felt so nice under her lips and who had given his word not to betray her shameful conduct to others, even though it meant sacrificing the definite glory he would otherwise have acquired among the rest of the staff.

She made up her mind. 'I cannot say.'

'Cannot, or will not?'

'Will not,' Nerina said, hopelessly.

Alcina paused again. 'There is no doubt in your mind that I will do what I say?'

'None.'

167

'Unless you tell me where you got that key, I shall whip you until you scream and faint with the pain. Then I will have you revived and whip you again. I will go on doing that until you do tell me.'

Nerina said nothing, her legs turning to jelly and her brain completely numbed by what was to come.

Alcina was insistent. 'Yet you still have nothing to say?'

Nerina shook her head. It was hard to speak, because her teeth were chattering so violently. 'No,' she whispered. She waited tensely for the first searing slash of the whip. Where would it come? On her back? On her buttocks? She hoped she could hold out.

'Get up!'

'What?'

'I told you to get up. Do so!'

Bewildered, Nerina looked around. Was this just another twist of the knife? Some ploy to put her off guard and make her beating harder to bear? Alcina was going back to the chest. She put the whip away and closed the lid. Nerina climbed to her feet, somewhat groggily. 'You are not going to beat me?'

Alcina was coming back towards her. 'No, I'm not,' she said. 'Do pull your knickers up, girl, you look ridiculous standing there with them round your knees.'

'But . . . but I don't understand? Why not?'

'Put on your dress and come and sit with me by the window. I will explain.'

When they were both dressed and occupying the armchairs, Alcina said, 'I have been waiting for an opportunity to put you to the test. That was a severe one, and you passed it.'

'I did? How?'

'Someone helped you to obtain that key. It is all

too obvious that you don't possess the necessary skills yourself.' Nerina opened her mouth to speak, but Alcina held up her hand for silence and continued. 'I do not know who that was. Frankly, I do not want to, although I have a shrewd idea. What matters is that you had the opportunity to save yourself from unbearable pain by betraying your associate. That you did not do so proves to me that your training is working. The moment when you return to rule Isingore drew just that bit closer today.'

Nerina found herself blushing and tears prickled in her eyes. How strange it was that just a short time ago she would have considered this woman to be far beneath her in status, yet now praise from her was something to be coveted and savoured.

She was not allowed to remain in her self-congratulatory mood for long.

'However,' Alcina said, sternly, 'there remains the matter of your disobedience to be dealt with. Do you deny that you stole things from the chest and used them unsupervised?'

Nerina shook her head. 'No,' she murmured, blushing again, but for a different reason.

'By doing so, you have severely disrupted a training programme which was most carefully planned. It will have to be revised now. For that, you will have to be punished. Do you agree that you deserve it?'

Nerina nodded. In fact, she truly did believe that she ought to suffer some penalty for what she had done. Perhaps, by that punishment, she could expunge some of the guilt and shame she felt when she recalled her recent experience.

'Very well. Today your training moves on, as you wished it to do. Part of the object of that training is to instil in you a complete understanding of what it feels like to be an underling: to serve without complaint when there is resentment in your heart and to know hunger and thirst. I cannot, without excessive cruelty, deprive you of food and drink. What I can and will do, however, is to deprive you of something else for which you have developed an undoubted appetite.'

Nerina was mystified. 'What do you mean?'

'For the next week, you will have no orgasms. None whatsoever, however induced. By the end of the week, you will know what it feels like to be starving.'

Nerina almost allowed the smile inside her to leak out onto her face. She had been prohibited from masturbation before and had found it all too easy to circumvent that prohibition. 'I understand, Alcina,' she said, humbly. 'I am most grateful to you for being so lenient. It is more than I deserve.'

'That is not all,' Alcina continued. 'That would simply be wasting valuable time. Concurrent with that punishment will be another, designed to teach you how it feels to serve others, so that when others are employed by you to serve, you will treat them with the appropriate respect. From tomorrow, you will take up your duties as a maid.'

'A maid! You want me to be a servant?'

'What's the matter? Still too much of a princess? Or perhaps you fear that the work will be too hard.'

Nerina braced herself. She would not allow this woman to best her. 'Whatever task you set me, I can do.'

That evening, she knocked rather timidly at the door of Leah's room. On being bidden to enter, she did so. She looked around. 'You are alone? I am not disturbing you?'

'Of course not, Princess. You are always welcome. What happened with Alcina? Did you get into trouble for using those dreadful things?'

170

Nerina nodded. 'Yes. That's why I've come to see you.'

'I did warn you, but you wouldn't listen,' Leah said, perhaps too smugly. A sudden thought crossed her mind. 'I say, you didn't tell her about me, did you?'

A twinge of guilt passed across Nerina's mind when she remembered how tempted she had been to do just that. To punish herself for that, she refrained from saying anything about her subsequent noble gesture. 'No, of course I didn't. I came to see you about something else. Alcina is going to punish me by making me act as a maid and I wanted to find out how bad that is likely to be, so that I can prepare myself for it.'

Somewhat bitterly, Leah said, 'So your dreadful punishment is to play for a while at being something I have been ever since I can remember.'

Nerina flushed, suddenly aware of how her question had made certain assumptions about her friend's life and previous occupation. 'I'm dreadfully sorry, Leah,' she said. 'That came out sort of wrong. I really do need your help, though. Tell me about being a maid.'

'That's not too difficult. You learn to speak when spoken to, not before. You keep yourself and your clothes clean and neat, even directly after performing the filthiest task. You assume a humble and grateful manner, even when you are seething with anger. You call your employer "Mistress" at every opportunity, to remind her that she is better than you and has the power to make your life a misery. You put her first in all things, even when that makes you unhappy. You eat scraps while she eats fine food. You sleep on a straw mattress in a garret while she sleeps in a soft bed. When she behaves outrageously or indecently or

171

unreasonably, you forgive her and never speak of it to others. You understand and accept that when she is angry with someone else, she will abuse you instead.' She grinned at the expression on Nerina's face. 'There's more. Do you want me to go on?'

'Oh, Leah! Was it really like that for you with me?'

'Worse,' Leah said cheerfully. 'It's a hard life for a princess to get used to.'

Now Nerina was feeling really guilty and her expression showed it. Her eyes filled with tears at the way she had maltreated this girl.

Leah took pity on her. She reached out and touched her hand. 'There's one thing I didn't tell you.'

'Oh,' Nerina said, miserably. 'What's that?'

'After you've been doing it for a while, you come to love your mistress; not because she is perfect, but in spite of the fact that she is flawed. When that happens, you accept all the bad things and do the job: not because you have to, but because you want to.'

That was too much. 'Oh, Leah! I didn't know! I'm so sorry!' Nerina put her face in her hands and burst into tears.

Leah put her arms round her and comforted her. 'There, there,' she said. 'It's been a trying day.'

172

Nine

'A uniform?' Nerina stared suspiciously at Alcina. 'You said nothing about having to wear a uniform.' Already, she thought, she had broken the pledge she made to herself after that salutary conversation with Leah: that she would try to be worthy of her friendship by being meek, humble and obedient throughout her period of punishment. Only thus could she understand and atone for the abuses she had unthinkingly heaped on her loyal servant.

'Didn't I mention it?' Alcina said, innocently. 'I thought I had. Why? Does it matter? Does her Highness not deign to wear one?'

Nerina coloured, remembering Leah's description of a good servant and suppressing her annoyance. 'It's not that, but why me? None of the other servants wear them.'

Alcina sighed. 'I have already explained to you that there are no servants in this house; only people who perform various jobs. You will be the only one. Your own servants wore uniforms, did they not?'

Nerina recalled the liveries of the footmen in the palace of Isingore. Was that really such a short time ago? It seemed like ancient history. 'Yes,' she admitted, grudgingly.

'And what do you suppose was the purpose of those uniforms?'

Nerina had never thought about it. It had been an accepted fact of life. 'To provide them with decent, tidy clothing if they had none of their own?' she hazarded.

'Quite wrong. They were dressed that way to mark their status in life. To distinguish them from their employers, in case there might be any confusion. The uniform sent out a message to all that here was someone who could be uncaringly abused and mis-used without risk of retaliation, would work long hours for a pittance and perform all the unpleasant tasks too tiresome for those dressed differently. That is why you will wear one. I want no one to be in any doubt as to how to treat you.'

That was fairly chilling information. Nerina gulped nervously, then set her shoulders. If Leah could put up with it for all those years, surely she could survive a few days. 'Very well. What sort of uniform?'

'I have it in this box,' Alcina said.

Nerina had been wondering about the contents of that wide, flat, cardboard box ever since Alcina had brought it in with her. Now she took it from her and removed the lid. The item that immediately struck her attention was a starched frilly cap: no more than a tiny linen tiara, really. It was a regular part of a lady's maid's uniform in some houses but Nerina had pre-ferred Leah to wear a long but simple, embroidered dress of her own design. Below the cap was a small, starched, frilly apron. When that was removed, she saw the expected black satin. That would also be a routine part of a maid's habit. She took out the dress and shook it, then held it against herself. 'It's awfully short, isn't it?'

'For a purpose. You'll see,' Alcina said. 'Now slip out of your clothes and try it on.'

Nerina went over to the bed, taking the box with

her. She took off her dress, her slippers and her knickers, which were the only clothes she wore.

She made as if to pick up the dress, but Alcina stopped her. 'First the stockings.'

Nerina had not noticed the black stockings in the box. She held them up and examined them. Made of sheer silk, they were very flimsy and transparent. She rolled them, slipped her feet in one at a time and rolled them up her legs, smoothing as she went. She was very pleased with them. She could not remember ever having such fine stockings, notwithstanding that the colour was a little dismal.

'Now the suspensory belt.'

That must be the ribbony thing in the box, with its projections of ruched black satin over elastic. She had heard of such things, but never seen one. This must be another Paris creation. She picked it up. 'How does it work? I've always worn garters.'

Alcina came over to her. 'Here, let me help. It goes around your waist and fixes with this hook and eye. Now you join the suspensors to your stockings by pressing this little rubber button into the material and putting this metal loop over it to hold it.'

From the black band around her waist, Nerina could see two lengths of black material stretched straight down the side of each thigh, straining the stocking tops into black, upward arrows. How ingenious! Much better than tight garters that tended to cut off the circulation and slipped anyway, leaving ugly wrinkles in even the prettiest stockings. She made a mental note to have several belts like this one made for herself. In a less sepulchral fabric, of course.

There was nothing else in the box. She checked the bed, shaking out the dress again in case she had missed something. 'I don't see any knickers. Do I wear my everyday ones?'

'No.'

'Oh? Then where are the ones that go with the uniform?'

'There are none.'

'Oh.' Nerina was baffled. 'Then what do I wear?'

'Nothing.'

'Do you mean that under my dress I shall be naked?'

Alcina's smile gave the answer before she spoke. 'You will have stockings and suspensory belt. Nothing else.'

Nerina opened her mouth to argue, then closed it again. Servants did not answer back. Leah said so. She picked up the dress and pulled it over her head. It settled on her shoulders, but the hem was so high that it barely covered her pubes. When she tugged it down, easing it away from her shoulders to give a little extra length, her breasts popped out of the deeply scooped neckline in a most disconcerting way. She pulled the material over them again. At this, the hem rose alarmingly until it revealed the whole of her pubes, on which the hairs were just beginning to show as stubble. She pulled up and pulled down, struggling with the stupid thing, only to give up in exasperation. 'It doesn't fit,' she complained.

'Yes it does.' Alcina came to her and grasped the sides of the dress. With a quick jerk, she pulled it down until Nerina's breasts were exposed and the hem came just below the junction between thighs and belly. 'There,' she said. 'That's how it's meant to go. Now put on the apron.'

The apron was no help, being hardly larger than a handkerchief. Nerina looked down at herself in consternation. Words bubbled out of her, despite all her good intentions. 'Like this? I can't go about like this!' She went over to the dressing table and looked at her

176

reflection, turning to inspect the back as well. 'Anyone could see most of my bottom, as well as my breasts,' she protested.

'Until you bend over,' Alcina remarked, drily. 'Then they'll be able to see all your bottom, not just a part of it. I can assure you that the work of a maid involves lots of stooping. No one said it would be easy, did they? If it were, you would learn nothing.'

Nerina bit back a sharp retort and put on the apron. That didn't help at all, being even shorter than the dress. When Alcina put the frilly cap on her head and adjusted it, Nerina found it odd that this seemingly innocuous article of apparel did more to humiliate her than anything the dress revealed. She eyed her reflection with distaste. She was a grotesque parody of a maid, deprived even of a decent, concealing uniform. It would be obvious to anyone that she had been dressed in that way to strip her of any pretence of pride or dignity. She felt the tears welling into her eyes at the sight of herself, blinking them back furiously before they could escape on to her cheeks.

'Here are your shoes.' Alcina held out a pair of patent leather shoes with very long, pointed heels. Nerina put them on and found that she teetered for a while before becoming accustomed to the sudden gain in height.

'Did you masturbate this morning?'

Nerina jumped guiltily at the suddenness of the question. She had, in fact, masturbated twice, just in case Alcina found a way of preventing her illicit pleasure. Since discovering some of the drawbacks of severe bondage, her masturbation fantasies had changed a little. She had not abandoned completely the phantom of Count Michael abusing her helpless body, but her mind had turned more and more often to Johann's penis and what she had done to it. It was not difficult to superimpose Prince Argan's face on Johann's body and that was highly satisfactory. She tried to imagine what it would be like to have that magical wand pushed hard up inside her, pulsing against the walls of her vagina, and to know the joy of hot, sticky juices bathing her womb as they had once bathed her throat. It was hard to know which image to choose, sometimes, and her craving flitted back and forth between them. On the one hand, total subjugation and all the lusts she knew that created in her. On the other, complete freedom to participate: to know at last the guessed-at bliss of a full sexual connection and to give to Prince Argan as much pleasure as she received. Alcina's question brought all these images rushing into her head simultaneously, stilling her tongue. In spite of that, her blush served in place of an answer.

'That's the last time for a week, remember.'

'Yes.'

Alcina frowned. 'Yes mistress, if you please. From now on, you will address everyone as "mistress", or "sir". Understand?'

'Yes . . . mistress.'

Alcina nodded approval. 'Good. Your first task is to clean out the grate and lay the fire.'

Nerina turned to contemplate the fireplace where last night's cheerful glow had been replaced by dead ashes and her face fell. 'I'm sorry; I don't know how.'

'Have you never watched it done?'

Nerina searched her mind, but could find no trace of such a recollection. Fires were things one did not have to think about. They burned and gave off heat. The next day, they did the same thing. She had never considered that at some time between one day and the next, while she was bathing, sleeping or otherwise occupied, the thing would need to be silently and unobtrusively attended to by someone. That was quite a novel idea and interesting in the abstract. However, now that she was that 'someone' who would have to do the job, the full extent of her lack of knowledge struck her with considerable force, leaving her bewildered and helpless.

'No, I'm sorry, I haven't.'

Alcina was staring at her in a most peculiar way, head back and eyebrows raised in interrogation, as though expecting her to say something else. Nerina looked about her for some clue as to what she might have overlooked which had made her statement incorrect or ridiculous. Finding nothing, she spread her hands, shrugged and said, 'Sorry,' again, rather lamely.

'Haven't you forgotten something?'

Nerina turned right round this time in her agitated determination to miss nothing. The grate, the ashes, the poker and the coal scuttle: these things stared back at her, their muteness mocking her stupidity. Suddenly light dawned and she spun round, words tumbling over themselves in her anxiety to repair damage which was, perhaps, already irreparable.

'I'm sorry, mistress,' she stammered. 'I really meant to say "mistress", mistress, but I forgot for a moment, mistress.' There! that was four 'mistresses'! Would that suffice? She gazed anxiously at Alcina, waiting for her reaction.

Alcina laughed – a good sign, surely. 'Very well,' she said. 'The transition from princess to maid has been abrupt enough for me to make allowances. Nevertheless, that is the only time I will show such forbearance. Your proper training demands that I should insist on the correct form of address on all occasions. To impress that on your mind, I will tell you that a new toy will soon be added to the chest. It even has a pet name. It is called the "chastiser". Any misbehaviour or error will mean that I will introduce your bare bottom to the chastiser. I don't think you will find the meeting a happy one.'

Nerina shuddered. 'Yes, mistress. I understand, mistress.' Would a curtsey be appropriately ingratiating? Couldn't do any harm! She bobbed a small one. Unfamiliarity with this movement when used as a token of deference conspired with her short skirt and high heels to make her singularly clumsy.

To her relief, Alcina laughed again. 'Fortunately, I anticipated your ignorance and have made appropriate arrangements. I have asked Leah to help you. Mark my words carefully: she has been told that she is not to do the job for you and is not to help in any way whatsoever, other than by giving instruction and advice. If my orders are not complied with to the letter, both of you will regret it.'

'I understand, mistress. Will you send for her, please?'

Alcina's friendly smile was deceptive. 'Of course. She is in the kitchen. I will send my maid to fetch her.'

'Thank you, mistress . . . oh! That's me, isn't it?'

Alcina nodded, still smiling.

'I'm sorry, mistress, but do you mean that I have to go out of this room dressed like this? What if someone sees me?'

'You will find that your duties call for you to move about the house a great deal. You had better get used to the idea quickly. Now get about your work, girl, before I form the opinion that you are dawdling.'

'Yes, mistress.'

Nerina made for the door, but Alcina called her back. 'You have forgotten the scuttle. It will need filling. Take it with you, otherwise you will have two journeys to make.'

'Thank you, mistress.' Nerina was not unhappy to have the scuttle to carry. Perhaps, by holding it with both hands in front of her she could remedy some of the shortcomings of her dress. She set off for the door again.

'Wait!'

'Yes, mistress?'

'Do you know where the kitchen is?'

'Er . . . no, mistress.'

Alcina shook her head sadly. 'The three P's, Nerina. The good servant, or the good statesman, always remembers them. Preparation and Planning make Perfection. I can see that the chastiser is going to be needed sooner than I thought. This time only, I will come with you and show you the way.'

They went out of the room together, Nerina holding the scuttle in a decorously strategic position in front of her. They had gone only a few paces when a young man came towards them along the corridor. Nerina half-recognised him as someone she had seen in the garden and involuntarily hunched her shoulders as if, by doing so, she could minimise the protrusion of her bare breasts. He smile broadly at her and winked. To her consternation, he raised his forefinger and pointed directly at her. She blushed hotly and turned her head away in disgust. He passed them and, although she did not look back, she knew that he was still staring at her. The thought that she was not wearing knickers and that the lower part of her bottom cheeks was in no way concealed by her dress caused her to blush again.

'That was very rude of you,' Alcina said. 'Don't do it again, please.'

Indignation overcame caution. 'But you know what he was suggesting by his gesture, mistress.'

Alcina shrugged. 'He is a young and vigorous man. You are a young and lusty woman, and a very beautiful one. What more natural than that he should pay you the greatest compliment that lies within his power? Your churlish spurning of that compliment was unnecessary. He was not to know that you are, at present, not available in that way. You had merely to smile pleasantly and close your fingers into a fist. That message is well understood and accepted without rancour.'

Nerina digested this. 'Is sex with many partners and in many different ways such an unimportant and casual thing in Paradon, then, mistress?'

'Absolutely not! It is taken very seriously indeed and great efforts are made to explore every nuance of the delights the body and the mind may discover. The understanding that it is a delight, and not a chore or a sin, is what makes Paradon unique and its inhabitants so at one with each other. Humans take pleasure in sex. They are designed that way. They also take pleasure in opera. No one thinks any the worse of them if they go to the opera on every possible occasion. They would be thought mad if they went only to one opera and heard only one singer every time. Why should the rapture of sex be different from the pleasure to be had from music or song? Also, to continue the analogy, sex takes many forms and embraces many techniques, as does music. It would be a dull composer who used only the white notes, when the black ones make the piece so much more interesting and enjoyable.'

That was a lot to think about and Nerina did so while they made their way downstairs. Alcina pointed to a door in the back part of the house. 'That is the kitchen.'

'Thank you, mistress.' Nerina pushed open the

door. The kitchen was vast, as the size of the house and the number of inhabitants dictated. Huge steel hobs, ovens and machines whose use she did not comprehend were scattered about in seeming disarray. There was a hubbub of noise from the ten or a dozen occupants who were going about their work with the frenzied order of ants in a disturbed nest, carrying their eggs to safety. The sudden silence and stillness which fell upon the place as she opened the door was disconcerting. It seemed that every eye was on her and she stopped, irresolute, poised for flight.

Then Leah was coming towards her, holding out her hands to greet her and the sight of her was reassuring in the extreme.

'Come in. Look, everyone. This is Nerina.'

The men and women who had stopped their work smiled and nodded in a friendly fashion; some men smiled more broadly than others and even pointed a finger at her. She was ready, this time: smiling, nodding and closing her fist in response.

Leah took her free hand. 'Come on! I'll show you where to get the coal.' She led Nerina through the kitchen and out into a small yard at the back. Opening a door in an out-building, she said, 'It's in there.'

Nerina peered into the black depths. 'You mean I have to go in?'

'Well, it won't come out to you. It's not really dark when you are inside. Your eyes get used to it. You'll find a shovel in there.'

'Do I use that to put the coal into the scuttle, then?' It was just as well to be absolutely sure of everything when one was in such unfamiliar territory.

'Yes. Go on in.'

'There aren't rats in there, or anything?'

Leah laughed. 'No, silly!'

'Spiders?'

'Oh well, naturally there are spiders. It's a coal cellar. Of course,' she added quickly, seeing the expression on Nerina's face, 'they are very tiny ones.'

Nervously, feeling her way with her feet, Nerina made her way into the darkness. What Leah had said was true. The light from behind her was sufficient to make out a huge heap of coal and a small shovel lying beside it. She picked up the shovel, grimacing at the gritty feel of coal-dust on her palm and stabbed tentatively at the heap. A piece of coal rolled down from the top, convincing her that she was about to be set upon by armies of hostile, giant spiders, but she stuck grimly to her task until the scuttle was full. Once filled, it was enormously heavy and she had a little difficulty in backing into the daylight with it.

Leah took her back into the kitchen. 'You'll need a newspaper, a bundle of wood, a dustpan and a brush,' she said. 'They are over there.'

Nerina looked and saw the things she needed. They were tucked well back between two large metal cupboards. An awful difficulty occurred to her. She lowered her voice and whispered to Leah, 'Will you get them for me? If I bend over in this skirt, everyone will be able to see . . . everything.'

'I'm really sorry. I mustn't. Alcina has given very strict orders about that and everyone here would see me doing it. You'll have to do it yourself, I'm afraid.'

Nerina made her way over to the cupboards. There really was no way she could reach that far in and still maintain a ladylike concealment of her posterior parts. She looked around, waiting for a moment when no one seemed to be looking her way, then stooped quickly, her bare breasts hanging and swinging, squeezing the upper part of her bent body into the gap while she stretched for the tools. She felt her

184

skirt ride up at the back and a coolness told her that her bottom was now completely uncovered. At that moment, a great cheer and a lot of clapping told her that her exposure had not gone unnoticed. Hideously embarrassed, she straightened, the things in her hands hampering her attempts to pull her skirt down.

'Let's get out of here,' she hissed to Leah. 'How am I going to carry all these things?'

'Pick up the scuttle with one hand and carry the other things under your other arm.'

Nerina did so, the huge weight of the coal causing her body to tilt the other way in compensation. She did not see how she could walk far without changing hands and resting. She felt Leah behind her, fumbling with her skirt, lifting it up and tucking the hem into the fastening of her apron so as to leave her bottom uncovered. 'What are you doing?'

'It's all right. Everyone has to do it first time. You'll be all right. Just take no notice. Make for the door and keep walking, no matter what.'

What did it matter? Nerina thought. This whole experience was so weird that one extra piece of weirdness, more or less, could not possibly make any difference to her misery. She trudged slowly forward, staggering a little on her high heels. Only then did she notice that the kitchen staff had formed themselves into a double line. To get to the door, she would have to run the gauntlet of their stares by passing between them.

They each held a dish-towel in their hands and those towels were wet. Each one, as she passed, flicked her bare bottom with the end of their towel, laughing heartily as they did so. Such flicks hardly stung at all, but the slapping noise and the encouraging cheers were difficult to endure. Loaded down as she was, she could not hurry, so that they had ample opportunity for several flicks each. She was thankful when Leah closed the kitchen door behind her and she could set her scuttle down.

'Why were they so beastly to me?' she asked as Leah fussed around her, pulling down her skirt and rearranging it.

'I know you don't understand, but they were really being friendly,' Leah said.

Nerina sniffed mournfully. 'What do they do when they're unfriendly?'

'It's just their idea of a bit of fun. They did it to me and they've all had it done to them. It's their way of welcoming you into the community. It made me laugh, because that's what I'm used to. That's the way ordinary people who are not princesses behave. They would be upset if they thought they had made you unhappy.'

She still didn't understand, but Nerina found that she was much happier now that she knew that what had just been inflicted on her was done in a spirit of friendly horseplay. She picked up her scuttle and trudged on in a better frame of mind. The stairs were particularly difficult and she thought her arms would never be the same length again by the time she plonked her burdens down in front of the dead fire.

With Leah's skilled knowledge, she quite quickly raked out the ashes, swept them up and wrapped them in part of the newspaper. Leah showed her how to lay the fire, putting wood on paper and coal on wood. When she finally lit the fire and could see it beginning to burn well without smoking, Nerina experienced a real thrill of accomplishment. For about the first time in her life, she had actually done something practical and useful. She sat back on her heels, watching the flames licking up through the coals and pushed a stray lock of hair out of her eyes with a grimy hand. She smiled at Leah who smiled back. The smile became a laugh and, before she knew it, they were clinging together, giggling helplessly about nothing at all.

Alcina's entrance went unnoticed by either of them until she spoke. 'What's this, then?'

Nerina scrambled to her feet. 'Leah showed me how to lay the fire. Look, Alcina! I did it all by myself. See how bright it burns!' Her bubbling happiness at her new-found mastery of the recondite rites of fire-laying had made her incautious. Far too late, she added, '. . . mistress.'

'Who gave you permission to speak of Miss Leah as "Leah"?'

'Why, no one. I thought . . . Do I have to call her "mistress", too, mistress?'

'You are a maid; than which there is nothing lower. You call everyone, "mistress" or "sir". Have you forgotten already that I told you that? And what sort of state do you call that? You are filthy!'

'But I've just done the fire, mistress.'

'Maids do not answer back.' From behind her back, Alcina produced a short, slender, leather whip with a silver handle. The tip, instead of coming to a point, had a flat flap of leather, about ten centimetres square. 'This is the chastiser,' she said. 'I think it is time for the introduction I spoke of.'

The skin of Nerina's bottom crawled as she looked at this instrument. 'Please, mistress . . .'

'Not another word. You have said far too much already. Go into the bathroom and wash your face and hands. When you have done that, come back here. I will be waiting for you.'

Dejectedly, Nerina slunk off to obey.

Turning to Leah, Alcina said, 'As for you, Leah, I am a little disappointed in you. I hoped that you would join in the spirit of what has to be done a little better than that. For the next week, it is necessary that Nerina's life should be as difficult as possible. For me to find you laughing together makes a mockery of that intention. You will go to your room and think yourself lucky that I do not choose to punish you for your foolishness. It will be sufficient punishment for you to know that it is entirely your fault that your friend, Nerina, is about to receive a whipping.'

'But that's not fair,' Leah burst out.

Alcina silenced her with a raised hand. 'Have a care,' she said. 'I may yet change my mind about punishing you in a more direct fashion. On your way to your room, send Zelda to me. What comes next will form a necessary part of her training as my deputy.'

As Nerina washed, she recognised Alcina's cruelty in making her take the time to do so. To be beaten at once, to be taken almost by surprise, would mean that there would be only the punishment itself to be borne. To be thus forewarned and have time to think about what was in store, was an additional ordeal. She extended her time in the bathroom as much as she thought was safe in order to delay her whipping, fully aware that by doing so, she was abetting Alcina's cruelty. The only possible consequence of delay was a longer period of apprehension.

Thus it was that, when she went back into the bedroom, Zelda was there with Alcina. Nerina instantly recognised that as a bad omen. She was afraid to ask what had happened to Leah, but had no need to.

'I have sent Leah to her room,' Alcina said. 'I shall deal with her later. Are your hands clean now?'

'Yes, mistress.'

'Show me!'

To be made to show her hands, front and back, like a child, was somehow even more humbling with Zelda in the room.

'Very well. Never let me see you in that disgusting state again. This is how your punishment will always be administered. I will go through it once for your benefit and for Zelda's should she have need to chastise you for some reason.'

Zelda! Zelda was going to be allowed to beat her! Nerina almost protested, but thought better of it.

'Pay attention! I shall say, "Get it up," and you will at once go down on all fours, wherever you happen to be. Do that now.'

Nerina sank to the carpet on hands and knees, very conscious of the shortness of her skirt in this position. 'Put your knees apart. No! Wider than that.' Alcina tapped her whip on the small of Nerina's back. 'Lower! No, not your head and shoulders. Keep your arms straight. Keep your bottom up as well and just let your back dip down. That's right! That is the position you will assume when I say, "Get it up". I will tell you the number of strokes you are to receive and you will count them aloud. If, during your punishment, you allow your back to straighten or, worse, if you allow it to arch up the other way, that will invalidate any strokes you have already received and I will begin again. When the required number of strokes have been given, you will thank me for correcting you.'

For Nerina, kneeling there, this was a completely shaming experience. It had, somehow, not been so bad to be tied in a particular position. To be forced to adopt this one of her own free will, impelled only by her desire to reach a level of accomplishment that would entitle her to couple with the prince of her dreams and fantasies, was something else, a different kind of subjugation. Yet, in spite of her mortification, there was yet that flame of lust flickering inside her, some perverted part of her personality that actually enjoyed that very shame. She had felt it most strongly when that unknown hand had slippered her naked bottom so thoroughly and, though she dreaded the whipping she was about to receive, she felt it now. Her vagina was letting down its juices and her nipples were erect. It was an upward spiral of appetite. Shame and humiliation led to sexual arousal. That was a humiliating thing to learn about herself and the shame of being aroused in that way led to even more sexual excitement.

Alcina was excited, too, although she took care to allow no trace of it to show in her manner or expression. To herself, but to no one else, she admitted that she enjoyed inflicting punishment. Standing there now, drawing her whip through her hands as she gazed down at Nerina's bare backside, she also felt the wetness within her and knew the cause. Sometimes she came to orgasm if the beating went on long enough and she had been obliged to control herself, exerting considerable discipline over her passions to ensure that she did not give way to them entirely and slash again and again with all her strength, simply to satisfy her own lust for greater sexual pleasure.

The pale, quivering buttocks before her were precious to Prince Argan. They had to be treated in just the right way: made to feel sufficient pain for the purpose intended, but not enough to cause inconvenient injury. She could cause no damage with her eyes and she used them, drinking in every detail of Nerina's vulgar exposure and rejoicing in her subservience. Her straddled posture and the way she had been made to distort her back caused her bottom to stick up in a particularly lewd, undignified fashion, completely open to any attack upon it. It also meant that her anus and the peach-shape of her vulva were just as exposed. Alcina bent down and flipped up the short dress which already concealed little. When she laid it along Nerina's back, it left her naked from the waist to the tops of her black, silk stockings; the long black suspensors against the soft, white skin of her thighs served only to accentuate her nudity.

Being that much closer allowed her a better view of Nerina's sphincter. That small, pinky-brown dimple drew her eyes like a magnet. Even as she watched, some involuntary nervous twitch caused it to pucker momentarily, as if in an attempt to kiss some spectral intruder. The knowledge of what she was going to be doing to that particular little treasure at some time in the near future caused a fiery worm to bite at Alcina's womb, contracting her vagina into an answering kiss. Allowing her eyes to drift lower, she observed that Nerina's pubic hair had started to grow in again, just enough to impart a delicate shade of brown to her vulva, from which her labia protruded enticingly. Alcina's sharp eyes detected the shine of vaginal fluid which told her that Nerina was not indifferent to what was happening. If those lips opened just a fraction more, she would be able to see right inside her vagina and she resisted a strong urge to order wider parting of those delicious thighs.

Clearing her throat a little, to avoid any chance of her aroused state from showing, Alcina said, 'On this occasion, it will be sufficient for you to receive only five strokes. Next time, you will not get off so lightly. Have you remembered that you are to count the strokes aloud?'

'Yes, mistress.'

'A nice loud, clear voice, please. I would hate to miss one and have to repeat it.'

Alcina raised the whip. This was a moment she much enjoyed. The flesh before her was white and unmarked. Knowing what it would look like when she had finished increased her arousal. Her first stroke landed squarely in the centre of Nerina's right buttock with a sharp, slapping sound. The soft skin wobbled under the impact and Nerina jerked forward. 'One,' she said, making every effort to speak distinctly.

A square patch of redness, slightly darker at the edges, appeared on the whiteness.

The second stroke was aimed at the left buttock. This time, Nerina grunted, her head jerking back. 'Two.' The pain was very real, but bearable. Nerina was grateful for the breadth of the leather tip. Had it been an ordinary whip, the force would have been concentrated on a much smaller area, with more painful and damaging results. Her bottom was already tingling, even though it had received only two strokes. She knew that her nipples were tingling, too, keeping pace with the tumult in her vagina. It had happened when she was slippered and now it was happening again. She longed to reach underneath herself and finger her clitoris but was aware of what the consequences of that would be, so she refrained.

'Three.'

Zelda watched Nerina's half-naked body jerk forward, her dangling breasts wobbling with her movement. Before the beating began, she had assumed that she would watch it with the same neutral feelings as she had experienced when seeing other servants punished in a more normal fashion. This was completely different. To start with, there was a ritualistic quality about it that was clearly designed to heap shame on pain and she found that much to her taste. More importantly, it was a princess whose bottom was being thrashed: one of those important people accustomed to command, not to obey. Zelda discovered that the sound of the whip and the grimace it provoked each time was moving her profoundly, providing sexual stimulation. She moved cautiously to a position slightly behind Alcina so as to have a better view and to be out of her line of sight. Satisfied that she was unobserved she hitched up her dress, little by little, drew aside the gusset of her knickers and explored the wetness of her sex with her finger.

'Four.' Now the abused area was burning with a throbbing heat and Nerina understood better Alcina's concern that she should continue to keep her bottom in the air. Without that warning, she had no doubt that she would have arched upwards so as to make it easier to tense her gluteal muscles and withdraw them from the whip that was causing her backside to glow so powerfully. She longed to reach back with her hands, not only to finger her sex, but to use them to shield her stinging posterior. She could sense a curious ambivalence in her relationship with the chastiser. The hurt it inflicted also induced intense sexual yearning for orgasm. She held on grimly. There was only one more to come.

'Five!'

Nerina collapsed forward, her elbows on the floor, taking deep breaths and attempting to regain her composure.

'I didn't hear that. What did you say?'

'I said, "Five!",' Nerina shouted, only just remembering to add ' . . . mistress.'

'Sorry. I didn't hear you. Get it up again!'

Again Nerina opened her mouth to protest, but thought better of it. Wearily she assumed the correct position and waited.

Alcina stepped to a position alongside her and to her right. She raised the whip again and brought it down. This time, she did not aim at the reddened buttocks. The stroke was precisely vertical. The thin part of the whip fell exactly on Nerina's anus in the stretched crease between her buttocks, while the leather flap slapped directly on her vulva. With a great shriek of surprise, she leapt forward and fell on her face, her breasts grinding into the carpet while her hands clutched herself between the legs, cupping the source of her discomfort.

'I didn't hear anything,' Alcina said.

'Five!' Nerina screamed. 'Five! Five! I said five, mistress!'

'But you moved from the position. Get it up!'

Hastily, Nerina scrambled back into the required pose. 'I'm sorry, mistress,' she whimpered. 'Please let me off. I won't do it again.'

'You also forgot to thank me for correcting you.'

'Thank you, mistress! Thank you for correcting me,' Nerina babbled.

'Very well. I will let you off, although you don't deserve it. No more chances, though. I think I am being much too lenient with you.'

Alcina had not had the slightest intention of inflicting any more punishment. In fact, she would have stopped at five strokes, had Nerina not shown an unexpected ability to deal with her whipping, There was a germ of intuition in Alcina's mind that told her that her victim was, at least in part, enjoying what was being done to her bottom. That had to be corrected at all costs if the threat of the chastiser were to be effective in the future as a deterrent. If it were, it would mean that there would be fewer whippings, which was a pity, but couldn't be helped. Her job was to carry out Nerina's training in the most efficient manner. She had thought that just one slap in the right place with the chastiser would do the trick and she had been proved absolutely right. She was convinced that Nerina would try just that bit harder from now on.

Ten

Completely unaware of the motivation behind Alcina's unexpected leniency, Nerina continued to kneel. After a while she plucked up the courage to ask, timidly, 'May I get up, please, mistress?'

'What? Oh yes, get up, girl.'

'Thank you, mistress.' Nerina stood for a while, uncertain what to do next. She did not have to wait long to find out.

'Go to the chest and bring me back the wrist cuffs and the knee spreader.'

Nerina paled, but dared not disobey. She went across the room with her mind in a tumult. Alcina had said that her punishment was at an end, but that was probably another of her cruel tricks. If not, what could she possibly want with those things? She came back and stood with them in her hands, looking from one woman to the other.

'Give them to Zelda and take off your dress and your shoes.'

The questions in Nerina's brain died still-born in her mouth. Mutely, she removed her dress and folded it neatly on a chair, placing the shoes beneath the same chair. As she came back to Alcina, she was longing to hunch her shoulders and cover herself with her hands, because of the embarrassment caused by Zelda's presence. She was careful to do neither of those things for fear of provoking Alcina to further anger. She kept her shoulders back and her hands at her sides. She was not quite sure why Zelda's eyes upon her should be any more difficult to deal with than all the other eyes that had inspected her body. There was something intuitive about the feeling. She had sensed it when Zelda had first seen her naked. On this occasion she was wearing stockings and suspensory belt but these garments seemed only to make her more naked, not less.

'Put the cuffs on her, Zelda.'

Meekly, Nerina held out her wrists and allowed Zelda to fit the leather cuffs around her wrists. She pulled the straps savagely tight and Nerina winced.

Alcina inspected Zelda's work. 'Not so tight, stupid girl! They may be there for some time. Loosen them.'

Zelda scowled, her head bent over her task so that Alcina should not see her expression.

Alcina inspected again. 'That's better.' She went over to the bed and piled up all the pillows against the headboard. She beckoned to Nerina. 'Come over here and get on the bed. That's right. Sit with your back against the pillows.'

Nerina did as she was told, worried and puzzled, while Alcina went to the chest. She came back with several lengths of chain. Taking one length, she passed it around the right side-frame of the bed near the head and padlocked two links together so as to leave a foot or so of chain lying on the coverlet. She pulled Nerina's right wrist to her and padlocked the ring on the cuff to the end of the chain. She did the same the other side so that Nerina's arms were extended on either side of her.

'Not too tight?'

Nerina wondered why she should care. She shook her head.

'Zelda, put on the knee spreader. Not too tightly, mind. I'm watching you.'

Nerina watched as Zelda strapped the spreader into place over her black silk stockings. Having Zelda so close to her parted legs was uncomfortable and Nerina wriggled uneasily.

Alcina had been fastening chain to the frame at the bottom of the bed, leading the end up over the foot board. 'Bend your knees!'

Nerina did so and Alcina padlocked the end of the chain around the spreader bar, adjusting the length with care. 'See that?' she said to Zelda. 'That is how it is to be done. Sufficient length to allow her to alter her position a little but insufficient to allow her to swing her body round so as to touch herself. That is to stop her from masturbating, which is what she will do unless prevented.'

Nerina's face burned fiery red. To be spoken about so casually as if she were not in the room was bad enough; to have Zelda told about her most private addiction was far, far worse. She felt her eyes fill with tears.

'You, Zelda, will help me to supervise her while she works about the house. You will not take your eyes off her for one single moment. That includes everything she does, including visiting the bathroom.'

It was impossible for Nerina's face to grow redder, otherwise it would have done. None of the indignities so far heaped upon her could compare with this last.

'If, for some reason, you have to lose sight of her, this is the only place she may be while you do. You will fasten her like this every time you leave her alone. This, also, is how she will sleep. I have decreed that she shall have no orgasms for a week and I am determined not to be thwarted by her, as I have been in the past. I have to leave you now. Don't fail me in this, Zelda. This is as much a test of yourself as it is of her. You have my full permission to punish her as you see fit if she gives you trouble.'

Alcina left the room and Nerina watched her go in sick despair, believing that her spirits could sink no lower. She had been shamed beyond all measure and was now tethered, naked, like some animal, completely dependent for everything on her captors. How mistaken she had been to believe that she could outsmart Alcina. The naiveté of her blithe assumption that she could continue her masturbation habit surreptitiously was now fully revealed to her and embarrassed her enormously. And she did want to masturbate, that much she knew. Her whipping had stirred her, as corporal punishment had always done from her first experience of it. In more normal circumstances, that excitement might well have led to the urge for self-gratification. On the other hand, she might have thought about it and then been distracted by something else. Left like this, with her hands immobilised away from her body and her thighs widely parted so that she could not rub them together, her mind was forced constantly to return to the reason for her confinement. Furthermore, the bondage itself, as it always did, was stoking the fire of her lust until it burned bright and hot. She tried hard to ignore her urgent need, but the horrifying prospect of seven days without sexual release lay before her. A tear trickled down her cheek untended. She had been deprived even of the power to wipe it away.

'So! The high and mighty princess likes to play with herself, does she?'

Zelda's voice broke abruptly into Nerina's self-pity. She jolted back to full awareness, suddenly conscious of a menace from a totally unexpected

199

direction. Zelda was sitting on the side of the bed, one foot on the floor and the other curled up beneath her. Nerina did not care for the way Zelda was staring at her and all her previous intuitions returned to her in full force. A sixth sense told her that any reply she made would be used as an excuse for increased animosity, so she made none, merely turning her head away in feigned disinterest.

She gasped in pain and surprise as Zelda gripped her right nipple, squeezing and twisting.

'I asked you a question!'

Nerina moved her upper body as far as she was able, trying to twist away from the torment being inflicted upon her, but it was useless. 'Ow! Ouch! I don't know what you want me to say.'

'The truth!'

'No, I don't ... Ow! Ow! That hurts! All right then, I do!'

Zelda released her grip and sat back. 'Do what?' she enquired.

Nerina looked blankly at her. 'I don't understand.'

'I'm asking you to tell me what it is that you do. I want to hear you use the words.'

Nerina blushed. 'I can't do that.'

Zelda reached forward again, stopping with her fingers only inches from Nerina's nipple. 'I'm sure you can. You can say, "I'm a dirty little girl who likes to masturbate", can't you?'

Nerina bit her lip, her blush deepening. Zelda was toying with her, as a cat plays with a mouse before the kill, and Zelda was a particularly dangerous cat – far more of a threat to her than Alcina. Alcina's motive was to train her. Nerina had a nasty suspicion that Zelda's lay in pure vindictiveness and sadism. She hung her head and mumbled, 'I'm a dirty little girl who likes to masturbate.'

Zelda sat back again. 'There! That wasn't so hard, was it? I wonder what else we could get you to say? No matter, for the moment. Now that we have the subject matter out in the open, we can discuss it, you and I. I expect you'd like to do yourself right now, wouldn't you?'

Nerina groaned in misery and closed her eyes again. Not simply because she realised Zelda's purpose in saying such a thing, but because it was true. She longed most urgently for an orgasm and the knowledge that it was Zelda's cruel interrogation that was increasing that longing was hard to bear. She raised her head and stared angrily at Zelda. 'Yes! Yes I would. All right? Is that what you wanted me to say?'

Zelda laughed. 'All right,' she said. 'No need to get so upset. Keep calm and, who knows, I may be able to help you.'

The bright spark of hope that flared inside Nerina at those words was as degrading to her as anything that had gone before. Was she truly so far gone in depravity that a half-promise from someone as odious as Zelda could excite her? 'What do you mean?' she asked, cautiously.

'Just that a little more enthusiasm for our chat might make me better disposed towards you. You notice that I am being nice to you. I don't insist that you call me "mistress".'

'What do you want to talk about?'

'Let's talk about what you do to stir yourself up. For instance, do you think about other women?'

Nerina did not in the least want to have this conversation. The idea of humouring Zelda was repellent, but her need drove her on to do so, all the time there was the slightest chance of that need being met. 'Sometimes,' she replied.

'Do you think about them naked?'

'Yes.'

'Would you like to see me naked?'

There it was again, that jolt of mortification. An indignant refusal sprang into the thinking, reasoning part of Nerina's brain, to be immediately submerged by the part that was under the command of her subconscious, fuelled by the symptoms within her body. 'Yes,' she said. She tried to tell herself that her answer was simply for the purpose of humouring Zelda and, thereby, obtaining the release she sought, but she knew that it was really driven by her obscene desire to see the private parts of another woman. Anyone, she now realised, anyone at all, even someone like Zelda, would do for that disgusting purpose, so low had she sunk into depravity.

'So you shall, Princess.' Zelda rose and took off her dress. Her breasts were large, white and soft; her nipples pink buds in the centre of extremely large, pink aureolae. She hooked her thumbs into the waistband of her knickers and paused. 'Would you like me to take these off, too?'

'Yes.'

'Now, now,' Zelda reproved. 'You must ask me nicely, then I might.'

Sick with shame, Nerina bit her tongue in an effort to prevent it from uttering the words but the power of her jaw was not equal to the power of the contractions in her vagina.

'Please, Zelda, will you take off your knickers?'

Zelda smiled brightly. 'Of course,' she said. 'Why didn't you say so before?' She pulled her knickers down and took them off, revealing that her pubic hair was as fiercely red as the hair on her head. Sitting down on the edge of the bed, she resumed her former pose, one leg tucked underneath the other. In this position, Nerina had a clear view of her vulva and the gaping divide of her sex. Her labia were very long and thick, suffused with redness and standing out from the thicket of red hair like the pages of a half-opened book.

'There. That's much friendlier,' Zelda said. 'You must understand that I know exactly how you feel.'

'You do?'

'Naturally. I like to masturbate frequently, myself.' She dropped her hand into her lap. 'For instance, I like to rub myself like this.' She put her right forefinger between her labia and moved it slowly up and down. 'Do you like to do this?'

Nerina licked her lips, her gaze fixed on Zelda's hand between her legs. Her cuffed hands twitched, grabbing at nothing. 'Yes.'

'It must feel awful, not being able to do this to yourself when you want to so badly.'

'Yes,' Nerina ground out.

'And then there's the best bit. That's when I touch my clitoris like this and rub it in tiny circles. Have you found yours?'

Nerina nodded. The intense contractions in her lower stomach were leading to a faint hope that she might be blessed with a spontaneous orgasm. It would be unsatisfying, but better than nothing.

Zelda was speaking again. 'And I just love to squeeze and pull my nipples like this while I'm doing it. Such a pity you can't do that, isn't it?' She stopped, suddenly. 'I know what,' she said. 'I've just had an idea. I've thought of something that will squeeze your nipples for you. You'd like that, wouldn't you?'

The truth was that Nerina would like that very much. Watching Zelda had driven her so far up the ladder which led to insanity that she was in danger of toppling off into uncaring mania. If her nipples were to be stimulated in some way, surely that would lead to the result she wanted so much. In spite of that, she was still sane enough to ask, suspiciously, 'With what?'

Zelda laughed. 'Nothing painful. With these.' She removed her jet pendant earrings and dangled them in front of Nerina's eyes. 'You'll like it. See; they have screw fittings.'

Nerina could see the u shape and tiny screw Zelda meant. When the screw was tightened, the earrings would be clamped on to her nipples. Surely, there could not be enough power in such a small thing to hurt her. Anyway, at that moment she felt that she did not really care how much she was hurt, as long as it led to fulfilment. 'Very well,' she said. 'You may put them on me.'

'Most gracious of you, Princess. Wait a moment. I'll get something else.'

Nerina watched her cross the room to the chest, her naked hips swinging as she went. She came back with a short length of chain.

'What's that for?'

'You'll see.' Nerina slipped a link of the chain over one earring's fitting, then applied it to Nerina's right nipple. She tightened the screw and Nerina felt the pressure as the earring was clamped into place. It was a little uncomfortable in the sense that she was constantly aware of its presence, but not otherwise painful. Zelda did the same thing to her left nipple, leaving the chain with some slack hanging down between them. The necessary touching that took place during this operation was delightful, but not enough to bring on orgasm. When Zelda resumed her former pose, Nerina looked down at her breasts. The juxtaposition of cold, metallic chain and soft breast-flesh was exciting, as was the compression she could now see being caused by the tiny clamps which held the earrings firmly on her nipples.

Zelda began to masturbate again. 'It pleases me to look at you, Princess,' she said. 'You look so helpless, sitting there like that. Do you like me to look at you?'

'Yes.'

'You know it's very unladylike to sit like that with your legs open. I can see your cunny.'

Nerina had only very occasionally and by inadvertence, heard that coarse word used for that particular part of the body. Zelda's unexpected use of it had two effects: one was to make Nerina squirm with embarrassment and the other was to increase her sexual tumult.

Zelda observed the effect of the word on her victim with glee. 'Oh dear, Princess, have I offended you? When I saw your cunny, I shouldn't have told you that I could see your cunny, or if I did, I shouldn't have called it a cunny, should I?'

Being assaulted repeatedly with the word was almost worse than being physically struck. Nerina turned her head aside and closed her eyes.

Zelda scrambled up and knelt with her face close to Nerina's. 'Look at me!' she screamed. 'You shall look at me!' She controlled herself and smiled. 'You want me to be nice to you, don't you?'

Nerina nodded.

'Then you have to be nice to me and do things to please me. Here!' she said, picking up the slack of the chain between Nerina's breasts. 'Hold this between your teeth and keep it there.'

She went back to her place, raised her knee again and resumed her masturbation, rubbing her clitoris and massaging her nipples. 'Look at me!' she commanded. 'Now let me see you raise your head.'

Nerina did so and the chain connected to her nipples tightened.

Zelda's movements increased in pace. 'Yes,' she panted. 'Yes! More. Lift your head more!'

Nerina obeyed, her eyes fastened on Zelda's masturbatory movements. The chain was tight enough to begin to lift the weight of her breasts and she felt the first faint pulsing that might have been the onset of orgasm. She tugged a little to increase the stimulation in her nipples.

Zelda was close to orgasm. Her mouth was open and her jawline tense with strain. 'Go on! Go on! Really pull! I want to see your nipples stretch! Do it! Hurt yourself! I'll teach you, you little . . . Agh! Oh! Ah!' She came to climax with a final, frenzied wriggle of her fingers on her clitoris, then relaxed, breathing deeply.

Nerina continued to tug at her own nipples, needing no instruction from Zelda to do so. What she was doing was having the desired effect. She felt that a few minutes more of this treatment would bring her off. Zelda watched her for a few seconds before she realised what was happening.

When she did, she sprang forward, trying to take the chain from Nerina's mouth. 'Here, stop that. Stop it at once! Let go!'

Nerina tried to fight her, but there was no way she could prevent Zelda from removing the chain from between her teeth. With deep disappointment, she watched the earrings being taken off and the chain along with them.

Zelda put the earrings back on her ears, then picked up her clothes. She put them on again and straightened her hair, looking down at Nerina from the side of the bed.

'What about me?' Nerina said.

'What do you mean?'

'You said you would help me.'

'In what way?'

Nerina knew that she was going to have to say the words. She took a deep breath. 'Please masturbate me, Zelda. I need it so badly.'

'Oh, I couldn't do that. Alcina wouldn't like it.' Zelda turned and walked away towards the door.

'No! Don't go! Don't leave me like this, I can't bear it. Please Zelda! Please! I beg you!'

The door closed and Nerina was alone. She allowed her head to fall forward on to her chest, utterly defeated. The first of many tears slowly made its way down her face and dropped on to her bare stomach.

The following days were purgatory for Nerina. She was awakened at dawn and worked hard until late at night. At first, the tasks she had to perform took a long time to complete and were difficult because they were unfamiliar to her. She was a quick learner, though. Once she had mastered something, her speed improved and her superior intelligence enabled her to find whatever short cut would get the job done without forfeiting the standard of her work. In a way, the fact that she had little spare time or energy was a blessing. It allowed her to tolerate the deprivation which would otherwise have broken her spirit within a matter of hours. As her personal tribute to Leah, she tried her best to perform her duties as cheerfully and as diligently as she could.

There was never a moment when she had the privacy to masturbate. When working, she was watched all the time, either by Alcina or by Zelda. If she were not being watched, she was secured to the bed, unable to touch herself. Her necessary visits to the bathroom were the times she hated most. She was not permitted to put her hands anywhere near her private parts, which meant that she had to bend over and grasp her ankles while all cleaning and washing in that area was done by her supervisor – a hateful process.

With Alcina watching, a bath was not something to be luxuriated in at the end of a long day. She was obliged to get on briskly with what she was there for. She was not allowed to put her hands below the surface of the water at any time. When she had washed those parts above the water line, Alcina took over and dealt with the rest. As she invariably bathed in the evening when she was very tired, it would have taken quite a lot of lathering of her sex to bring about orgasm and Alcina took care that her attentions in that area were the minimum necessary for cleanliness. One blessing, at least, was that Zelda never bathed her. Neither did she get the opportunity, for a while, to repeat her taunting torture. By good fortune, Alcina seemed always to supervise Nerina's chaining to the bed and either left at the same time as Zelda or sent her away first, so that they were not alone together, as they had been on that first day. Nevertheless, Nerina sensed that Zelda had not finished with her and was looking for the slightest excuse to resume her harassment. In consequence, she took care not to make any errors when supervised by her and to perform her work conscientiously and quickly.

Her attitude was subtly different when Alcina was her warder, particularly when she had to work in her own room. Although she had little hope of a climax without clitoral or vaginal stimulation, she did, from time to time, make deliberate mistakes or dawdle over her work, just so that Alcina would beat her bottom with the chastiser. Her hope was that this stimulus, plus just one more slap anywhere near her clitoris would result in orgasm, so hungry was she for one.

Sometimes she believed that Alcina was aware of her motive, because she never gave her more than five strokes – not nearly enough to bring about a peak. Neither did she allow the pad of leather to fall anywhere but on her buttocks.

Measured in units of work, sleep, shame and apprehension, the days passed until Nerina lost count of them. She knew only that she had been in this predicament for what seemed a long time. Thus it was that when she found herself chained to her bed one lunchtime, it might as easily have been a week later, or a month, as far as she was concerned. Tethering was customary during the lunch hour. In a little while, Alcina or Zelda would come and release her, taking her to the kitchen for a plate of scraps before her work began again. When she heard the door open, she expected to see one or other of them. Instead, it was Leah who poked her head around the door.

'Psst! Is it all right? Can I come in?'

Nerina was so pleased to see a friendly face that she felt tears in her eyes and had trouble in controlling her voice. 'Oh, Leah! How wonderful to see you.'

Leah came over to the bed and sat down on the side of it. 'Oh, Highness! What are they doing to you, my poor baby?'

'It's all right, Leah. Don't cry, otherwise you'll set me off. It's not so bad, really. Remember what you said. I am only playing for a few days at something you have been doing ever since you can remember.'

'Did I really say that, Highness? How unthinking of me. I made no allowance for the fact that I was brought up to it while, for you, the change was sudden and cruel.'

'Never mind. That didn't occur to me, either. It's so nice to see you. Why have you come?'

Leah giggled. 'Mostly because I was forbidden to. I find it's the things I'm forbidden to do that I just can't resist. You've no idea of the rumours that have been spread of the dreadful things that happen to you in this room. I just had to come and see that you were all right.'

'Yes I am, thank you. Quite all right.'

Leah sniffed. 'I don't believe that for a minute. I know you too well. I can see it in your face. Anyway, if you're all right, why are you chained up like that?'

Nerina coloured a little. 'Well, I wouldn't tell anyone else, but I don't mind telling you, old friend. They do it to stop me from masturbating.'

'They do? That's awful! How long have they been doing that?'

'Since the last time I saw you.'

Leah was incredulous. 'You mean to say that you haven't had a thrill all week? How dreadful. I'd just die if that happened to me. Well, we can fix that. I'll unstrap you and you can do it now.'

The Devil tempted Nerina, but she resisted. 'No, Leah! You mustn't do that. If Alcina or Zelda came in, you'd get into the most awful trouble. I can't have that.'

'Let me do it for you then.'

'Well ...' Nerina never found out whether this second knock of Satan at her door would have resulted in his stern dismissal again, or whether she would have allowed him to push past her. At that moment, she heard Alcina and Zelda in conversation outside the door. 'Quick!' she hissed. 'They're coming back! Hide in the bathroom.'

Leah had only enough time to dart into the bath-room and half-close the door behind her when Zelda came into the room. She was alone, which was unusual. She came directly over to the bed and,

210

instead of releasing Nerina, as was normal at that time of day, she sat down on the edge of it in the pose Nerina remembered so well and disliked so much.

'Alone together in private again at last,' Zelda said. 'Want to play another game? Would you like me to clip a chain to your nipples again? Perhaps this time you'll be able to pull hard enough to get off.'

'Leave me alone, Zelda, or I'll tell Alcina how you've been tormenting me.'

Zelda laughed. 'And do you think she'll believe you? After what I'm going to do to you today, she'll think you're just trying to get me into trouble to get your own back.'

'What are you going to do?'

'I'm going to whip you for being so careless as to tear your stockings.'

'I haven't torn my stockings.'

Zelda leant forward and dug her sharp nails into the sheer black material covering Nerina's right calf. She pulled sharply and the flimsy silk gave way, leaving a gaping hole. 'Yes you have,' she said. 'And you heard Alcina give me the right to punish you if I thought fit. Well I do think fit.'

Nerina knew she could not win this battle. 'Very well,' she said, resignedly. 'Let me go and I will kneel down for you.'

Zelda laughed and her laughter was not pleasant to hear. 'Don't trouble yourself, Princess. I can manage very well without moving you.'

'How can that be?' Nerina asked, but Zelda was already moving away to the chest against the far wall. She came back with the chastiser in her right hand, casually slapping the flat pad against her left palm.

'Have you ever had your breasts whipped, Princess?'

Nerina pulled madly at her wrist restraints, then

stopped, realising the futility of that. 'Please don't, Zelda,' she said.

Zelda laughed again. 'But you'll love it. They'll jump and wobble and get all red and tingly. I promise to pay special attention to those long nipples of yours. Wouldn't you enjoy that?'

'No!'

'Well it's going to happen, anyway. Now put your head back. All the way back. Stretch them nice and tight and lift them up for me.'

Nerina bent herself backwards as far as she could and gazed at the ceiling, praying that she would be able to stand the pain. She saw Zelda raise the whip high and closed her eyes, bracing herself for the first stroke across her unprotected breasts.

That stroke never came. Instead there was the rustle of clothing, a wheezing gasp and a thump. Nerina opened here eyes to see Zelda rolling on the floor. On top of her, pummelling, clawing, biting and spitting like a wild cat was Leah. The fight did not last long. In a short while, Leah had her adequate bottom planted firmly on Zelda's chest, while Zelda's upper arms were trapped under Leah's shins.

Leah looked round at Nerina, her eyes shining in triumph. 'Didn't stand a chance,' she panted. 'Too much practice with too many saucy kitchen boys for that.'

Before Nerina had a chance to thank her, Alcina came into the bedroom. She took in the scene at a glance. 'Just what's going on here? Get up at once, Leah. And you too, Zelda.'

Zelda scrambled to her feet. 'Leah was masturbating Nerina and when I tried to stop her, she attacked me.'

Alcina turned to Leah, who had also risen and was trying to rearrange her clothing. 'Leah, is that true?'

212

'No, it's not. She was going to whip Nerina's breasts, so I stopped her.'

Zelda interrupted. 'She's making it up! They said that if I interfered, they would try to get me into trouble.'

Leah attempted to intervene, but Alcina signed to her to remain silent. 'Tell me Zelda, why is the chastiser on the floor when it ought to be in the chest?'

'Oh, I'd got that out before. I was going to punish her for tearing a hole in her stocking. You said I could punish her.'

'Quite right, Zelda. I did. And I can see the hole in her stocking. How did she do that?'

Zelda looked around the room. 'On the coal scuttle.'

'You're quite sure Leah was here and masturbating her when you came into the room?'

'Oh yes, Alcina, quite sure.'

'That presents a bit of a problem, doesn't it? You and I left this room together and there was no hole in the stocking then. We had lunch together and stayed together until I left you just outside the door of this room. How did she get across to the scuttle? How did you find out about the hole while you were lunching with me?'

Zelda made no answer but her expression was answer enough.

'I think it's time you undressed, Zelda.'

Zelda wrung her hands. 'No Alcina, please . . .'

Alcina stooped and picked up the chastiser. 'Off, Zelda! Everything! And be quick about it.'

Zelda stripped quickly, fumbling in her haste. When she was naked, Alcina said, 'Go and fetch Nerina's dress from the chair.'

Zelda went to the chair on which Nerina's dress

had been folded when she was tethered and picked it up. She went with it to the bed, but Alcina called her back. 'No, not there, Zelda. Bring it here.' Zelda came obediently, the dress in her hands.

'Put it on.'

'What? You want me to . . .'

'Indeed I do. You are about to take up a maid's duties and you'll need a uniform. Nerina has finished with hers. We won't bother about the stockings for now – they're torn, anyway. Leah, you can release Nerina. Her term as a maid is over.'

As Zelda struggled into the dress, Leah released Nerina by unbuckling the knee-spreader and the cuffs. Nerina got up and came to stand beside Alcina, rubbing her wrists. 'It's not a cruel joke, is it, mistress?'

Alcina laughed. 'No, Nerina, it isn't. You can stop calling me "mistress" and revert to "Alcina" now. As for Zelda here, what would you like me to do with her?'

Nerina looked at Zelda. She was taller and thicker in figure than Nerina and the dress looked ridiculously small on her. Her large breasts hung over the top of it, while the hem was not long enough even to cover the top edge of her flaming red pubic hair. Nerina knew how it felt to be wearing such a garment and, in spite of what had happened, she felt sorry for Zelda. She shook her head. 'I don't want you to do anything with her.'

'Nevertheless, I'm afraid I shall have to. Inflicting pain for the purpose of correction or tuition is acceptable in Paradon. However, inflicting pain for the purpose of personal gratification is not and has to be discouraged. Get it up, Zelda!'

'No, please . . .'

'Get it up at once and receive ten strokes or dawdle over it and receive twenty. It's up to you.'

Zelda fell to her hands and knees immediately and posed with her bare buttocks in the air. The dress was so short on her that there was no need for Alcina to flip it back. The target area was completely clear.

Alcina beat her bottom with steady, regular strokes, first on one cheek and then on the other. Zelda screamed and yelled throughout, twice losing control to such an extent that she forgot to count, which meant that she received twelve strokes altogether. When it was over, she thanked Alcina in a tearful voice and was sent to her room to await further instructions.

Alcina turned to Nerina who had watched the beating with interest and some small satisfaction, in spite of her sympathy. 'And now for you, my dear. This long, weary week is over and I can tell you that you have done very well. I am pleased with you. I am pleased with myself, too, because I achieved what I intended, in spite of the minor hitch I have just begun to correct. You were successfully deprived of orgasms. I am not going to intrude upon your privacy by prying into how that made you feel. I am content that you will, at some time in the future, understand better how someone else truly feels when they say they are hungry. So, the drought now being at an end, so to speak, you are at liberty to refill the well. Would you like us to retire, so that you may do what needs to be done in private, or would you like me to stay? Perhaps Leah would join me if you asked. That might be exciting for us all. I don't think you have experienced two attentive women at the same time, have you?'

'I'd like you both to stay, if you don't mind,' Nerina said, a little shyly.

'I'd like to,' Leah said.

Alcina said, 'I must confess that I am rather

curious to see what happens when a highly sexed woman who has had no orgasm for a week comes to the boil for the first time.'

Nerina took off the hated suspensory belt and stockings. She rearranged the pillows and lay down on the bed which had been her prison for so long, watching Alcina and Leah strip. They came on to the bed and lay on either side of her, kissing and stroking her face, breasts and belly. It was wonderful after so much deprivation and she felt her juices let down almost at once.

Alcina raised herself on one elbow, tracing patterns with her finger around Nerina's right nipple. 'I don't think we should keep the poor girl waiting any longer, do you, Leah?'

Leah shook her head, smiling while her finger performed a similar dance on Nerina's left breast.

Alcina went on, 'Since she has been working so hard, perhaps she should lie back and let us perform the required rites?'

'No, please,' Nerina protested. 'I want it to be fun for you, too.'

'As it will be, I assure you. Well, we will compromise with you. Leah likes to be licked, so she can squat above your face. I, for my part, will be very happy to service your own lower parts with my lips and tongue. Is that satisfactory to you?'

'Oh, very!' Nerina exclaimed, with deep feeling.

The last time she had licked Leah's sex, it had been covered with hair. This time, because she had continued to shave, it was totally bald. When Leah squatted above her, the necessary spread of her legs stretched her vagina until it gaped, the pink petals of her labia far apart. Nerina raised her head a little and lapped eagerly at this treasure. Her mind whirled with a confusion of memories and emotions. She remembered the first time she had seen Leah's pubis after her shave and had longed to touch it and lay her cheek against it. What she was privileged to do now was far better than that and that good feeling was multiplied by the fact that she was again indulging in an act of sexual liaison. There had been moments in the past week when it had seemed to her that she was fated never to do so again.

Then Alcina began her ministrations with lips, tongue and fingers. The knowledge that this heavenly treatment was going to continue until inevitable completion was a joy in itself. Alcina's warm, wet tongue poked at the entrance to her vagina while her fingers manipulated her clitoris in such a knowing and sensitive manner that she was held on the brink of orgasm for many delightful minutes before exploding like a rocket. Only a small pause, then the treatment recommenced. Every orgasm Nerina received, she faithfully passed on to Leah. She lost count of them and eventually they subsided into small ripples of ecstasy. Finally, she could manage no more and allowed her head to fall back, completely exhausted.

Eleven

The resumption of the lifestyle of a guest, rather than
that of a maid, was not a particularly smooth transition. When Nerina woke in the morning, the sun was
already high. With a single glance, she took in the
amount of light and the tall figure of Alcina at her
bedside. In a panic, she threw off the bedcovers and
knelt bolt upright; hair askew and eyes still bleary.
'I'm so sorry, mistress,' she said. 'I must have overslept. Please excuse . . .' The broad smile on Alcina's
face stopped her in mid-sentence and, as her wits
returned, she remembered her restored status.

'It's all right,' Alcina said, pushing gently at her
shoulders. 'It's over. Lie down again and wake up
more slowly. I'll get Leah to bring you breakfast in
bed. I just came in to bring you more civilised
clothing than you have been wearing.' She indicated
a small pile at the foot of the bed.

Nerina lay back against the pillows and stretched
her arms luxuriously. 'Mmm! How nice this is. I
didn't appreciate it before.'

'Just part of your training. We never recognise the
full worth of something until we are deprived of it.
That is as true of everyday life as it is of sex. After
last week's experience, I expect you would be willing
to swear to the truth of that.'

Nerina blushed a little, recalling exactly how it had

felt to be brought to orgasm in such a delightful way after a long period of deprivation. 'You said you would make me understand hunger,' she said. 'Now I truly believe I do.'

Alcina sat down on the edge of the bed and stroked her hair fondly. 'Good. That means that you know more than any previous ruler of Isingore. Now why don't you go back to sleep? I'll sit with you awhile.'

'Thank you. That would be nice.' Nerina snuggled, but there was something wrong, something missing. After only a few seconds, she opened her eyes again. 'Isn't this silly?' she said. 'For the past week, I have been dreaming of being able to lie in bed in the morning and now that I can, I don't want to.'

Alcina laughed. 'You're a free agent now. What do you want to do?'

Nerina thought hard, exploring her feelings. What on earth was making her so restless? There was a totally strange impulse within her, yet she could not put her finger on it. The closest she could come was the frustration she used to feel back in Isingore when she was ordering supper. She knew that she was hungry, but could not decide what she wanted to eat. It was most annoying. Quite suddenly, she knew what she wanted to do, but hesitated to put it into words.

'You're going to think I've gone out of my mind if I tell you.'

Alcina laughed again. 'Perhaps. Tell me, anyway.'

'It's absolutely ridiculous, but I think I want to clean out the fire and light it.'

'That's not ridiculous. It's wonderful. It's called the work ethic. The feeling that, unless you are doing something useful and productive, you are wasting your day. Everyone in Paradon has it and now your training has brought it to you. It will stay with you always, I hope.'

'So I haven't gone mad. There is a small problem, though. Although I know I want to light the fire, I also know I don't want to fetch the coal. It's not just the heavy scuttle, it's the spiders in the coal cellar. Does that mean I don't have the work ethic after all?'

'Not at all. It only means that you prefer to choose the work you do with care, so that it is a pleasure to you. That means that it isn't work at all. Would you like me to have one of the men bring you the things you need?'

That idea was inexpressible luxury for the ex-maid. 'Oh yes, please!'

'I'll go and see about it. Take your time over getting up.'

While Alcina was away, Nerina tried hard to stay in bed, but it was quite impossible. She got up and investigated the clothing on her bed. There was a long robe which she put on over her nightdress before sitting at the dressing table to brush her hair. She was still doing that when there was a tap at the door. She got up and answered it, recognising the young man standing there as one of the kitchen staff.

'Your things, Nerina,' he said, nodding his head at his several burdens.

'Oh, thank you so much, Helmut.' She gave him a bright smile. 'Can you put the scuttle by the fire, please. Here, I'll take those other things.' She took the tools and fire-lighting materials from under his arm and followed him across to the fireplace.

He put the scuttle down in the hearth. 'I'll come back for those other things later, shall I?'

'No, that's all right. I'll be going past the kitchen, anyway. I'll drop them off when I've finished.'

'I really don't mind,' he said. 'I'd do more than that for you, Nerina.' He gave her a broad grin and pointed his finger.

220

Smiling, she closed her hand into a fist then, on a sudden impulse, moved it up and down in an impudent gesture reminiscent of masturbation. 'Go on with you, cheeky monkey!' she said, and pushed him out of the door. She closed it behind him and leant her back against it, laughing. Life was suddenly very good. The sun was shining, men fancied her and she had a fire to light!

She went to the fireplace and knelt down, then paused, frowning. This was rather a messy job and she didn't want to spoil her clothes. She got up again, went over to the bed and took off her robe and her night-dress. Naked, she went back to the fireplace and knelt down again. Picking up the poker, she began raking out the dead ashes. In a little while she began to sing, a silly little song that she had learned as a child at Dorcas' knee.

She had just set a match to the kindling when Alcina returned with a large box under her arm. 'Well!' she said. 'There's a sight! Is that your new fire-lighting uniform?'

Nerina laughed. 'No, of course not. I'll have to get a pinafore or something if I'm going to do this often.' She gestured at her nudity. 'This just seemed to make sense for today. I was going to take a bath, anyway. Oh, it's all right,' she said, pulling a mock-serious face, 'I'm not going to play with myself. You can come and watch again if you like.'

'Actually I will, but just to talk to you, not to stop you from being naughty. That's up to you, now. If you do, though, you might wish you hadn't. You're having supper with Prince Argan tonight and who knows what that might lead to! It would be a shame to take the edge off your appetite.'

Nerina jumped up, her eyes ablaze with excitement. 'Really! You're not just teasing? It's really tonight? When did you find out about it?'

'Yesterday afternoon.'

'Oh! You knew yesterday! And you didn't tell me!'

'Would you have slept well last night if I had? I can't have my Prince entertaining a woman with big bags under her eyes.'

Suddenly, Nerina's face fell. She ran to the dressing table and stared at her reflection. 'Oh no!' she wailed. 'I look a sight. Look at my hair! I'm sure there's a pimple coming on my nose. And as if that's not enough, I haven't a thing to wear.'

'Yes you have,' Alcina said, pointing at the box under her arm.

Nerina clapped her hands. 'Is it a dress? It's a dress, isn't it? Is it nice? Let me see!'

'With those grubby paws? I should think not indeed. Just calm down and have your bath. We'll talk about what needs to be done and who's going to do it; then, if you behave yourself like a grown-up lady instead of like a five-year-old, I may let you see the dress.'

Alcina sat on the edge of the bath and watched her protégée with fond eyes as she soaped herself and chattered ceaselessly. When the excited flow slowed a little, she managed to get in a calming word here and there until she had made space enough to discuss the arrangements. Leah would come and wash Nerina's hair, then arrange it in a pleasing fashion. Alcina herself would attend to her face with cosmetics, so that Nerina could be secure in the knowledge that no trace of the imagined pimple would be visible, even on the most minute inspection.

Finally, a much quieter Nerina lay at full length, gently swishing water over herself with her hands. 'Tell me,' she said, 'Do you really think he's going to do . . . it to me, tonight.'

Alcina smiled, trailing her hand in the soapy water. 'I'd be very surprised if he didn't after Leah and I have finished with your appearance. He's not that strong-willed. But let's not talk about him doing . . . it to you. Let's talk about you and he doing . . . it to each other. That's much more fun.'

'I've thought about it a lot,' Nerina said, passing soapy hands over her nipples. 'In my dreams it was always lovely, but now that it's real and the time is nearly here, I feel all wobbly inside. I wish I knew what it was going to be like. Can you tell me? For instance, you said there was something to be broken through. It sounds painful.'

'That's hard to say. It's different for different women. It depends on how you are made and on the man who does it. If he is gentle and considerate and takes his time, that helps a lot. If he isn't and rams at you before you are completely lubricated, it can hurt enough to put you off the whole idea for a long time. I can tell you that it is impossible to find a more gentle and considerate man than Prince Argan.'

There was a catch in her voice and Nerina looked up, amazed to see tears welling in Alcina's eyes. 'Alcina,' she said. 'You're crying. What is it?'

Alcina blinked and impatiently brushed her eyes with the heel of her hand, shaking her head as though to dislodge some image from her mind. 'Just silliness,' she said. 'I was just thinking that if I were a few years younger and a little more beautiful and a virgin princess . . .' Her voice trailed away with the same catch in it.

Nerina reached out and caught her hand. 'Why Alcina, you really love him, don't you?'

Alcina collected herself, pulling her hand away and straightening her shoulders. 'Hah!' she said. 'What woman in this house doesn't? I go unnoticed among such a crowd. Let's get on with what concerns you.'

'All right,' Nerina said slowly, unwilling to pick at a half-healed scab and cause further pain. 'Will you tell me what it was like for you, first time? Perhaps that will help.'

Alcina laughed bitterly. 'Somehow I don't think so. It was very romantic. I was employed on the land at the time, working in the hayfield. It involved a haystack, a large flagon of cider and a great clod of a farmer's lad with hands like legs of mutton and a brain composed of the same meat. Need I say more? However, it does allow me to give you one sound piece of advice. Don't be drunk when it happens to you. The moment is too precious. And don't be with someone you don't love, either.'

'Oh Alcina, I'm so sorry.'

'Spare your pity. I got over it,' Alcina said, shortly.

There was an awkward pause. Nerina felt that she could not reach through the defensive barrier that Alcina had erected around the soft centre she had glimpsed. 'So you can't tell me how it will be for me,' she hazarded, timidly.

'Not without knowing how you're built inside. I could put my finger inside you and feel what's there, if you like, then make a more educated guess. Would you like me to do that?'

Nerina nodded, shyly. 'I think I would, if you don't mind.'

'Very well,' Alcina said, briskly practical. 'Slide your bottom down a bit and lift your knees up.'

Nerina positioned herself as requested and parted her knees. Alcina knelt down beside the bath and put her hand into the water between the spread thighs. She probed with her forefinger and Nerina gasped as she felt it slide between her labia.

'It's all right,' Alcina said. 'Just relax. I'll be very careful.'

224

The finger advanced a little and Nerina felt her vagina pulse into life. The finger moved around a little, pushing very gently.

'Feel that?' Alcina asked.

'Mm! Sort of funny.'

'That's it. That's your maidenhead. That's what is going to go missing tonight, unless I'm much mistaken. The gap is wide enough for me to get my finger past it. Keep absolutely still, now.'

As Alcina's finger intruded just a little further, Nerina felt the contractions inside her vagina increasing in quantum leaps. She longed to squirm forward to increase the penetration but held herself still, mindful of Alcina's caution.

Alcina withdrew her finger slowly and carefully, making Nerina gasp again. 'You should be all right,' she said, swishing her finger around in the water, then shaking her hand to dry it. 'It's not too big or too tight. Quite normal, in fact. There may be a little pain but, if everything else is going well, you won't have much attention to spare for it. Judging by the way you nearly bit my finger off, I estimate that Prince Argan will be a bit preoccupied, too.'

'Is that what it will feel like when he does it? Like your finger, I mean.'

'Better! Infinitely better! We have enjoyed sex with each other in a variety of ways, as you know, but to have a lusty man who knows what he's doing between your legs, thrusting himself into you . . . well, that's a different thing entirely.' She pressed her hands into her lap. 'I think we'd better stop this conversation, now. I find myself getting too heated for comfort.'

Later that afternoon, Nerina sat at her dressing table and stared at her reflection. She hardly recognised the person in the mirror. She had never experimented with more than the barest minimum of cosmetics, so that what Alcina had done so skilfully was a revelation to her. This new woman was incredibly beautiful. Her skin glowed with a healthy vibrancy, her eyes were large, dark and mysterious, her lips full and rosy-red. Leah was putting the finishing touches to her hair, piling it high on her head so that the back swept up in all the glossy splendour a hundred passes of the brush could impart.

Alcina opened her box at last. She took out the dress and shook it, holding it up for inspection. It was pure white and adorned with a myriad sparkling traces of gold thread.

Nerina's mouth fell open. 'Oh Alcina,' she breathed. 'It's the most beautiful dress I've ever seen. May I try it on?'

'First the foundations of the structure.' Alcina delved into the box again. 'All white, of course, as befits a virgin. Shoes, stockings, knickers and suspensory belt.'

Nerina stood up and slipped out of her robe to stand naked. Alcina advanced on her with a small phial in her hand.

'A little dab of perfume here and there. Here and here, behind each ear. A little dab on each wrist. A tiny bit under each breast. Remember that for the future: not on the nipples – it might sting his mouth a little.'

Nerina blushed.

'Part your legs. Just a suggestion on the inside of each thigh, like this and this – hardly more than a wave of the bottle. Not anywhere more personal; it would not only sting his mouth, it would sting you, too. Now turn round. That's right. Feel where I'm dabbing? Right down here, just above your bottom. Not on it: you can guess why.'

Nerina blushed again.

Once into the white stockings and suspensory belt, she inspected herself in the mirror. Her pubic hair had grown back very well and was now not a bit scratchy, just an attractively light fluff, yet still dark enough to show through the silk of her white knickers when she put those on as well.

Leah held the dress for her to step into then pulled it up until Nerina could wriggle her hips and settle into place. When Nerina lifted the front part of it, she felt the stays which gave it shape.

'It would be inconvenient to wear a corset on such an occasion,' Alcina said. 'This has a corset incorporated into it for that reason. Once securely buttoned behind, it will stay up by itself.'

Leah worked at fastening the long row of buttons while Nerina inspected herself in the mirror. Although floor length and all-concealing below, the dress had no top at all, not even the narrowest of straps to keep it up. It was quite the most outrageously daring thing she had ever seen, let alone worn. The stays supported her breasts, pushing them up and out from below, so that they appeared to be much bigger than they really were.

'Are you quite sure it will stay up?' Nerina asked anxiously, picturing potential disaster.

'During supper, at any rate,' Alcina said. 'After that, I would be surprised if it did.'

Long white evening gloves with small pearl buttons at the wrist, a thick choker of pearls, a matching pair of pendant earrings and a small white evening purse to match the dress, completed the ensemble. As a finishing touch, Alcina produced a little posy of white violets attached to a white satin band which she slipped over Nerina's wrist.

Nerina raised them to her nose and sniffed. 'Thank you, they're lovely. Do I look all right?'

'You'll do,' Alcina said, shortly. 'Now stop preening and come along.'

Leah kissed Nerina lightly on the cheek. 'You're lovely,' she whispered. 'Good luck!'

Alcina led the way out of the room and Nerina followed her down the stairs. They went into a wing of the house Nerina had not visited before and seemed to walk a long way. At every step, she grew more and more nervous until, when they stopped outside a door, her knees were trembling so much that she was sure that they would soon make an audible knocking sound.

Alcina turned to face her and took both her hands, holding her at arm's length. 'Let me look at you,' she said. She nodded approval, then surprised Nerina by drawing her towards her and giving her a little hug. In a husky voice, she whispered, 'Be good to my Prince.'

Giving Nerina no time to reply, she released her and stepped back, then turned and knocked at the door. She opened it and announced, 'Her Highness, the Princess Nerina of Isingore, by your own invitation, sir.'

She stepped aside for Nerina to enter the room. Prince Argan was already on his feet and coming forward. He was wearing the same clothes that she had seen in the garden, except for the addition of a black jacket and cravat. Nerina's knees turned to jelly and she could feel her heart attempting to escape from the constriction of her dress. In a daze, she extended her hand and he bent to kiss it, murmuring a welcome.

Still holding her hand, he looked past her. 'Alcina, you are well?'

'I am well, my Prince.'

He nodded, smiling. 'I know whom I have to thank for this lovely gift and I do so now.'

'I am yours to command, sir, now, as always.'

'That may be, but there are some things that go beyond mere obedience to commands. You should know that I am aware of that.'

'Thank you, sir. Goodnight.'

'Goodnight, dear Alcina.'

Nerina, still in a stupefied daze, heard the door behind her close, then the Prince took the hand he was still holding and turned, tucking it naturally into the crook of his elbow. 'Come, my terrified little mouse. We have many affairs of state to discuss, you and I. We will do so over a good supper. See; there is a table already laid just for us.'

Nerina saw ahead of them a small table spread with a snowy white cloth on which were arranged two place settings. She was having a little difficulty in remembering the complicated procedure by which one made forward progress by putting one foot in front of the other. 'Forgive me, Prince,' she said. 'I am not quite myself. I find everything a little strange.'

'Of course it is. How could it be otherwise. But not "Prince". Not tonight. Tonight, you shall call me "Argan", for that is my given name and I, by your gracious leave, will call you "Nerina". Agreed?'

She smiled up at him, a fragment of confidence returning. 'Of course, Argan.'

They reached the table and he drew out a chair for her, tucking it in behind her as she sat. He took his seat opposite her while she submerged her nervousness beneath the trivial ritual of removing her gloves. When she looked up again, she was disconcerted to see that a large centrepiece of fruit almost completely blocked her view of him. She leant a little sideways to restore her line of sight, only to find that he had leant the other way. For a moment or two, they swayed back and forth, missing each other each time, until he rose to his feet and looked over the top.

'Ah! There you are! I thought you had taken fright and run away.'

His smile was infectious and she returned it. Her smile became a giggle and provoked his smile to become a laugh. She laughed with him and the ice was broken. He picked up the offending table decoration and put it on the sideboard, then returned to his seat. Hitching his chair, he observed, gravely. 'Nerina's face in exchange for a pineapple. I think that's a fair trade, don't you?'

She inclined her head in acknowledgement of the compliment. 'If it pleases you, Argan, then I am pleased, too.'

'Your face pleases me very much,' he said. He picked up a tiny bell from beside his plate and shook it.

For a week, Nerina had been jumping at the sound of such bells and the habit died hard, particularly in her tense condition. She jumped now. Only a trifle, just enough to cause her hands to move to the arms of her chair as though to rise. She blushed. 'I'm sorry. I thought I saw something moving.'

Fortunately he did not appear to have noticed her slip. 'I thought I did, too,' he said. 'I do hope it wasn't a fly. We have had a little trouble with them lately.'

A young man came in with a soup tureen and served the first course. He left at once and they dawdled over the soup while Argan engaged her in informative conversation. She was completely fascinated. He knew everything there was to know about Isingore and its affairs, things from the past which she had not even guessed at. For the first time, she learnt all the details of the invasion and its outcome.

During the main course, he told her about Isingore's progress towards democracy and, over dessert, about the new Council of Isingore's plans for the future. Among other thing he told her that her palace was destined to become a hospital. Oddly enough, she could find nothing in her which regretted that decision. The palace was part of an old life to which she no longer found herself suited.

Such was her enjoyment of the meal and his company that she quite forgot about their proposed liaison, recalling it with a start only when he offered a liqueur to follow coffee. That reminded her of Alcina's admonition about drunkenness and she flushed at the recollection.

He frowned a little at her reaction to his simple offer of a drink. 'Something is wrong, Nerina? Have I inadvertently given offence, perhaps?' His frown gave way to a smile. 'Ah! I know what it is. The meal is over and you have suddenly remembered the arrangements for this evening. By the way, you paid me a great compliment by forgetting about them during supper. Now you think that I will leap up and hurl myself upon you to wreak my terrible will upon your frail body.'

She blushed and hung her head. 'No, I don't think that.' That was the truth. Nothing could be less likely to happen with this gentle man. 'It's just that it's all so . . . so strange and businesslike, if you know what I mean.'

He reached across the table and took her hand. 'I know. I feel that myself. It was a wretchedly poor plan from the start. I can't think how I allowed myself to be caught up in it. Now that we are both so deeply involved, I see no way of extricating ourselves from the trap we have laid. You have come here, feeling under some compulsion to surrender your virginity to me. I, for my part, cannot express any wish for intimacy without appearing to be a tyrant slaking his lust upon a poor, defenceless girl. Worse than that, I cannot avoid expressing that wish, either. I cannot tell you the truth, which is that I already know enough about you to put you back on the throne of Isingore without further training or tests. I cannot say that, lest you should think that I am attempting to avoid intimacy because I find you unattractive.'

She thought about this. 'I see,' she said. 'It is a problem, isn't it? One that is just as difficult for you as it is for me.' There was a long silence until she went on. 'What you seem to be telling me is that any future relationship we may or may not have has nothing to do with establishing my suitability to rule Isingore. It has to do only with personal preferences.'

He nodded. 'I think that sums up my feelings very well.'

She remained silent for considerably longer this time. His hand on hers was warm and friendly. She made up her mind. 'I think,' she said, 'that the answer to this impasse lies right under our noses in this very house.'

'It does?'

'Certainly!' Was a little teasing in order? Of course it was! He deserved it! 'Please give me back my hand, sir.'

'Of course!' He let go at once, folding his hands into his lap, embarrassed. 'I beg your pardon.'

She sat for a few seconds, enjoying a woman's power, then very slowly turned her hand over and laid the back of it flat on the table. She saw his eyes fixed upon it and, with exquisite cruelty, she prolonged his agony for several seconds more before extending her thumb as widely as it would go.

232

Her hand seemed to have mesmerised him and it was a while before he could drag his eyes from it and look into her eyes. 'Really?' he murmured, hoarsely.

She nodded and smiled. 'Yes, really!'

His hand came forward again, forefinger extended. Slowly and carefully, he placed the tip of it on the ball of her thumb. A giant force seemed to leap between them and she remembered Leah's account of how Michael's touch had seemed to leave a permanent mark. Her nipples were prickling, while her knickers were already soaked through. To judge by his expression, Prince Argan was not insensible to the feel of her skin, either.

'That seems to be settled, then,' she said. 'I presume you have a bedroom close by?'

'Er . . . yes!' He indicated a door. 'Just through there.'

She rose gracefully from the table and he, by force of custom, rose with her. 'I shall go there, then,' Nerina said. 'If you wish to accompany me, there is a price to pay.'

'Oh?'

'Yes. I cannot permit a gentleman to take me into a bedroom unless he has kissed me first.'

He took her into his arms and kissed her on the mouth. His lips were warm and dry, as were his hands on her bare back. She had never been kissed by any man, let alone one with carnal thoughts, therefore she had no measure by which to judge its quality. It seemed to her, however, to be a masterpiece among kisses. It dug down deep inside her, searching out nerve-endings she did not know she had and seemed to go on for a very long time. For a fleeting second, she brought to mind Leah's expression, 'tongues and everything'. Well, no matter. She could wait. Probably that would come later, with a little encouragement.

Twelve

Prince Argan's bedroom was large and decorated in a distinctly masculine fashion. Nerina's first impression could be summed up in two words – plain and simple. The unpatterned green carpet toned with the darker green of the wallpaper, the plainness of the latter relieved to some small extent by unobtrusive, gold fleurs-de-lis. The ceiling of lighter green was bare of painted or plaster decoration. A bright fire burned in a grate with a surround of green marble. What little furniture there was matched the mahogany of the doors and window-frames. There was a tall secretary bookcase, a long mirror, a brass-bound military chest (which, by virtue of the mirror and brushes on top of it, must, she thought, serve Argan in the office of a dressing table), a very plain, but well-made table and some chairs. Only two portraits of rather severe looking gentlemen adorned the walls and that was all, apart from the bed.

The half-tester bed was huge! Large enough, probably, for four. The plain fabric of its curtains matched the ceiling, but what mostly caught Nerina's eye was the coverlet. Made of long, black fur – most likely that of several bears – it dominated the room and made it difficult to look elsewhere. How white her skin would appear against that background. She wondered if the fur would be tickly or sensuous when it touched her. She dragged her eyes away from the counterpane and regarded Argan, who was standing to one side just behind her.

Her tongue locked. So far, all had seemed light and easy. Now it had become suddenly difficult. What was she supposed to say. 'How do you want me?' sounded ridiculous and forward.

Argan solved the problem for her. 'These moments are always tricky,' he said. 'I suggest that we kiss again, just in order to pass away the time while we decide what to do next.'

She grinned in a rather unsophisticated manner at that suggestion, then closed her eyes and put up her lips to be kissed. She felt his arms about her again and that felt very cosy and safe. Their lips met and she thrilled all over again at the contact. Then she felt his tongue against her lips, tapping at them to ask permission to enter. This was 'tongues and everything' as described by Leah. It seemed a wicked and dangerous thing to do and she was in a mood to be wicked and risk danger. She opened her mouth a trifle and felt the tip of his tongue slide inside. She was quite unable to think why she had ever described this procedure to Leah as disgusting. It wasn't at all! It was perfectly delicious, in fact. Argan's tongue was warm and strong. The way it intruded into her mouth reminded her strongly of her experience with Johann, except that this was more arousing. Greatly daring, she flicked her own tongue around the intruder, then pushed to demand access to Argan's mouth. This being chivalrously granted, she explored within, only to find that he was sucking on her and making it difficult for her to draw back. So that was how it was done! She awaited her opportunity, then drew his tongue back into her mouth and sucked on it with enthusiasm.

She was a little breathless after that – whether from the exertion or from sexual excitement, she could not tell. She had thought herself thoroughly aroused before they entered the bedroom, but had moved several notches up the scale in the last few minutes. She could feel something pressing against her stomach. Because of her inexperience in these affairs, it took her a while before she realised what it was. She dropped one of her hands from its place behind Argan's neck and caressed the front of his breeches, feeling the taut hardness of him move beneath the material. She took that as a pretty compliment and kissed him all the harder in lieu of thanks.

He pushed her away gently and held her at arm's length, his hands on her upper arms. He seemed to be just a little breathless himself. He looked hard at her, as if trying to read some message in her expression. Apparently satisfied, he pushed with one hand and pulled with the other, turning her so that she had her back to him. She felt his kiss on the back of her neck and shuddered with the impact of the forces that welled up in her because of it.

'May I help you with your necklace?'

She nodded assent. His fingers at the clasp were not entirely steady and it pleased her to think that perhaps he was not as fully in control of himself as a very experienced man ought to be. The table was within reach, and he put the pearl choker on it.

'And your gown?'

Her heart skipped a beat in a curious manner, causing her to draw in her breath sharply. The expansion of her chest made the top of her dress grip her breasts more closely. It was as though her body were deliberately trying to protect itself by making the unfastening of the buttons more difficult. She brought it under the control of her will again by letting out her breath. That wasn't easy and it emerged from her mouth fitfully, in little trembly sighs. Now his fingers were busy with the long line of buttons at the back. She felt the security of her stayed bodice diminish little by little and she fought her body again to prevent it from bringing up her hands to hold up the front.

The full-length mirror was before her and in it she could see her own reflection. Argan was partly hidden behind her, his head bent intently to his work. Now the buttons were undone as far as her hips and the front of her dress fell down of its own weight, swinging away from her and leaving her breasts bare. She was surprised to see her reflection allow this to happen, taking no action at all to prevent it but just standing there with its hands loosely at its sides. Now all the buttons were undone. One twitch of his hand and the dress would crumple to the floor about her feet. She watched her reflection with interest, to see what it would do about this. It did nothing and the dress was on the floor. She stepped out of it and he picked it up, draping it neatly across the table.

Her white stockings with their embroidered clocks were hardly more white than her thighs, against which the white silk of her suspensors delineated a curve that pleased her. Her white silk knickers, dainty and fragile as a cobweb, clung to her body and caused the dark shadow of her pubic hair to become a place of infinite mystery. Now he was behind her again, his lips on the side of her neck this time. She could see his finger tips on the tops of her shoulders and his blond hair alongside her face in the mirror. She bent her head to the other side, stretching her skin under his lips and making access easier. She had never thought of anyone's neck, least of all her own, as a place which could harbour thoughts of sex. Now she found that this was so and those thoughts, liberated by his kisses, went scurrying off around her body in a most pleasing manner to play 'hide and seek'. They lodged in her nipples, her vagina and in a dozen or so less expected places, calling, 'Come and find me, Argan!'

She felt his hands leave her shoulders and slide a little way down her arms. In the mirror, she saw them creep across the front of her body until he had one of her breasts cupped in each hand. He pulled her towards him, pressing her back against his body until she felt the hardness of him against the top part of her buttocks.

His hands seemed to burn her like fire as they gently squeezed and relaxed, squeezed and relaxed, palpating the soft flesh within their grasp. She longed for the natural facility all cats had of of purring when they were contented. She could only express herself by way of a long, sighing hum. He changed his grip. Now he had one forefinger beneath each nipple and his thumbs on top. Holding the fingers steady, he pushed the thumbs forward, squeezing the elongated buds of flesh very softly while rubbing their upper surfaces forward. For this treatment, a hum was inadequate. Her mouth opened to change the sound to a long 'Aaah!', while her head rotated slowly, to maximise the offerings her neck was continuing to receive.

He appeared to accept the sound she made as acquiescence. He brought his thumbs back to their starting point and did it again, obliging her to increase the volume of the sound. It seemed to her that each of her nipples was connected directly to her vagina by taut guitar strings. Every time he made that rubbing, milking motion, the strings vibrated and her vagina vibrated with them. Something very strange was happening to her breasts; she could feel it. She dragged her eyes away from the mirror and looked down. Behind his tormenting thumbs, she could see that the whole area around her aureolae was swollen, as from a bee-sting. Her nipples were longer and harder than she had ever known them and, even as she watched, a tiny teardrop of clear fluid emerged from the tip of each, glistening on his fingers.

Try as she might, she was unable to sustain the length of the sounds she was making. Against her will, they shortened into a staccato 'Uh! Uh!' while her bottom gyrated, grinding itself backwards against his erection. Part of her mind wanted this delicious torture to go on for ever. Another part screamed 'Stop! Please stop! I can't stand any more.' The coolness between her legs told her that her juices were evaporating on the silk of her knickers. She found that she didn't care. She felt the symptoms of approaching orgasm. Part of her mind regretted that, thinking it might spoil what was to come. Another, more robust part did not care at all. Let it happen, if it must.

Just in time, he released her nipples and she returned her gaze to the mirror to see his hands pass down over her stomach with little stroking movements. It was a long, slow way down to the waistband of her knickers and she watched his fingers pause awhile before the tips of them disappeared inside. He pushed outwards, stretching the material away from her heaving belly. She could see him looking down over her shoulder and knew that he was inspecting her pubes. She pushed her hips forward so as to afford him the maximum possible opportunity to admire her pubic hair. His hands described horizontal arcs on either side of her hips, with the backs of his hands pressing outwards on the silk of her knickers.

Each pass was a little lower until, bit by bit, the semi-transparent silk descended and she could see her own pubic hair uncovered in the mirror. He continued his movements, except that now his palms were in contact with her thighs, stroking them as he forced her knickers slowly to her knees. Once they reached that point, he knelt and tugged at them so that they fell to the floor. With elegant and precise movements, she stepped out of them and they joined her dress on the table. For a moment, she saw him behind her again, admiring her reflection in the mirror, then he pushed her gently so that she was obliged to made a half-turn to the left. His right arm went across her back as he stooped and gathered up her knees over his left arm, sweeping her off her feet. He held her there for a second, supporting her weight in his strong arms as easily as a child holds a doll. She put up her free hand to stroke the side of his face and smiled up at him. He smiled back and with long easy strides carried her to the bed. He put one knee on it and deposited her gently in the centre of the black bearskin coverlet.

It felt every bit as good as she had hoped it might and she stretched luxuriously, feeling the soft hairs massaging her bare back, bottom, thighs and calves, before putting her hands under her head, completely relaxed.

He began to undress and she watched him do it with huge interest. There was nothing hasty about his movements, almost as though she were a deer he was stalking and he feared to startle her into flight. With leisured slowness, he divested himself of his garments, placing them tidily on the chair at the side of the bed. During the whole of this operation, his eyes never left her face. His chest was even more pleasing to her than Johann's had been, she decided. She much admired the blondeness of his chest hair. When he sat down to pull off his boots, she knew that what she most wanted to see would soon be revealed to her. He stood and unbuttoned the flap of his breeches and she noticed that he made no attempt to turn away from her, but continued his examination of her face.

When he took off his light cotton drawers, she almost exclaimed with pleasure. His pubic curls were as fair as the rest of his hair. His member stood out from this mass in full erection, yet there was no menace for her in it. Not as thick as Johann's, yet longer, it curved up and away from his body in a graceful arc so that she thought she could already feel how that shape would so admirably fit inside her.

She held out her arms to him and he came to her, first kneeling over her and kissing her lips, then lying beside her to do it again. She ran her hand down his bare body, rejoicing in the feel of his nakedness beneath her palm, then groped for her special treasure. The heat and hardness of it surprised her and she gasped. She felt she could wait no longer. Her vagina was wet with longing and she pulled on the springy flesh in her hand, pointing it at the place where she most ardently wished him to lodge it. In her brain, a voice was shouting, 'Do it to me, my love! Please, please do it to me!' Shyness prevented that thought from emerging as words. The best she could manage were little whimpering, mewing sounds of entreaty and encouragement.

She felt his knee come across her body and rest between her legs. She opened them as wide as they would go and he rolled over on top of her, supporting himself on his elbows so that his chest hair brushed her nipples lightly, inflaming them all over again. He inched forward and she groped for his organ again, seizing it and guiding it towards her eager vagina. She felt it probe between her labia and her head shot back as though in orgasm at the thrill of it. He nudged forward a fraction and the thickness of his glans forced her labia further apart. Then his penis was rubbing mischievously at the very entrance to her vaginal passage. Her teeth were chattering – not with cold, but with sexual tension. The sensation inside her was fantastic as he nudged and rubbed his way further in. She felt the strong contractions of her young, healthy muscles grip and suck at the intruder. They had made such movements before, but then had only emptiness to work on. To be filled and stretched by hot, male hardness was suddenly to understand what those muscles were really for and there was a satisfactory rightness about the fact that they were at last fulfilling their proper function.

The ridge of his glans reached a point just beneath her pubic bone and he arrested forward progress there, pumping in and out with gentle, teasing strokes. His organ's curve caused it to exert greater pressure on this spot than on others and that was bliss. She felt her orgasm coming, but tried to hold out against it. She longed to feel the full length of him inside her before that happened but she was not strong enough to stem the tide of love and lust that overwhelmed her. Her orgasm was upon her and that delicious, teasing, glorious part of him was going to bring it about. She gasped and tensed, her mouth open and every muscle taut before convulsing into glad climax, her arms pulling him close as she murmured, 'Oh, my sweet love! My lovely Prince!'

She lay still for a moment, then felt him stir. He leant forward to kiss her lips and she felt his penis begin to withdraw from her slowly with an easy, pumping movement. Desperately, she clung to him, crushing him to her breast while she smothered his face with kisses.

'No, no! Don't stop! Go on! I can do it again!'

'You can?'

'Yes! Oh, yes! Please go on!'

She waited, tense with anxiety until she felt him nudge forward again. His hardness pushing inside her filled her with joy and she uttered a deep sigh of contentment. Now his flesh was rubbing against surfaces made a thousand times more receptive to touch by her first orgasm; every centimetre of her vaginal canal was a source of delight to her. Further and further he penetrated until she felt the tickle of his pubic hair against her own and knew that she possessed all of him. Now his pumping became more urgent, driving his penis into her with long, full strokes that excited her beyond measure. At every forward thrust, she could feel his testicles slapping against her bottom and that was an additional stimulation. He twisted his head round and took her left nipple into his mouth, sucking hard. She screamed and her hands beat on his back and his bottom, her nails scrabbling at him. She wanted to eat him with her vagina, to consume him absolutely so that there would be nothing left but ashes and to suck him dry of all his sperm. She could feel herself nearing her peak again as every bump of his pubes against her own jolted her, causing her breasts to judder and her head to nod. A voice began to call out, hoarse, inarticulate, animal grunts of lust that she recognised as her own. Her orgasm rose up within her, terrifying and magnificent. She hung on the brink until he, too, gave a great cry and she felt his hot ejaculation deep inside her, burning and lubricating. That was enough to loosen her precarious grip on herself and she climaxed with him, jerking and sobbing her way through a swamp of sheer bliss.

For a long time they lay in each other's arms, their

cheeks close together. He stroked her face and her hair, whispering soft endearments in her ear while his organ slowly softened inside her. She was still on a sweet cloud of contentment, totally fulfilled. It had been even more marvellous than her most exciting dreams and she recalled the apprehension she had expressed to Alcina. Was it only that day? It seemed much longer ago than that. With a start, she remembered the discussion about pain when her hymen was broken. She grinned to herself and almost giggled aloud at the thought that it must be now the most severely fractured hymen in history. Had she felt pain? For the life of her, she could not remember doing so. Alcina had been right again. If there had been pain she had found no spare part of her mind or body to give it attention.

When Argan finally got up, Nerina continued to lie on the black, bearskin counterpane, making no attempt to cover her nakedness but rather rejoicing in it. In her many dreams about this night, she had wondered about that. Would she feel ashamed afterwards and wish to cover herself with all possible haste? It was pleasant to experience no desire at all to do any such thing. She was content to let him look at her, if he wished. He did not seem embarrassed at his own nudity, either. He put on a striped robe, but not with the nervous, rapid moves of a man who was in any way ashamed of what had taken place.

He came to the bedside and smiled down at her. 'Don't move,' he said. 'The picture you make is far too charming.'

She returned his smile. 'As my Prince commands.'

'Not a command, my little mouse, but a humble plea. Only do as I ask and you shall be rewarded with champagne. I will be only a moment.' He kissed his finger-tip and blew the kiss towards her. She reached

244

up her hand and caught it, then impishly placed it between her legs and rubbed at it to make sure it stayed there. He laughed and went back into the outer room.

He was as good as his word. In a very short time he came back bearing a tray on which there were two tall flutes and an ice-bucket containing a bottle of the finest of the Widow Cliquot's product. She sat up, cross-legged as he set it down carefully on the bed. He removed his robe before climbing on to the bed with her and copying her pose. 'This is cosy,' he said. 'A champagne picnic for two.'

Nerina had never had a picnic in bed and the picture it conjured up was amusing. She watched him twist the bottle away from the cork, admiring the movements of his strong, brown hands against the green glass. She took the foaming flute he offered her. 'What shall we drink to?'

He filled his own glass. 'The health of the restored ruler of Isingore?' he suggested.

She wrinkled her nose. 'How dull! I'd rather drink to our next meeting on this lovely coverlet.'

He frowned. 'Perhaps not.'

'Oh?'

He set his glass down. 'It is probably better that we do not do this again. It would not be right for us to become too attached to each other.'

Nerina's world fell apart around her. How could he be saying such a thing. 'I don't understand,' she said. 'Didn't you like me?'

He could see the hurt in her eyes and it damaged him. 'Oh, my sweet little mouse. How could you think such a thing? You are adorable in every way.'

She sniffed. 'But not good enough for you to want a second encounter, apparently.'

He caught her hand and held it. 'Think about it,

Nerina. I thought you understood. If you are to rule Isingore, it must be in the Paradon way. To do that, you need to be self-supporting, yet you have no working skills that would enable you to be that, nor could you acquire them in a short time. The only possible solution is that you should marry some worthy farmer or businessman who can live with you and teach you what needs to be done, supporting you while you learn. He would be your consort and adviser. Believe me, it is the only way. That being so, it would be wrong for you and me to continue our liaison.'

'You would so willingly give me up to another man?'

'Not willingly, but with an empty heart. In affairs of state it is often that way. Power brings responsibility. We have to give up the things we treasure most. If either of us pursued our own selfish pleasure, it would be at the expense of people we are destined to serve.'

She put down her glass. 'Forgive me, Prince. I find that I have no appetite for champagne. If you will excuse me, I will return to my room now.' She got off the bed and crossed to the table. Suddenly, she felt naked and ashamed. She dressed quickly, not bothering to attempt to button her dress, but merely holding it against her breasts.

He put on his robe and attempted to detain her. 'Nerina, please don't go like this. At least let me escort you to your room.'

'Thank you, sir. You are very kind, but I can find my own way.'

He followed her into the outer room and opened the door that led into the corridor. 'I beg you to think about what I've said. Sleep on it. In the morning, you will see that it makes perfect sense.'

She was still enough of a princess to remember her manners. 'Thank you, Prince Argan, for an excellent supper and for your sound advice.' She held herself together until she heard the door close behind her. The tears came then and she fled up the stairs, sobbing and clutching her dress to her. In the comparative security of her own room, she threw herself face down on the bed and cried broken-hearted tears.

She was still in the same position next morning when Alcina found her. Nerina raised her head when she heard her come into the room and turned her reddened, tear-stained eyes towards her mentor.

Alcina sat down on the side of the bed and took in the situation at a glance. 'It did not go well, then? I'm so sorry. I could have sworn ...'

'Oh no, Alcina. It's not that. It was lovely. He was lovely. That's just the trouble. He doesn't want me, Alcina.' Her voice dissolved into a long wail of misery. 'He wants to marry me off to some fat old farmer! Oh! Oh!' She got up on her knees and threw her arms around Alcina, burying her face in her shoulder and sobbing bitterly.

Alcina returned her embrace, patting her on the back and rocking her like a child. She waited for the violent paroxysms of grief to subside a little before she pushed Nerina gently away. 'Here, take this handkerchief and blow your nose. Now tell me exactly what he said to you.'

Nerina recited Argan's declaration, which she knew by heart, and Alcina listened patiently. At the end, she said, 'Men are such fools, aren't they? With them, it's all logic and reason. They never listen to what their heart tells them. Noble self-sacrifice is all very well, but sometimes it amounts to sheer stupidity.'

Nerina sniffed and hiccuped, wiping her eyes with

Alcina's handkerchief. 'You don't understand. He just doesn't want me.'

'You are quite wrong. I have reason to know that he does want you very much.'

'He does? Then how can he let me go?'

'I told you. Through sheer idiotic nobility of spirit, carried to ridiculous excess. That's just the way he is.'

'But he has made up his mind,' Nerina said, mournfully. 'There is nothing to be done about it.'

'Yes there is.'

'There is?'

'Yes. We shall have to unmake it for him.' Alcina got up, extending a hand. 'Come on. Let's clean you up and make you look half-human, then we must plot and plan as only women can. What man's decision can survive against the determination of two strong women of contrary opinion?'

Nerina gave her a watery smile, much heartened at this prospect of hope; then her face fell again. 'But why should you help me, Alcina? You, who want him so much for yourself.'

Alcina met her eyes unflinchingly. 'If I thought there was a chance that my Prince would ever think of me as he thinks of you, I would kill you before I let you near him. There is no such chance, not even of the most remote kind. I love him dearly and I seek only his happiness. You are the best thing that has come into his life and you could give him that happiness.'

Nerina came to her and hugged her. 'Alcina, I believe I love you almost as much as I love Prince Argan.'

Alcina pushed her away quite roughly, clearing her throat. 'Enough of that nonsense,' she said, gruffly. 'We have no time for it. There is too much to do.'

Thus it came about that there began what has to

be recorded as the vilest act of treachery in the history of Paradon. Almost every single member of staff in Prince Argan's household was subverted to the cause and conspired to bring about their master's downfall. Their motivations to do so were varied: Alcina was a respected figure and Nerina had also made herself popular by her good humour and resolution in the face of adversity. More than that, by her stint 'in service', she had become identifiable as one of their own, an underdog deserving of their help and sympathy. What also had to be considered was the opportunity to meddle in great affairs of state and alter the course of history. Overriding all these, though, was the more attractive aspect of the ambush. It was seen as a vast practical joke and the best sort of practical jokes, as everyone knows, are played upon those one likes and admires.

Leah was quickly recruited and joined in with a will. She used her growing influence on Count Michael and also provided Alcina with valuable tittle-tattle and gossip. Before very long the whole house and, indeed, the surrounding countryside, was rife with rumour and speculation. By a word here, a carelessly flung sentence there and a titter and stare elsewhere, Prince Argan became aware that he may have been mistaken in casting aside a toy before he had fully explored all its potential for amusement.

The rumours were flavoured with just enough of the spice of truth to be credible. Leah told Alcina about Johann and his pledge not to reveal Nerina's prowess in one particular aspect of the art of arousal. That promise was now counter-productive and Alcina saw to it that Johann broke it comprehensively.

'It was not easy,' she reported to Nerina. 'He had to be persuaded and the man drives a hard bargain.' There was a complacent and far-away look in her eyes as she said it. She passed her hands over her breasts and belly thoughtfully. 'I'm not altogether certain that he got the better part of the bargain in the end.' Nerina, recalling the dimensions of Johann's private parts and his great strength, thought that could well be true.

The things Prince Argan was hearing were alarming because they threatened political stability. It was only natural, therefore, that he should turn for counsel to his most trusted advisers. When he did so, they all deceived him in a most shameful way.

He called for Count Michael's counsel, intending to raise the matter of Nerina's growing reputation with him. Before he could do so, Michael broached the subject himself.

'Have you heard, sir, what is being said of the Princess Nerina?'

'Indeed I have. No one seems to talk of anything else. It is most worrying.'

'Oh, I don't think it's anything to worry about,' Michael said, airily. 'Quite the opposite. Have you heard that she even ...' He leant forward and, shielding his mouth with his hand, whispered in the Prince's ear.

Prince Argan was truly shocked. 'No! I don't believe it!'

'My source was not first-hand, but reliable, nevertheless. Apparently it was the most incredible experience of his friend's life.'

'What on earth am I to do about her, Michael?'

'I know what I intend to do, which is why I was happy to come to see you today. I need to be sure that you have finished with her in that way. I wouldn't like to trample on your garden, as it were.'

'What? No! We are no longer ... I mean that I have no further ambition in that direction.'

'Excellent, sir. With your permission, I will make trial of her myself at the earliest opportunity.'

'You? Oh no, Michael, I don't think that would be a good idea.'

'Why not? The wench is unattached and seemingly happy to be so as it allows her to play the field.'

'It would be politically inadvisable at present.'

Michael regarded the Prince quizzically. 'It is just politics? You're quite sure you have finished with her?'

'Quite sure!' Argan said, in some irritation. In a calmer voice, he added, 'I cannot give orders to you or to her on such a matter. I can only advise against it.'

'I hear your advice, sir.'

The unsettling nature of that conversation led Argan to his greatest error of judgement. He turned to another trusted adviser for help and Alcina betrayed him more thoroughly than anyone.

It was in consequence of Alcina's advice that he summoned Nerina to his room for a conference. To mark her lack of respect for him, she did not come immediately and he had to send for her again. When she did come, she was haughty and serene, offering her hand to be kissed. He did so and showed her to a couch. She settled herself into it, arranging her limbs gracefully and gathering about her the folds of her dress. Her beauty was as stunning as an hour or so of Alcina's artifice could make it and his heart caught in his throat as he took his seat in an upright armchair opposite her. The soft white skin of her bare shoulder seemed to beckon to him, calling his name.

He sought to cough away the obstruction to his breathing, failed and swallowed it instead. 'I don't have a great deal of time. I am going away today and my coach is waiting, yet there is something I must settle before I go. I have asked you to come here . . .'

'Ordered me to come here,' she interrupted.

'Asked? Ordered? Let us not play with words. You are here because I have been hearing certain ... things about you and ...'

'What things?'

'Well, let us just say certain ... things and they won't do, Nerina. They simply won't do at all.'

'You said that we should not play with words. Very well, let us not. You have heard that it pleases me to disport myself with others. Why not? You had your pleasure of me, then rejected me. Would you deny that pleasure to others who find me more attractive?'

'But you must see that it makes the political position very difficult.'

She tossed her head angrily, shaking her hair away from her face. 'Pooh, sir. Why should I care a fig for politics? Did you think you could awaken feelings in my body, then have me ignore them like some ageing widow, just because you cast me off as casually as you would throw away an old shoe. No, sir, I won't! You don't own me. It may be your intention to marry me off to some clod of a farmer, but I will have my fun in the meantime. And probably afterwards as well.'

His heart went out to her. He could see, now, how deeply he had wounded her. As a kind and considerate man, that would have affected him very much, even if he had not loved her as he did.

'I have been told of your concern over this proposed marriage and I assure you that I understand it. I have taken advice which seems to me to be sound. Perhaps you will agree. I can promise you that you will not be forced to marry anyone who is not to your liking.' He reached into his breast pocket and drew out a piece of paper, offering it to her. 'I have had a list drawn up for me of several men who would be politically suitable. They are all worthy individuals and none of them is old or fat. I will have you introduced to all of them, if necessary, and you shall choose. If that list proves inadequate, I will have another list made.'

She took the list from him and looked at it. He was pleased to see that she appeared to be responding to the idea. Alcina had been right, as always. It was time to press home this slender advantage. 'Please think about it, Nerina, and believe that I have your true happiness at heart. Any of these men can be yours.'

She looked up at him sharply. 'But what if I find a man whose name is not on this list. I suppose you would find him politically unsatisfactory and forbid me to marry him, even though he filled all my heart?'

He thought about this. 'No, I don't think so. We must, of course, bear in mind the political significance of such a marriage. It would be important that the man be financially stable – a farmer, say, or a merchant. Someone in a good way of business who can support you while you learn to support yourself. With that proviso, you are free to choose as a husband any man in Paradon, or elsewhere, for that matter.'

She gazed at him as though trying to read his mind. Finally, she shook her head. 'No, I dare not. I cannot trust you. I would give my love to someone and, just when I had come to care for him deeply, you would interfere for some reason known only to yourself and break my heart.'

'I would not!' he protested. 'I promise you that I would not.'

'You would break that promise.'

He was offended. 'I am a man of my word.'

She studied him through half-closed eyes, appraising his sincerity. She leant towards him and pinned his eyes with hers. 'Swear to me!' she said. 'Swear on your honour as a gentleman and on your oath as a prince that you will allow me to choose my own husband, provided that he is a farmer, a merchant, or in a good way of business, and that, whether you like my choice or not, you will never force me to marry anyone else.'

He laid his hand on his heart. 'I so swear it, by all I hold sacred.'

'And you will never break that oath, no matter what?'

'Never! May I be forever damned if I do!'

Nerina sat back, smiling. 'That seems to be satisfactory then. We appear to have reached agreement.'

He smiled back at her, infinitely relieved. 'I'm so glad. When you have made your choice . . .'

'Oh,' she said, casually, 'I have already made it.'

'You have? Who is the fortunate gentleman?'

'You.'

He started back, his hand to his head. 'What?'

'I choose you for my husband. You qualify; being not only a farmer, but a merchant in a good way of business besides. You will suit me very nicely.' She enjoyed the sight of his mouth opening and closing. It reminded her of a pet goldfish she had once owned.

'But . . . but . . . I did not intend . . .' The pit that had been dug in his path became clear to him. 'You tricked me!' Slowly, the depth and breadth of the pit made itself apparent. 'Alcina tricked me! Alcina! I don't believe it! My God! Michael? Not Michael too?'

She nodded, laughing at his discomfiture. 'Almost everyone you know, and many you don't, my darling Argan.'

He glared at her. She was so beautiful, sitting there and laughing at him. Her teeth were so white, her lips so red and her skin so soft and inviting. His gaze softened. It was impossible to be angry with her. He

254

smiled, then laughed with her. A little flicker of lust nagged at his loins. She was adorable and would make a good wife. But he would have to do something very speedily about her triumphant gloating. He could not have her thinking she could manipulate him in this cunning way and escape unscathed.

'Very well, madam,' he said. 'I am a man of honour. I swore an oath to you and I will keep it, no matter what devious means were used to extract it from me. You must be married and there is now no other possible spouse for you. I will marry you. That being so, it seems that I have yet another training programme to undertake and I will see to it personally. If I have to mould you into the shape of a dutiful and obedient wife, I must start immediately. Go forthwith into the bedroom and remove all your clothes. All of them, mind – not a stitch left on! I shall be in presently to attend to you.'

She rose and made him a deep curtsey, bowing her head while she looked up at him with smouldering eyes under lowered lids. 'As my future husband, the Prince, commands,' she said. She moved gracefully towards the bedroom door, exaggerating the swagger of her hips for the benefit of the eyes she knew would be certain to be fixed on that portion of her.

When he opened the bedroom door a little while later, she was waiting for him. She had chosen to stand facing the door, so as to allow her body the opportunity to wreak maximum havoc with his emotions. She stood with her legs slightly parted, her hips thrust forward and her hands behind her back in token of her submission to his will. She was delighted to see his eyes widen and his pupils dilate as they drank in her nudity; then he was coming towards her. Her vagina twitched in glad expectation and she closed her eyes, putting up her face to receive his first

255

passionate kisses. She felt him take her right wrist in his left hand, then squeaked in panic as he pulled her forward and his right shoulder drove hard into her midriff, toppling her over his back. In a second, she was off her feet and over his shoulder, with her knees trapped by his right arm, while his right hand replaced his left in gripping her wrist, leaving him one hand free.

She struggled, beating on his broad back with her free hand and kicking her legs. 'Argan! Argan! What are you doing? Let me down at once!' He took not the slightest notice, but strode to the bedroom door and into the outer room with her alternately laughing, squeaking and protesting. It was only when he opened the door into the corridor that she realised that he intended to take her outside his room into a place where anyone might see them.

Her stomach lurched and she screamed, 'No, Argan! Not outside! Stop! I forbid it! I'm serious!' This latter statement might have carried greater weight had she not immediately followed it with a helpless fit of the giggles.

He used his free hand to give the bare bottom against his right ear a little love-slap. 'Shut up, woman! Someone might hear you and come running to see what's the matter.'

The warning was too late. Someone had already seen them and passed the word, which spread like wildfire. The Prince was not walking slowly. Nevertheless, by the time he got to the front door with his delicious burden, a small crowd of people had gathered to see the show. Becoming aware of the front door looming, Nerina renewed her giggling, screaming and struggling. 'No darling! Not outside the house! Oh God, I shall die of shame!' The sound of cheering and clapping that greeted her emergence into the daylight did nothing to decrease her embarrassment.

Argan strode across the gravel to his waiting coach and opened the door. He bent forward and shoved Nerina inside, releasing her so that she sprawled over a seat. He closed the door on her, then turned to his coachman at the head of the lead horse. 'All right, Konrad. I shan't need you for a while.'

Konrad touched his top hat, his face as immobile as though the sight of his master flinging a naked woman into his coach were something that happened every day. 'Very good, sir.'

Argan sprang lightly on to the box at the front and picked up the reins and the whip. Nerina reached for the catch of the door to get out, then, seeing the increasing number of faces in the crowd, hesitated to display her nude self to them. The hesitation was fatal and the opportunity was lost. Argan whipped up the horses and the coach lurched forward, quickly achieving a speed at which it would have been folly to jump out.

Nerina let down the window and put her head out, clinging to the frame to support herself against the coach's mad lurching. She could not see Argan on the box, so she leant further out, the wind chill on her bare breasts. 'Argan!' she shouted. 'What are you doing? Where are we going?' She might as well have saved her breath. It was by no means certain that he could hear her. Someone did. Too late, she saw a traveller on the road turn to stare, attracted by the sound of her voice. She saw his jaw gape open in surprise at the sight of the top half of a naked woman hanging out of the window, then the coach was past and gone.

Nerina shrank back inside, ducking down below window level. After a while, she felt the coach slow and stop, then heard Argan climbing down from the box. He wrenched open the door. 'Out!' he commanded, jerking his thumb.

'What? Why? Where are we?' She looked past him. There was nothing to see except meadowland.

'Out!' he said again. 'Or must I come in there and drag you out?'

She came timidly to the door, uncertain whether his stern manner was pretence or genuine anger. He grabbed her wrist and pulled her out bodily, so that she stumbled on the steps and would have fallen if he had let her go. He did not. Still grasping her wrist, he pulled her after him into the meadow. The grass felt strange beneath her bare feet and she was acutely conscious of her naked state. She laid her weight back against him and dragged her feet, half-laughing, half-apprehensive. 'Where are we going? What are you going to do to me?'

He stopped abruptly and pushed her down on to the grass. Immediately, she rolled on to her belly and flattened herself as far as possible, grabbing at the too-short grass and attempting to pull it around her in lieu of clothing.

'Do to you?' he said. 'What else should I do to you but that which a good husband does regularly to his wife?'

She felt her heart lift up at these words, even as her bowels squirmed with lust. She peered over her shoulder to see him unfastening the flap of his breeches. 'But not here, dearest Argan? You can't mean to do it here, where anyone who passes by can see us?'

'Indeed I do mean to do it here. You may be ashamed of yourself for your trickery, but I have no reason to be. Now turn over and show yourself to the world.'

These words were definitely wicked and exciting.

She could feel the cool wind of the open air on her back and knew that it would be deliciously naughty on her breasts and belly. She wriggled even closer to the ground, holding on to tufts of grass. 'No, please! I'm shy!'

'Must I spank your bottom into obedience?' he growled. 'Turn over at once!'

Her already erect nipples ground themselves into the grass and her pubes moved against the same coarse stimulus in sympathy. For a moment, she was tempted by the enticing prospect of having her bottom spanked, but decided against it. Not only would it increase the time she was on naked, public display. More importantly, it would delay the moment when she would again feel his hardness pushing up inside her and that was unthinkable. She was fully lubricated and more than ready for such an encounter. She rolled over, spread her legs wide and held out her arms.

He came into her without preamble, his penis thrusting far up into her vagina. He was punishing her with it, using it as a club to beat her inside in places where no whip could possibly reach. His mastery of her was complete and she succumbed to it gladly, clinging to him with happy little cries of contentment. The feel of the grass below her, the breeze on her skin, the sound of birds and all the other evidences of the open air made her feel vulnerable and increased her sex-drive. The knowledge that at any moment someone might see how she was being punished and debauched drove her into an ecstatic frenzy. She locked her ankles behind his back and pulled him to her, using her own leg muscles to add to the force of his already powerful lunges. Her orgasm coincided with his and she screamed with joy at the force of it, her hands beating a tattoo on his back.

He lay on her for only a short while before getting up and taking both her hands to pull her to her feet. 'Let that be a lesson to you not to irritate me again in the future,' he said.

She laid her cheek against his chest. 'Are you saying that if I make you angry, you will punish me like that again?'

'I am!'

'Dearest,' she said, with sweet innocence, 'I have learnt the lesson well, I promise you. You must make a long list of the things that make you angry. I would not want to do them by accident.'

He laughed and put his arm around her waist to lead her back to the coach. He reached up and took Konrad's long cloak from its place below the box. 'Here,' he said. 'Cover yourself with this.'

She put it on and he opened the door of the coach for her. She put her hand on his arm. 'Please may I ride on the box with you?'

'Why not?' He grabbed her slim waist with both hands and swung her up so that she could scramble into place on the seat. He climbed up beside her and shook the reins, turning the horses homewards. He drove in silence for a while, then looked down at her fondly. 'Having you alongside me starts a train of thought,' he said. 'Now that I know you are so good at intrigue and deception, I have to reconsider your value to me as a politician and stateswoman. Perhaps your place beside me in the driving seat of Paradon should not be merely that of a figurehead – beautiful as that figurehead may be.'

She put her arm through his and snuggled, her head on his shoulder. 'Whatever you decide, dearest Prince of my heart,' she said. 'I would be honoured to serve Paradon in that way. I would only ask that we separate council chamber from bedchamber. I think I would like you to make most of the decisions there. For instance, my recent punishment was not as effective as I had at first thought. It seems to be wearing off already. You may have to teach me another lesson when we get home.'

He smiled at her. 'As you wish. On that very subject, one of the first decisions of state we must make together is the appropriate punishment for those who aided you in your treachery.'

She sat up and looked at him, not yet knowing him sufficiently well to be able to judge if he was serious. 'Not Alcina! You can't punish Alcina. She loves you too much and wished only your happiness.'

He threw back his head and laughed. 'Punish Alcina? I wouldn't dare! She is far too important and powerful to antagonise. Sometimes I wonder who really rules Paradon, I or she. No, I was thinking of Count Michael. Don't you think he deserves to pay some small price for his part in the affair?'

Nerina clapped her hands. 'Ah! That's a different matter.' She thought for a while, then laid her head back on the Prince's shoulder. 'Darling,' she said, softly, 'how does "The Countess Leah von Selfingen" sound to you as a title?'

He nodded admiring approval. 'Such cunning! Excellent! A most fitting life sentence! She would keep him in order admirably. I'm sure I can leave that to you and Alcina and all the others whose names I do not know.'

She smiled up at him and squeezed his arm. 'It will be a pleasure, sir, to obey that command. She will be Countess von Selfingen and I will be . . . let me see . . . I'll be Her Royal Highness, the Princess Nerina of Paradon.'

'And Isingore,' he reminded her.

'Oh yes! So I will. Do you realise what this means?

When we are married, we will be joint rulers. The principalities of Paradon and Isingore will become one. It will need a new name.'

'So it will,' he said, turning his head to kiss her. 'I hadn't thought about that.'

'I had,' she said, laughing. 'We must call it "Paradise".'

NEW BOOKS

Coming up from Nexus and Black Lace

The Castle of Maldona by Yolanda Celbridge
April 1997   Price £4.99   ISBN: 0 352 33149 6
When a twist of fate brings the fun-loving and disciplinarian Jana and her lover Cassie to a remote castle, they willingly submit to the whims of its Master, only to regret it when his cruelty becomes all too evident. Returning, they ingratiate themselves again with the Master – little does he know that the women have revenge in mind.

Nymphs of Dionysus by Susan Tinoff
April 1997   Price £4.99   ISBN: 0 352 33150 X
Ancient Greece. Acantha has a tough job: to guard the sexually insatiable Chryseis' virtue before her arranged marriage. The two have little in common apart from an enormous appetite for debauchery and, when they are shipwrecked on their way to the wedding, their desires come close to being sated. But there are also dangers to be faced – not least those posed by the mysterious and orgiastic followers of Dionysus.

Emma's Humiliation by Hilary James
May 1997   Price £4.99   ISBN: 0 352 33153 4
When Emma's masterful lover Henry comes back into her life, she is keen to resume their delightful disciplinary dalliances. But they are soon discovered by Emma's Mistress, Ursula, who sends her to a rehabilitation centre to ensure she remains an obedient slave. Under the tutelage of the Headmistress and the Major, Emma soon learns total subservience to her Mistress's strange desires. This is the fifth volume in the highly popular 'Emma' series.

Web of Domination by Yvonne Strickland
May 1997   Price £4.99   ISBN: 0 352 33154 2
The Villa Rafaelo in Tuscany caters for the special tastes of guests keen to make use of their fully equipped dungeon and the other bizarre delights on offer. All goes well until three young travellers lose their way and see things they were never intended to see. The secrets of the villa must be guarded, and the three become pawns in a game of lust and perversion guaranteed to ensure humiliation and silence.

Avenging Angels by Roxanne Carr
April 1997   Price £4.99   ISBN: 0 352 33147 X
Karen is dismayed by the lack of respect shown to women in the sun
and sex-soaked Tierra del Sol holiday resort, and decides to tackle
the problem by becoming a dominatrix – with surprising results.
There is only one man in the resort who will not succumb to her
charms – and this is the one man she must have, at any price.

The Gallery by Fredrica Alleyn
April 1997   Price £4.99   ISBN: 0 352 33148 8
WPC Cressida Farleigh is working undercover in an art gallery whose
owner, Guy, is suspected of faking old masters. Her boyfriend is
starting to get jealous, and with good reason – not only is Cressida
powerfully attracted to Guy, but she is also in the process of seducing
a young artist who supplies the gallery with disturbing and powerful
erotic images. In striving to crack the case, she runs the risk of finding
out things about herself she dare not admit to anyone.

The Lion Lover by Mercedes Kelly
May 1997   Price £4.99   ISBN: 0 352 33162 3
When the darkly sensual missionary McKinnon tires of his women,
he sends them to a Sultan's harem. Mathilde Valentine, a medic in
his East African mission post, is warned to be wary of her new employer, but ignores the advice and soon has to accomodate the lusts
of the demanding Sultan, his sadistic brother and his naive son.
Meanwhile Olensky, her 'lion lover', is plotting her escape. Will he
succeed?

Palazzo by Jan Smith
May 1997   Price £4.99   ISBN: 0 352 33156 9
When Claire and Cherry visit Venice, they soon succumb to the se-
ductive charms of the city – and the men who inhabit it. Claire meets
the mysterious Stuart MacIntosh who encourages her to explore
strange new sexual avenues, but before long she finds herself trapped
in a web of conflicting desires and dark intrigue.

Past Passions: an anthology of erotic fiction by women
May 1997   Price £4.99   ISBN: 0 352 33159 3
This unique anthology features historical fantasies from the female sexual imagination. Bizarre sexual excesses from days gone by collide with worlds of secluded passion and scintillating characters delight in the thrill of total surrender to pleasure and decadent indulgence.

NEXUS BACKLIST

All books are priced £4.99 unless another price is given. If a date is supplied, the book in question will not be available until that month in 1997.

CONTEMPORARY EROTICA

AGONY AUNT	G. C. Scott	Jul
ALLISON'S AWAKENING	John Angus	Jul
BOUND TO SERVE	Amanda Ware	
BOUND TO SUBMIT	Amanda Ware	Sep
CANDIDA'S SECRET MISSION	Virginia LaSalle	
CANDY IN CAPTIVITY	Arabella Knight	
CHALICE OF DELIGHTS	Katrina Young	
THE CHASTE LEGACY	Susanna Hughes	
CHRISTINA WISHED	Gene Craven	
CONDUCT UNBECOMING	Arabella Knight	
DARK DESIRES	Maria del Rey	
DIFFERENT STROKES	Sarah Veitch	
THE DOMINO TATTOO	Cyrian Amberlake	
THE DOMINO ENIGMA	Cyrian Amberlake	
THE DOMINO QUEEN	Cyrian Amberlake	
EDEN UNVEILED	Maria del Rey	
EDUCATING ELLA	Stephen Ferris	Aug
ELAINE	Stephen Ferris	
EMMA'S SECRET WORLD	Hilary James	
EMMA ENSLAVED	Hilary James	
EMMA'S SECRET DIARIES	Hilary James	
EMMA'S SUBMISSION	Hilary James	
EMMA'S HUMILIATION	Hilary James	May
FALLEN ANGELS	Kendal Grahame	

- -

Please send me the books I have ticked above.

Name ....

Address ....

....

....

.... Post code ....

Send to: **Cash Sales, Nexus Books, 332 Ladbroke Grove, London W10 5AH**

Please enclose a cheque or postal order, made payable to Virgin Publishing, to the value of the books you have ordered plus postage and packing costs as follows:

UK and BFPO – £1.00 for the first book, 50p for each subsequent book.

Overseas (including Republic of Ireland) – £2.00 for the first book, £1.00 for each subsequent book.

If you would prefer to pay by VISA or ACCESS/MASTER-CARD, please write your card number and expiry date here:

....

Please allow up to 28 days for delivery.

Signature ....

- -